HER
DEADLY
TRUTH

BOOKS BY L.A. LARKIN

L.A. LARKIN

HER DEADLY TRUTH

bookouture

Published by Bookouture in 2023

An imprint of Storyfire Ltd.
Carmelite House
50 Victoria Embankment
London EC4Y 0DZ

www.bookouture.com

ISBN: 978-1-80314-694-2
eBook ISBN: 978-1-80314-693-5

To Phil Patterson, friend and agent extraordinaire

ONE

JULY 22, 2016

Sally Fairburn was being extra careful—the killer knew that.

She had installed deadbolt door locks so that she and her son, Paul, could sleep soundly, lulled into a false sense of security by a set of shiny new keys. But Sally hadn't thought to update a third-floor sliding door to the roof terrace, and that was her mistake.

The house next door was empty, and the killer had a key. The row of townhouses with nothing but a glass divider between each terrace made it easy to hop from one house to the next. If the killer got lucky, it might not even be necessary to pick the sliding-door lock. The night was warm, and after a scorching-hot day, most people slept with the sliding doors open. Tonight, Sally had a friend sleeping in the room the killer must walk through. This friend, Margie Clay, was an unforeseen complication. It would mean creeping past the sleeping guest, then heading down one level to Sally's bedroom.

Dressed in black, with a balaclava covering their hair and most of their face, the killer stood outside the sliding doors, not unduly worried that they were, in fact, closed. The air-conditioning unit on the roof terrace hummed. The drapes were drawn halfway across the glass, so the sleeping woman was visible. Margie lay on her side, curled up under a sheet. It was 1:23 a.m. and hopefully she was in a deep sleep.

Picking the lock was easy, but as the lever disengaged from the latch plate, it would make a clank. How light a sleeper was Margie? The killer could handle Sally, no problem. But if the friend screamed, the son, Paul, would wake up, and three against one was not good odds. Slowly the killer inserted the lock pick and wiggled it about until it hit the right spot. Now to turn the mechanism that held the lever in place.

Clank.

The killer waited and watched. Margie didn't move a limb. Now to slide the glass door open. Fortunately, the thrum of the air conditioning drowned out the rattling sound of the door shifting on runners. Stepping into the room, they pulled the door shut. The air inside was cool on the skin and smelled of red wine and a pungent perfume. The carpet dulled any footfalls as the killer crept past the bed and opened the guest room door. The landing and stairs were polished pine. The killer's sneakers squeaked. It was best to remove the shoes and creep down the stairs to where Sally and her fifteen-year-old son had their bedrooms.

No turning back now.

The killer felt for the long-bladed knife, wrapped in a hand towel and hidden inside their jacket. The previous murders had been more distant and therefore less personal. No blood was spilled. Sally's death might get messy. What's more, she had a gun safe right next to her bed. The killer knew that she had handed over her Glock 19 to the detective, but what if she owned another gun? That was why surprise and speed were everything, catching Sally before she had time to reach for a weapon.

A light came on. The killer froze on the landing. A slit of light seeped under the door of the boy's bedroom. What the hell was he doing awake? The door opened and the boy was silhouetted, lit from behind by the bedside lamp.

The killer stepped back. One step. Two. Three. Then slowly closed Margie's door, leaving just enough gap to watch the boy switch on the landing light.

Would he notice the sneakers abandoned one floor up?

Paul's bare feet made slapping sounds as he went downstairs. The killer looked around at Margie, who was still asleep, her breathing now a regular snore. Beneath the jacket and the balaclava, the killer was sweating. How long would the boy stay downstairs? The sound of humming reached the killer. And a suction noise that suggested he'd opened the refrigerator. A pause. Then a suction sound again, perhaps taking something from the freezer? Then the whirring sound of a microwave and the aroma of mac and cheese. Who ate mac and cheese in the middle of the night, for Christ's sake! A kitchen drawer banged shut. More slaps of bare feet as Paul came back upstairs, clutching a plate and fork, and into his bedroom.

Paul left the door half open. This was going to ruin everything. One sound and he would come to his mother's aid. The killer really didn't want to have to kill a child. What to do?

Wait, the killer decided. Wait until the boy had eaten and gone back to sleep. As long as Margie didn't stir, that plan should still work.

The killer's leg muscles grew tight. Eyes sore from peering at the bright light. The smell of the mac and cheese made the killer's mouth water, and a stomach rumble was a reminder that no food had passed the killer's lips for over twelve hours. A clank of a fork. Then muffled sounds of voices and *boom, boom, boom*. Was he watching a movie?

2:07 a.m.

The killer's patience was wearing thin. Creeping out of Margie's room, and down the stairs, it was possible to see Paul wearing headphones and playing a video game: some kind of military rescue mission by the look of it. This was good. He was unlikely to hear the killer move about or Sally scream.

It was time.

TWO

Sally Fairburn paused just inside the entrance to the bookstore-cum-café where she worked, inhaling the smell of freshly baked sponge cake, coffee, and old books. Olivia's Bookstore stocked rare, used, and out-of-print books. The exception to this rule was the shelf of newly released crime and fantasy novels, and it was this that tended to bring people into the place. Olivia, the store owner and baker of delicious cakes, was a fan of these genres, and as she had so succinctly declared, "It's my store, so I can sell what I like."

With Sally's help, Olivia had positioned the tall bookcases to create several private nooks with tables and chairs, none of which matched, so that customers could browse and eat at their leisure. Nothing happened fast here. Even the ceiling fans whirred lazily and the cat, named Pajamas, ambled along the bookshelves as if she had all the time in the world.

Olivia, who had green hair and glasses, sat on a tall stool behind the counter, sipping her first coffee of the day. To her right was a commercial espresso machine that made two coffees at once and beyond that was a revolving cake refrigerator, where her cakes were displayed. "Going to be busy day today. I can feel it."

It was a Tuesday and customers generally didn't visit the store until after eleven.

"Would it be okay if I take a half-hour break at ten? My neighbor asked to meet me here," Sally asked.

"Sure. Pajamas and I can handle the rush." Olivia grinned, knowing full well that the only rush was on Saturday and Sunday lunchtime, and even then it was a languid rush, if such a thing existed. "Do try and get her to buy a book, will you? Does she like crime? The new Karin Slaughter thriller's just in."

"I'll do my best. Truth is, I don't actually know why she wants to meet. She and her husband moved into the house next door a few months ago and we sometimes wave and say hi, but that's about the sum of it."

Sally thought about Carolyn Tate, twenty-seven, successful brand director, blonde, pretty. Then she considered herself—a forty-six-year-old mom with hints of gray in her short brown hair, a former victim support advocate with the district attorney's office, jaded and burned-out. Life had kicked Sally in the gut one too many times. Why would someone like Carolyn want to have coffee with Sally? Was she simply being neighborly? Paul sometimes played his music too loud, until Sally asked him to use his earbuds. But Paul was on vacation with his second cousin, David Sinclair, and Sally was very quiet, so it couldn't be a noise issue.

"Maybe she just wants to make friends?" Olivia said, stroking the cat's back as he lay on the countertop purring. Sally put her purse in a cupboard behind the counter. She had no coat. It was a hot July morning and Sally wore a simple blouse, three-quarter-length pants, and pumps on her feet.

Olivia gave her a sly look. "Everyone knows who you are. It's half the reason why people come into the shop. They want to meet *you*."

Sally groaned. "I've walked away from anything to do with criminal justice. The whole process is broken. Cops protect cops." She knew she sounded bitter. But she couldn't help it because that's how she felt. Sally changed the subject. "Boxes need unpacking?"

"Yeah, three, in the back. Hey, Sally, I'm sorry I brought it up. I didn't mean to upset you."

"It's okay. It's my issue and I have to deal with it. I just want to forget all about my past and focus on the future."

"It must have been terrible, hunted by those evil men. At least one's dead and the other one is in jail. He can't hurt you ever again."

Yes, Sally wanted to forget about Richard Foster—aka the surviving Poster Killer. But there was a whole other aspect to her past life that she wanted to obliterate: her former husband, who was responsible for their daughter's suicide. And she had good reason to believe that he'd sexually assaulted their daughter's friend. But what galled Sally the most and still drove her crazy was the fact that Scott Fairburn was a cop, and because of that he got away with it all. The suffering she endured at Scott's hands was a tightly held secret, known only by her son, her best friend, Margie Clay, and Detective Fred Clarke, the only honest cop at Franklin PD. The burden of that secret was like a constant throbbing pain that no amount of painkillers could diffuse.

"This job, my new life, friends like you"—Sally smiled warmly—"it's all about starting again and creating a positive environment for Paul to flourish in. He's had a tough few years."

"Paul's a fine boy. Well, he's hardly a boy anymore, is he? Fifteen going on twenty. He's a credit to you, Sally."

"Thanks, Liv."

Sally wove her way through the meandering bookcases to the back of the store, where a room doubled as an office and storeroom. Beyond that was the kitchen, where Olivia baked cakes each morning before the sun rose, and a staircase that led up to the space where Olivia lived. Sally kept herself busy stocking shelves and serving a couple of customers until Carolyn walked into the store a little early, her perfume reminding Sally of tiger lilies.

"This is gorgeous," Carolyn said. "I've walked past the shop so many times and wanted to take a peek." Her long blonde hair fell over her tanned skin and the straps of her boho sundress. "It's like *Alice in Wonderland*'s rabbit hole."

Her English accent was pronounced.

When Carolyn ordered a rooibos tea from Olivia, Sally was surprised. She knew she shouldn't use stereotypes, but she had imagined Carolyn drinking English breakfast tea. Sally asked for a short black coffee. They hovered near the counter while Olivia prepared their drinks and made small talk, then they found a table for two tucked away in the history and travel section.

"It's great to get a chance to get to know you," Sally said. "How are you finding Pioneer Heights?"

The location of their adjoining townhouses.

"I love it. It's very different from England, but it has the same kind of village-y vibe, and I love the mountains."

"Where in England are you from?" Sally asked.

"Bishopstone. A village about two miles from Brighton."

"I guess you met your husband here?"

"Yes, Matt was born and raised in Franklin." Franklin's city center was five miles from Pioneer Heights. "The company I work for transferred me here from the UK. Then I met Matt, and well, everything happened so fast. Married in nine months, our own house within a year." There was an exaggerated levity in Carolyn's voice, as if it were put on.

"Nine months, wow! I guess you're still in the honeymoon phase?" Sally said. As soon as she said it, Sally felt a hypocrite. Scott changed from a charming and selfless lover to a domineering and manipulative narcissist almost as soon as Sally had said *I do*.

"Not exactly." That didn't sound good. Perhaps Sally should move on to another topic.

"Is Matt away? I haven't seen him for a while."

"At a convention in Las Vegas until Saturday, although it seems an odd location for a pharmacy convention. I mean, why there? It's full of gambling machines and showgirls with their tits out, and lurid pole dancers. Disgusting place." Her pretty face was a snarl. Carolyn caught Sally staring and her features softened. "How is your son? Has he gone to summer camp?"

"Not summer camp. Paul's visiting cousins in Tampa Bay. They're teaching him to sail. He's coming home tomorrow, as a matter of fact."

"Lucky boy. I'd rather be anywhere than here," Carolyn said, then stared down at her hands. "I guess I should come clean about why I asked you to meet me."

The black coffee in Sally's stomach churned. Carolyn clearly had a problem, and she was going to ask Sally to solve it. Since the high-profile arrest of Richard Foster and Sally's involvement in the case, she had been inundated with requests for her to solve anything from a stolen cat to a missing child. The missing-kids cases were the most difficult to turn away. Sally took care to reply to every email and letter, because she knew how heartbreaking the loss of a child was, but she politely declined every request. She wasn't a cop or a private investigator and she had stumbled on Foster's lair almost by mistake. She was no hero.

Please don't ask for my help, Sally thought.

Carolyn rolled her lips together and her eyes danced from shelf to shelf. Sally waited, sensing that this was very difficult for Carolyn. Finally, she said, "I... I need your help."

Sally waited a few seconds before she replied so she could

ask the right questions and then, she hoped, let Carolyn down gently.

"In what way?" Sally asked, studying Carolyn's face.

Her skin was unblemished. No dark bags under her eyes. She sat upright and composed. She appeared neither worried nor afraid.

"This will probably sound bizarre..." The words trailed away. She picked up her cup and sipped her rooibos, then put the cup down. "Let me take a step back. You were a police officer, I believe?"

"A long time ago, yes. Then I moved into victim support advocacy. Why do you ask?"

A year ago, when Sally had helped capture the infamous Poster Killer and shot dead his accomplice and son, Aiden Foster, Sally was later caught up in a whirlwind of media coverage that made her out to be a hero. She had succeeded where the cops had failed, the media said. Detective Fred Clarke had been working the case and was slammed by the press for failing to do his job. Franklin's homicide department had egg all over its face.

"You solved the Poster Killer case. I need your—"

"I don't mean to be rude, but do you mind if I stop you there?" Sally said. "I want you to know that I didn't solve that case. I blundered into Foster's house like a fool. I was his prisoner. When I escaped, I sought refuge in a stranger's house, and, because of me, a father died."

That man's tragic death was a burden Sally would carry for the rest of her life.

"I don't understand. You were given an award for bravery. You found the killers. You did what the police couldn't."

"That's true about the award, but I don't have the skills of a detective or PI. I'm sorry to disappoint you."

Carolyn shook her head. "Please hear me out. I don't trust

PIs and the cops will think I'm imagining it. You see, I'm bipolar. Do you know what that is?"

Margie, Sally's friend, was director of a mental wellness charity and she had raised the topic of bipolar disorder in a past conversation.

"Is it an imbalance that can cause extremes of mood from euphoria to depression?"

"That's as good as any description. There's more to it than that, but I won't bore you with it now. It's a mental illness, Sally, and I have to take medication. The police will say I'm paranoid because I'm bipolar. They won't believe me."

Sally could sympathize with Carolyn's situation. She knew what it was like to need help and have everyone treat her as if she were insane. Scott had a way of convincing everyone around Sally, even her parents, that he was the kindest, sweetest husband and father. But to Sally he was a cruel mental and emotional abuser, always twisting the truth so that Sally was the issue, never him. It had taken years of therapy with a psychologist to help her recover from Scott's gaslighting.

"If it's any consolation, I know what it's like not to be believed," Sally said. "But whatever you need, I'm the wrong person. I'm just a mom who works in a bookshop."

"Please, I have nobody else. I can't trust our friends. They'll tell Matt."

Sally furtively glanced at her watch. She could make an excuse that she had to get back to work, but Sally felt sorry for Carolyn. She seemed isolated.

"What is the issue you need investigating?" Sally asked.

"My husband's trying to kill me."

Sally's jaw dropped. The newlyweds. The parties. The laughter passing through the shared house walls. To Sally, her neighbors' lives seemed idyllic. "What makes you think that?"

"It started a few weeks ago. Little things. He'd work late even though the pharmacy was shut. Matt owns a pharmacy, by the way. He'd smell different, like he'd had a shower with somebody else's shower gel." Carolyn stared at her hands, clenched together on the table. "The band practice sessions got longer and longer, then I discovered that Lachlan, the drummer and Matt's business partner, was home hours earlier than Matt. When I challenged him, he said he needed time alone to work on new songs." She shook her head. "He's having an affair, I know he is." Carolyn fiddled with her diamond ring.

"I'm so sorry to hear that," Sally said. "Do you know who he's having an affair with?"

"No."

"And what makes you think he's trying to kill you?"

"Please, let me explain. We had a whirlwind romance. I still don't know why he wanted me. He's a daredevil and I'm, well, I guess I'm not. He finds reasons to go out alone. I get the feeling he doesn't want to be with me anymore." Carolyn's jaw muscle tightened. She looked as if she had swallowed a bitter pill. "He wants me out of his life. I'm sure of it."

So far, Sally was hearing a lot of conjecture. Was Carolyn imagining this?

"And so... I'm sorry to ask again, but why would Matt want you dead? If your marriage isn't working, he could always file for divorce."

"I've felt so ill. The doctor says there's nothing wrong with me, apart from my bipolar. But there has to be. I've always been clearheaded and energetic. Recently I've barely been able to get out of bed. I'm confused, forgetful. I vomit every day."

Sally's cursory understanding of bipolar was that it could have you depressed and unable to leave your bed one day, and then hyper and feeling invincible the next.

"Have you changed your medication recently?"

"No! You don't believe me, do you?" Carolyn shouted.

"It's not that. I'm just making sure I understand. You

mention the vomiting. Is there perhaps a chance you're pregnant?"

"I took a test. It was negative. Look, you have to believe me. Matt is poisoning me."

"How do you think he's doing it?"

"I don't know. He's a pharmacist. Maybe he's switching my medication or something." Carolyn sounded shrill.

"But... why? Why would he do it?"

"Because he wants me out of the way. Oh, I don't know." She stared at the polka-dot teapot on the table, then back to Sally. "Don't you see? Matt is the perfect killer. There's no other explanation."

Matt would certainly know which medications could be lethal at the right dosage. Still, just because he was a pharmacist, it didn't mean he'd use his knowledge to kill. The more Carolyn talked, the more Sally wondered if her bipolar was behind her current state of mind.

"Forgive me for being blunt, but if you really believe he's poisoning you, why don't you leave him?"

"Because I love him. I know it's pathetic. But I do. And what if I'm wrong? These days I'm so confused. I don't trust my own judgment. That's why I want you to find out if he's poisoning me. So I can be sure that's what's happening."

Carolyn was right about one thing. She was very confused.

"I'm not the right person, Carolyn, I'm really sorry. I have no training as a detective. I was a beat cop many years ago and that's very different to being a detective. And you need someone who's more positive than I am about the criminal justice system. It failed me with my abusive husband." Her voice was strangled with emotion. She waited a few seconds to recover her composure. "I'm the wrong person for this job."

"No, wait—"

"I can help you in other ways. I'd urge you to focus on your health. Seek a second opinion. Get blood tests done. My doctor is very good. I can give you her details. If you are in fear for your life, tell Matt you are going to stay with a friend, so you have time to think, time away from him. See if you get better when you are away from him."

Carolyn's eyes were watery. "I can't. I don't have any real friends here."

Sally found that strange. She had seen women come and go from Carolyn's house often and they all seemed very chummy. Nevertheless, Carolyn clearly felt friendless, and Sally sensed her loneliness.

"If you want some company, pop around anytime," Sally said. "You can always talk to me."

Carolyn clasped Sally's hand. "Thank you, I'd like that."

THREE

Zelda's grave was marked by a marble statue of a girl reading a book, leaning her back against part of the headstone. The girl was no more than three feet high, and she had her legs folded to one side, just as Zelda used to sit. The sculptor had done an amazing job of capturing her likeness, and every time Sally saw it, she felt her heart almost burst with love. There was the briefest of moments when Sally would always think that she were real. A second later, the living, breathing Zelda in Sally's imagination was gone.

When Sally's daughter had taken her own life at the age of thirteen, Sally lost a part of herself too. She blamed herself for missing the signs and hated herself for allowing Scott to thwart her attempts to get help for their daughter. "There's nothing wrong with her," Scott would say. "Just teenage tantrums. You're too soft."

Later on, when she began to unearth the truth behind Zelda's suicide, her guilt turned to fury, directed at her ex-husband, Scott. He had faked her suicide note, shifting the blame from himself to a school bully. He put his daughter through hell when he intimidated her into keeping his filthy secret—he had sexually assaulted one of her best friends, and if she told anyone, including Sally, he would kill her. Zelda had taken her own life, Sally believed, because the burden of that secret was too much. Sally didn't learn about this until years after Zelda's death. There wasn't a day that went by when Sally didn't ask, *What if I had done this?* or *What if I had said that?*

People told her that time was a healer. It wasn't. After six years, Sally's grief was just as sharp. She still cried when an object, word, sound, or place reminded her of Zelda. However, Sally had found a way to allow joy into her life again and that way was her son, Paul. He was her life now.

It was 5:30 p.m. when Sally reached the cemetery, and the sun's heat was dissipating a little, for which Sally was thankful. She meandered between the headstones until she reached Zelda's grave, a route she could complete blindfolded she had taken it so often. Next to the marble statue of Zelda, a vase contained some flowers. Sally had placed them there two days ago. In her hand was a new bunch—all yellows, including some sunflowers, which Zelda always adored. Sally fondly remembered that her daughter's favorite painting had been Van Gogh's *Sunflowers*.

Sally kneeled, removed her backpack from her shoulders, then carefully removed the pink flowers in the vase and lay them on the ground. They were a little faded but otherwise okay, and Sally would take them home and pop them in a vase until they withered. Sally liked to make sure that Zelda always had fresh flowers, and therefore Sally's visits were frequent. From a water bottle she filled the vase and then put the yellow bunch in it, placing it next to the marble girl's hip. To the girl's left, the words on the headstone read:

Zelda Ellen Fairburn

1997–2010

Every day

Every place
Every thought
Is connected to you,
Beautiful girl.
Like sand
Dancing in sunlight
You drifted through
Our lives
Captivating our hearts.
You are forever loved.

Sally shifted position, so that her back was against the left side of the headstone and next to "Zelda" on her right.

"What are you reading today, beautiful girl?" Sally asked, touching the statue's cold hand.

Sally liked to imagine that her daughter replied. Mourners visiting the surrounding graves had gotten used to finding Sally there, talking to a marble statue. They understood her grief and left her to it.

"We have some new books in the shop. I think you'd like one of them. It's called *The Weight of Feathers*. We don't normally have young-adult books in store, but this one captured Liv's heart and mine too, so we made an exception. I think you'd like the Romeo and Juliet characters. One has feathers and the other has scales and their families don't get on. Would you like me to read it to you?"

Sally took the book from her backpack and opened it at chapter one. She began reading. She only managed to reach page two before her eyes were so watery that she couldn't see the words. A tear hit the page. Sally quickly brushed it away, but the paper had a small round soggy dip where the water had seeped through.

Sally closed the book. "I'll read you some more tomorrow. What do you think so far? Good, huh?"

Sally laid the book on the grass. "Last visit I told you your brother's in Tampa Bay with his cousins. Having a great time too. I find home very empty. I walk around feeling like I'm the only kid in the playground. I was thinking about you as I ate my dinner last night. You'd be nineteen now. Tall and beautiful, I'm sure. Studying literature or art. You'd have lots of college friends—creative people like you. I imagine you would still live at home, and we'd chat about your studies and maybe you'd have a boyfriend and we'd laugh like we used to do before..."

Sally blinked and heavy tears trickled down each cheek.

"I'm sorry. I know I say it every time, but I am. I wish I had done more. I wish you had told me. I wish Scott had walked out long before you passed. Know that I love you, and I think of you every single day."

Sally cried for a while, then she blew her nose and watched the treetops sway in the breeze as she composed herself. "Paul says he has a present for you. He's bringing it back from Tampa Bay. They have lovely beaches there. Maybe it's a shell? He's home tomorrow. We'll come visit you together when he's settled in."

She touched the petals of a sunflower. "A woman met me at work this morning. A neighbor. She thinks her husband is poisoning her. Yes, I know, it's scary. But it happens. I don't know what to make of her. She seemed... well, very confused and perhaps a little paranoid. But I liked her. I said I couldn't help her establish the truth about her husband, and now I feel guilty. But how can I help her when I couldn't even help you? *And* I failed to prove Scott's guilt. We know, don't we, Zelda? We know what he did to Stacy Green. But I can't prove it. You know I've tried. The system is stacked against us. One day, though, he'll make a mistake. One day, he won't be a cop anymore and then he's fair game. One day, I'll get justice for you, I promise." Sally paused. "Do you think I should try to help Carolyn find out what her husband's up to?" Sally waited for an answer. She imagined Zelda telling her to do what she could. "You're right, I could've been more supportive. I know of some private investigators. I'll ask Carolyn if she'd like their numbers."

Sally gathered her belongings and left the cemetery.

FOUR

Carolyn Tate's RAV4 was nowhere to be seen when Sally pulled up outside her townhouse at a little after 6 p.m. She had wanted to knock on Carolyn's door and offer the contact details for a couple of private investigators.

Back in May 2015, when Clarke had closed the file on her husband, Scott, Sally had considered employing a PI to follow him. If Scott was true to form, he would pursue another young victim. Sally had spoken to three investigators who had initially seemed interested in the job, then a few days later they each rang to make an excuse as to why they were unable to take her job. Sally was convinced that Scott had somehow got wind of her plan and found a way to scare them off. He was a cop and therefore he could make life difficult for anyone that he took a dislike to. Now that he was working for Chicago PD, he was equally invincible. Sexual perverts like Scott got away with their crimes because they had a PD badge.

She didn't blame the private investigators for being afraid of Scott and perhaps Carolyn would find one of them useful. However, Sally's plan would have to wait until Carolyn was home, although Sally would need to also be sure that Carolyn was alone.

Sally's house faced west, which was great in winter but in summer the living room and the front bedroom could get very warm. As she slid the key in the lock, the steel cylinder was hot to the touch.

"Paul! I'm home!" she called out, entering the house.

Paul wasn't there. It was a habitual call, just as Paul always announced himself with "Hey, Mom!"

Paul was flying home tomorrow. Sally had missed him more than she imagined possible. Part of her wished that she had gone with him to visit David Sinclair and his family in Tampa Bay. But Paul needed some time away. It was just the two of them now and Paul had become overly protective of her. He had also inherited his father's short fuse, and any sign of a threat or an insult to Sally and his temper would flare.

Sally dropped her purse on the armchair, then opened a window to let some cooler air into the house. The rumble of a diesel engine caught her attention. A van from Charlie's Flowers came to a halt across the street and a young woman hurriedly got out, then opened the back of the van. Taking a bouquet of red flowers from the back, the doors slammed shut and she crossed the road.

Sally stepped back, her hands over her mouth, the room spinning. *Not again*, she thought.

The florist glanced at the street number on the gate and walked up the path to Sally's house, then rang her doorbell.

Sally could just see a flash of red cocooned in brown paper tied with string, which was Charlie's distinctive packaging. She knew exactly which flowers were in the florist's arms without having to see them close up: a dozen red roses.

"Hello? Anyone home?" the florist called out.

"Take them away. I don't want them," Sally shouted, loud enough for Charlie to hear.

Charlie's eyes met Sally's through the living room window. "Sally Fairburn?"

"Yes. No. I mean. Give them to somebody else."

"I can't do that. They are bought and paid for. I can't have the word get out that I don't deliver the flowers."

"No! I don't want them!" Sally heard the fear in her voice. "I won't accept anything from him."

Charlie scratched her head. "I'll leave them on the doorstep. Chuck them in the trash if you like, although it's a pity. They are such a perfect deep red."

Sally backed away some more, shaking her head, her mouth and throat scratchy. There was a rustling sound and the florist walked away, got in her van, and drove off, no doubt wondering why Sally didn't want the beautiful flowers. And Sally knew they were beautiful because a month ago he had sent Sally the same dozen red roses with a card. The car had only two words on it. His name.

Richard Foster.

Serial killer. Pedophile and rapist.

A shudder ran up her spine and the outrage burst from her lips: "How do you know my address, you bastard?"

Sally clenched her fists, her feet glued to the spot. Foster wanted her attention. He would not get his way. She would leave the bouquet on her doorstep. She imagined the afternoon sun wilting them. Tomorrow, when they were dead, she would wear kitchen gloves and throw them in the trash. But even the thought of touching his gift made her nauseous. They were from *him*! That evil man had been trying to get her attention ever since he was incarcerated at Franklin's maximum security prison, the Walla Walla State Penitentiary.

Sally's eyes traveled to her purse. She took a step. Then another. Opening the purse, she took out her phone. Her hand trembled as she found Margie's contact details.

"Hey, there," Margie said. "Are we still on for dinner?"

"He's... It's..."

Sally sat in the armchair before she fell.

"Sally? Has he tried to contact you again?"

"Flowers. The same as last month."

"Oh my God," Margie said. "It's the tenth of July."

"Yes. He sent flowers on the tenth of May and the tenth of June too."

"And the tenth of May is the date you brought him down."

"I know." She swallowed. "I can't bear it."

"Foster's a sadistic psychopath and he's messing with your mind. Don't let him do it. You're stronger than him."

"Am I?"

"Sure you are. The question is how Foster managed to place an order for flowers from jail. I thought they couldn't purchase items online, and there is absolutely no way that he should be contacting you at home. What the hell are the prison guards doing? They're supposed to vet his visits, phone calls, everything, right?"

"Clarke's already spoken to the prison warden about it. They don't know how he's doing it."

"That's not good enough," Margie said. "Oh, honey, I can be with you in thirty minutes. We'll make another complaint. This time I'll come with you. I'll kick up one hell of a stink until they take action."

"No point, Margie."

"Did you keep his letters?"

"I burned them."

Margie sighed. Sally should have kept them as evidence, but she couldn't bear them to be in her house. She didn't even read them. She had seen Foster's name and the Walla Walla address on the back of the envelope and set fire to them.

"And where are the flowers now?"

"On the doorstep. I can't go near them."

"I'll deal with them when I get there. And do me a favor.

Don't burn the card. You know how it goes. We need to prove to Clarke that Richard Foster's harassing you."

Sally promised.

Feeling better for knowing that Margie was on her way, Sally went to the kitchen and gulped down some cold water, spilling some drops on the kitchen floor because her hand was trembling so much. Half an hour wasn't long to wait, but it felt like hours. Sally tried to distract herself. She turned on the TV and watched the news, but she didn't hear a word the newsreader said. She went to the kitchen and tried to think about what she would cook for Margie tonight. She stared into the refrigerator for so long it beeped a warning to shut the door. She looked at the half-drunk bottle of white wine, longing to forget what lay outside her door, then she decided drinking alcohol wasn't going to help because it would only make her more emotional. Sally returned to the living room, sat in the armchair, and stared at the front door. All she could think about was what was on the other side.

He was invading her world. Making her feel unsafe. He knew her address. He could get to her anytime he liked.

Don't let him get under your skin, she thought. *That way, he wins*. The truth was that he had already won. Revulsion and fear battled with her desperate need to know Foster's message. Just a signature? Or more? What was the evil man up to?

Sally stood so fast the room swayed and she almost lost her balance. All she had to do was open the front door, look down, read the card, shut the door. Simple. She didn't have to touch the flowers.

She had defeated him. Surely, she could do something as simple as looking at the note.

Sally turned the latch and pulled the door open. She squinted at the sunshine in her eyes, then she looked down. The deep red roses hadn't faded yet, their heads hadn't wilted, the petals and leaves hadn't become limp. It was as if they were as enduring and pervasive as Foster. The white card was poking out between the leaves of brown paper. Words and then a name. The name was Richard Foster. But this time there was a message:

I know what you want, and I can help you get it.

FIVE

Sally drank too much wine last night, despite her best intentions, and her head throbbed this morning as she got ready for work.

The flowers were gone from her doorstep, as was the note. Margie took both away, promising to trash the flowers but to keep the note in the hope they could convince the prison warden to do more to protect Sally from Foster's attempts to torment her. Or so Sally and Margie saw it, but as Sally hadn't actually read Foster's letters, it was more of an assumption that torment was Foster's intention. Margie had encouraged Sally to send an email of complaint to the warden with a JPEG of Foster's note as an attachment.

Sally sat in her car, about to leave for work, and bristled with fury. How dare that murdering psychopath assume he knew what she wanted! How dare he think that she would come running. He had tried to kill her, for God's sake!

Don't let him win. Sally took some deep breaths.

Carolyn left her house, dressed in a skirt suit, and headed for her RAV4, which was parked across the road. Foster had totally occupied Sally's mind since his flowers arrived, but upon seeing Carolyn, a rush of guilt swept over her. She hurriedly unclipped the seatbelt, opened the door of her Honda Civic and raised a hand to catch Carolyn's attention. Sally would suggest the private investigators and share their contact details.

Carolyn's phone rang and she answered. Sally got out of her car, then waited for Carolyn to end the call.

"Are you sure? He's not meant to be back until Saturday," Carolyn said to her caller as she unlocked the RAV4 and laid her purse and laptop bag on the passenger seat.

Sally wavered. Perhaps she should talk to Carolyn later? She decided to leave Carolyn to her phone conversation.

It was the sound Carolyn made that halted Sally in her tracks. A moan, long and low, as if she were in terrible pain. Carolyn had her back against the side of her car. All the color in her cheeks had faded.

"I can't believe it. The scheming bastard!" Carolyn sobbed. "What do I do?" A pause. "I don't know. Oh my God, I suspected, but now it's hideously real." The caller must have spoken because Carolyn nodded. "I think I can. But facing him? Oh God, I feel sick." More silence as Carolyn listened. "You did the right thing. Don't apologize, and you're right. I have to see it for myself." Carolyn was quiet as the caller talked. "Yes," she said, her voice fractured by gulping sobs. "I'll see you there."

Sally was caught in that awkward moment when, if she went to Carolyn to comfort her, Carolyn would know that she'd been listening to her phone call. At the same time, Sally couldn't bear to walk away from someone clearly so upset. Carolyn hadn't moved. Crying alone in the street.

Sally left her car and approached her neighbor. "Hi. Has something happened? Is there anything I can do?"

Carolyn's mascara was smudged and her nose ran down her upper lip. She shook her head, unable to speak. Sally took her in a hug and Carolyn's body jerked with each sob.

"I'm sorry I wasn't more helpful yesterday," Sally began, then Carolyn pulled away.

"I can't deal with this right now," Carolyn said. "Maybe tomorrow, okay?" She got into her car and rifled through her purse for a tissue.

"Are you okay to drive?"

"I have to be." Carolyn blew her nose. "Oh, this is for you." On the passenger seat was a book. "It's my apology for sounding like a looney yesterday." Carolyn held out the book for Sally to take.

Sally took it. *All the Light We Cannot See* by Anthony Doerr. "Thank you, but it's me who should apologize."

"Not at all. You were honest with me. It was refreshing. Sorry, I have to go," Carolyn said, and drove away.

The scene Sally had just witnessed bothered her. Perhaps a private investigator was no longer necessary. Sally may have heard wrong, but it sounded as if Carolyn had found out something unpleasant about Matt, perhaps proof of the affair? To suspect it was distressing enough, but to know for sure, was devastating.

———

Sally left work early and drove to Franklin Airport. Paul's flight from Tampa was landing at 4:20 p.m. and she couldn't wait to see her son. Having parked in the multistory parking lot, she headed for the domestic terminal.

Her phone rang. It was her cousin, David.

"Hey, David! Thanks so much for having Paul to stay. I hope he wasn't any trouble."

"He's a fine boy and an excellent sailor. He's welcome to stay anytime, as are you, Sally. We'd love to see you." Over the airport's intercom a flight boarding announcement drowned out

David's voice. He stayed quiet until the announcement was finished. "I guess you're about to pick him up?"

"That's right."

"I don't want you to worry, but I thought you should know that Paul and Harry got into a fight." Harry was David's seventeen-year-old.

Not again, she thought.

Last semester, Paul had punched a boy his age in the gut because he had called Paul a mommy's boy. Paul had had to apologize to the boy and was warned by the school principal that if he did it again, he might be expelled. The principal also suggested that Paul see a child psychologist to deal with his anger issues. At the time he was already seeing one because of what happened to him at a safe house that turned out not to be safe at all. The sessions with Dr. Kaur had ended in June when the psychologist had suggested that Paul was doing so well that he might only need ad hoc visits.

David continued, "The boys wouldn't tell me what it was about. One minute Paul was with Harry taking down the sail, the next, Paul had Harry on the deck and was punching the bejesus out of him."

"Oh, David, I'm so sorry. Is Harry okay?"

"A few bruises. Nothing to worry about. I thought you should know, that's all."

"It's been a difficult few years for him."

"I hope you don't have a problem with me saying this, but he gets real angry when anyone mentions Scott."

"Scott was a cruel father. Paul carries a lot of emotional baggage as a result."

"I'm not criticizing. He's a good kid, but he's built like a bulldozer. You get my meaning?"

"I do. I'll talk to him."

Sally sat on a bench outside the arrivals hall, where a

smoker wandered up and down, a cigarette in one hand and his phone in the other.

In May last year, Aiden Foster had tried to kill Paul. Paul had proven remarkably resilient afterward, seemingly bouncing back and basking in his brief moment of fame at school when all the kids wanted to know about his encounter with a serial killer. Then Paul's football coach noticed that Paul was behaving aggressively toward his teammates. If Paul got into another fight, he'd risk losing his coveted place as linebacker for the Pioneer Panthers, the high school's football team.

Sally sighed, knowing that she would have to broach the subject of his fight with Harry at some point, but she didn't want to do it straight away. She just wanted to enjoy having her son back home.

Sally entered the arrivals hall. The flight information board confirmed that the American Airlines flight from Tampa International Airport was on time and the passengers would disembark in Hall A. She checked her watch—twenty minutes until the plane touched down. Thirsty, she stopped at a vending machine and bought a bottle of sparkling water. Taking a few sips, she watched people coming and going. A flash of long blonde hair and a familiar blue blazer caught her eye. What was Carolyn doing at the airport? Today was Wednesday. Hadn't Carolyn said that Matt would return from the convention on Saturday?

Carolyn wasn't alone. She had three women with her.

A petite Asian woman, her hair in a braid, wore baggy cheesecloth pants and had her arm looped through Carolyn's. Trailing slightly behind them was a tall dark-haired woman in a tan leather jacket. Walking next to her was an expensively dressed woman with flawless skin that had a plastic quality to it and fair hair styled in perfect waves that only curling tongs and masses of hairspray could produce—she reminded Sally of a fashion store's mannequin because she was too perfect to be real. Sally had seen these women come and go from Carolyn's house.

The four women were on a mission and strode past Sally without noticing her. Carolyn's face was puffy and blotchy—she'd been crying. This had to be related to the phone call Carolyn received earlier, and the three women were with her for emotional support. When they had met up at the bookstore yesterday, Carolyn said that she didn't have friends she could trust. Was that a lie to persuade Sally to investigate her husband or were these women the closest Carolyn had to a friendship group?

The arrivals hall funneled disembarking passengers through a narrow space lined by steel railings. Friends and family had to wait in the hall for the passengers to walk through some sliding doors and follow the narrow walkway to the hall, as if they were cattle being corralled. The hall was crowded, but Sally was tall —five feet eight inches—which meant she could see around most people's heads.

The four women huddled together in a conspiratorial manner. Carolyn's shoulders and back were slumped as if she carried the weight of the world. The tall dark-haired friend, who was almost six feet in height, appeared to be telling Carolyn what to do, carving the air aggressively with her hand as if to emphasize a point. Whatever they were discussing, it was upsetting Carolyn, who pulled a tissue from her clutch purse and dabbed her eyes.

Carolyn's petite friend cried too, then dashed into the ladies' bathroom. Then Carolyn positioned herself so that she was at the front of the arrivals hall but partly hidden by a big man who stood alone and was clearly a stranger since Carolyn and the man didn't exchange greetings.

The two remaining women had separated. The mannequin-woman pushed her way through the crowds, then stopped at the point where the railings ended. The tall friend remained stationary. From her position, she was most likely to spot a disembarking passenger when they first appeared through the frosted sliding doors. It felt to Sally like the women were laying a trap, although one of them had fled to the bathroom.

Sally checked her watch. Nine minutes before Paul disembarked.

Carolyn peaked out from behind the man she was hiding behind. When Matt walked through the sliding doors, Carolyn went white. Accompanying Matt was a man Sally recognized as mannequin woman's husband. A glance at the mannequin and Sally was in no doubt that she was angry with him—her lips were pressed together tightly and her eyes flashed.

Matt and his friend were chatting and unaware of the scene unfolding around them. It was obvious that Matt hadn't expected to be met by Carolyn because he didn't search the crowd. The men were almost upon Carolyn, who stood stock still as if afraid to show herself. Out of the corner of Sally's eye, she noticed a girl make a beeline for Matt. She looked to be in her late teens with straight blonde hair except for the tips, which were dyed lily pink. She wore faded and distressed denim shorts, a sleeveless top, and large hoop earrings. Her long tanned legs ended in strappy flat shoes, the ties of which criss-crossed up her lower leg, all of which gave her a sixties hippie look. Her eyes were locked on Matt, and she raised a tattooed arm and waved at him.

Sally felt a plunging sensation in her stomach. Was this Matt's supposed lover?

"Oh no," Sally said.

Matt's wife and his lover were at the airport at the same time? This had to be bad. Sally was watching people's lives unravel and it made her feel queasy.

Just then, Carolyn stepped out from behind the man she'd used as a screen and locked her sights onto Matt like a missile. Matt's head was turned to face his pal and so he didn't see

Carolyn until he almost collided with her. He jolted to a stop and stared at his wife as if she were a ghost.

It was like time froze around Carolyn and Matt. Disembarking passengers flowed around them while the couple didn't move or speak.

Matt's buddy kept walking, unaware that Matt had stopped. When he looked behind him, he also looked shocked. He muttered something. The mannequin stormed up to her husband and slapped him across the cheek so hard the *smack* reached Sally, and several people turned their heads and stared.

"What the hell, Nicole!" he said.

"Fuck you, Lachlan, you devious shit! You knew he was meeting Daisy. How could you do that!"

"What is wrong with you?" Lachlan said, rubbing his cheek.

"You're coming with me."

Nicole took hold of Lachlan's wrist, which he yanked free. "What about Matt?"

"Leave Matt to Carolyn."

Lachlan finally appeared to understand what was going on. "Oh fuck!" Glancing back at Matt for a second, then at Daisy, he followed Nicole out of the airport without further argument.

"Hey, babe!" Matt said, smiling at his wife as if there were nothing strange about their meeting.

He tried to kiss Carolyn on her lips, but she pushed him away.

"How could you lie to me like that! She's here." Carolyn swung her arm around and pointed at the girl who had waved at him. "I know all about your sordid little plan."

"Come on, babe. We left the convention early. So what?"

"Don't you dare! I know about the affair. And I know you're trying to poison me, you bastard!"

Matt shook his head vehemently. "What?" He noticed the crowd of onlookers. "We can't talk here. Let's go home. We can sort it all out, I promise. I love you."

Daisy spun on her heels and stomped away, her hips sway-ing, the overnight bag over her shoulder bumping. Sally was relieved, at the very least, that Carolyn hadn't had to confront Daisy as well.

Transfixed by the sad scene before her, Sally almost missed the public announcement that the flight from Tampa was disembarking. By the time the announcement finished, Carolyn and Matt were heading for the exit in awkward silence. The girlfriend who had dashed to the bathrooms hadn't reappeared and the tall woman in the tan jacket had walked away, shaking her head in obvious disapproval.

Paul was one of the first to come through the double doors, dragging his wheeled suitcase behind him.

"Mom!" he yelled, waving.

———

That evening, Sally was on the rooftop terrace barbequing steak kebabs and enjoying her son's company as he told her about his sailing adventure in Tampa Bay. He watched her as she turned the kebabs over, drinking from a can of Coke, while Sally sipped at a glass of red wine.

"The dolphins followed us for miles."

He loved his vacation so much that he was already asking her when he could do it again. Until this holiday, Paul hadn't shown much interest in sailing, but now it was all he could talk about. And the sea life too.

"I remember doing a summer camp job when I was seven-teen in Tampa Bay," Sally said. "On my day off, I'd snorkel and swim and go shelling." She smiled at the happy memory.

"I made something for you and Zelda." He put his hand in his shorts pocket and pulled out two necklaces, both on leather strings with a colorful tulip shell per necklace. One shell had rings of yellow, orange, and gray. The other shell was pinkish-gray, cream, and black. "I found them when we sailed to this amazing island, which has the best shells, and then I made the necklaces. Don't worry, they were dead shells."

"They're lovely." She kissed him on the cheek. "Thank you. Are you talking about Anclote Island?"

"Yeah. How did you know?"

"I've been there. It's beautiful." She was touched that Paul had gone to the trouble of making them necklaces, especially for his sister. The other kids would have probably found that weird. "I won't get to visit Zelda today, but we could take her necklace tomorrow. What do you think?"

"Sure."

Sally was loath to ruin his good mood, but she couldn't ignore David's phone call. Holding her shell necklace in her hand, she ran a finger over the shell's ridges.

"And what do you think of Harry?" she asked.

Paul gave her a suspicious look. "He's okay, why?"

"I hear you had a bit of a fight with him."

"Ah, David's been on the phone to you. It was nothing, Mom, just messing around."

"What was the fight about?"

"Nothing."

"It has to be something."

"There's nothing to talk about, Mom. Seriously. We threw a few punches, that was all."

Paul really was a master of avoiding answering questions. Sally hazarded a guess. "Did he laugh at you?"

Paul didn't look her in the eye. "I messed up when we were sailing. The boat almost capsized, but I righted it in time. He just wouldn't shut up about it. So, I hit him. It wasn't hard."

Sally didn't want him to follow in his father's footsteps. Scott's method of policing had been about using brute force, although Scott always had an explanation as to why the arrested person had bruises.

"It's more powerful if you just walk away. You know that, Paul. You're a big strong boy. One day you could hurt someone badly. Brute force is never the way to resolve issues."

Paul sighed. "Yes, Mom, got the message. Can we get on with dinner now? I'm starving."

Sally hesitated for another moment and then sighed. "Fine. Can you take the garlic bread out of the oven, and bring it up here?"

"Yep," Paul said, finishing the last sip of his Coke and hopping down the stairs.

It was a hot June night and she, and her neighbors, had their windows wide open to let the breeze into their homes. Carolyn and Matt had argued for over two hours, but now the house was quiet. Sally knew they were there—she would have heard one or both of them leaving.

The kebabs were almost ready and the rich meaty smells made Sally's stomach rumble. She had threaded pieces of sirloin beef, mushrooms, onions, and peppers onto skewers, and when they were just cooked enough, she had poured hot garlic butter over them.

The evening breeze carried Carolyn's weary voice across the roof terraces. Sally looked through the glass fence separating her terrace from theirs. They were just visible in the room adjoining the terrace, which they used as their master bedroom. Sally's bedroom was down a level, near the bathroom.

"Carolyn, please! Give me another chance," Matt pleaded.

"Why should I? We've only been married six months and you're already screwing around."

"I've told you, babe, it was a mistake. It meant nothing. I'll tell her it's over, okay?"

"How can I trust you? You lied. You even involved Lachlan in your plans. How could you!" Carolyn shrieked.

It made Sally's skin prickle.

"I've been a fool—"

"You don't love me, do you?"

"Sure I do. Of course I do."

"How can you say that when you planned to spend three days with Daisy in a cabin in Little Harbor, all the time telling me you were in Las Vegas!"

"It was her idea."

"Was it *her* idea to poison me or did you concoct that together?"

"Honey, nobody is poisoning you. I had a fling. It was wrong. I'll end it tonight. But I'd never, ever hurt you."

"You *have* hurt me, Matt! I loved you so much and you betrayed that love. You're making me ill. You're doing it to kill me!"

"This is your bipolar talking."

"Don't you dare do that. You don't get to blame my mental illness! No way. I'm getting weaker and more confused each day. I want you to leave. Go stay with Lachlan."

A whooshing sound of a sliding door and Carolyn stepped out onto the roof terrace. She was closely followed by her husband. Carolyn sat heavily on their outdoor couch and burst into tears. Matt saw Sally watching them.

"What are you looking at?" Matt said, his eyes angry.

Sally didn't want to get embroiled in their argument. She turned her head and concentrated on turning the kebabs.

Paul stepped out onto the terrace with oven mitts on his hands, carrying hot garlic bread in a baking tray. "Hey, Matt!" he said cheerfully.

Matt glared at Paul then left the terrace, leaving Carolyn alone, crying. Paul looked at Sally and mouthed, "What's going on?"

Sally hadn't told Paul about the strange scene she'd witnessed at the airport or about Carolyn's request for help. If Sally was honest with herself, she felt ashamed that she hadn't agreed to help her neighbor.

"Pop the garlic bread on the mat next to the salad," Sally directed Paul, nodding at the coffee table where she'd placed a heatproof mat. "Then can you give me a moment?"

Paul glanced at Carolyn weeping, then he did as he was asked. When he had gone, Sally put down the BBQ tongs and went over to the glass partition.

"Carolyn, is there anything I can do?"

Carolyn sniffed back a tear. She shifted her position on the couch so that she could see Sally more easily. "I don't know what to do. I feel crushed, but I still love him." She shook her head. "I'm pathetic."

"No, you are not pathetic. And I'm sorry I haven't been helpful."

"Maybe Matt's right. I could just feel sick because of what he's done. My stomach's been churning for days."

Sally glanced at the sliding glass doors. They were shut but how much could Matt hear of their conversation. She didn't want to inflame the situation, but at the same time she wanted to be supportive. "If you suspect you are in danger, you must get out of there."

"I'm not leaving. He can go."

The glass doors flew open and Matt glared at Sally. "This is a private matter, so why don't you mind your own business?" he demanded. His voice was cold.

SIX

JULY 14, 2016

Sally was in her running gear and her sweaty tank tap clung to her skin. She and Margie had completed their ten-mile forest-trail run and they were on the final one hundred yards back to Sally's house. Paul was still asleep, and Sally wasn't due at the bookstore until 10 a.m., so she had plenty of time to make him breakfast. Paul was old enough and sensible enough to make his way by bicycle to Reilly's house, where Paul was going to spend the day.

Carolyn's distress had played on Sally's mind throughout the run.

It was 7:30 a.m. when Sally reached home. She was stretching out her calf muscles as Matt left his house. If he noticed Sally, he didn't let on. He got in the RAV4 and drove away. Was Carolyn inside or had she gone to stay with a friend? Sally finished her stretching exercises, and when she was certain that Matt had gone, Sally knocked on Carolyn's door.

No answer. She waited.

A deep sense of unease had her staring up at the windows. The drapes were drawn. Carolyn usually left for work around this time. She usually drove the SUV, dropping Matt off at his pharmacy, then driving to the corporate park where the company she worked for was located. Sally tried the doorbell again, keeping her finger on it a little longer.

Again, no answer. Nobody called out.

She took her phone from its pouch on her arm and sent a brief text message to Carolyn:

> *Good morning. I just wanted to check in to see how you are. I rang your doorbell but there was no answer. Please let me know you're okay.*

If Carolyn was in the house, was she resting after her traumatic day yesterday or... was she sick?

Sally continued to feel ill at ease as she showered and then made Paul pancakes, bacon, and syrup for breakfast. Carolyn still hadn't answered Sally's text message. By the time she arrived at the bookstore, a sense of foreboding hung heavily over her. Olivia noticed Sally was distracted, and when Sally told her that she was concerned about a neighbor who was in a bad way, Olivia suggested Sally pop around to Carolyn's place on her lunch break.

This Sally did.

Sally walked up the path and had her finger hovering just off the doorbell when the door suddenly opened.

Carolyn was in a thin cotton mini-length nightie that was almost transparent. Her feet were bare. Her hair was messy, and her eyelids were only open a few millimeters as if she was drugged. Carolyn stepped outside and passed by Sally as if she wasn't there. She stumbled on a paving stone and Sally instinctively reached out to catch her. The woman's skin felt strangely cool.

"Leave me alone!" Carolyn slurred, like she was drunk.

"Carolyn, it's Sally. I think we should get you inside."

"Tired." Carolyn swayed again and leaned heavily on Sally.

Sally suspected that Carolyn had taken an overdose. She needed medical assistance. If Sally could get Carolyn inside, she could dial 911—she couldn't leave her out on the street.

Across the road was a three-story apartment block. A big-bellied gardener employed to maintain the lawns and hedges was mowing the grass at the front of the block. Sally found him creepy: he spoke only to women, especially attractive ones, and his eyes wandered over their bodies. He stopped what he was doing, although he left the mower's engine running, and stared at Carolyn, no doubt finding her semi-transparent nightie fascinating. He didn't, however, offer to help Sally, who was struggling to hold Carolyn upright.

"Can you help us? Call 911. We need an ambulance."

The caretaker turned his back and continued to mow. *What is wrong with people?* Sally thought.

"Don't!" Carolyn said, slapping weakly at Sally's hands. "I have to get out of here."

What in God's name had Carolyn taken? Or had Matt given her something?

Carolyn wriggled free of Sally's grasp and almost fell—she was shaking as if she were out in the snow in her nightie. But today was approaching eighty degrees Fahrenheit. Carolyn lurched between two parked cars. A truck delivering appliances was speeding toward her: he must have been doing fifty miles per hour in the thirty-miles-per-hour street.

"No!" Sally shouted and grabbed the hem of Carolyn's nightie, only just managing to clench a fist of cotton.

Sally succeeded in stopping Carolyn's forward momentum just in time. The delivery truck rumbled by with a gush of hot air and diesel fumes.

Carolyn's hair was blown back by the delivery truck. More aware of her surroundings, she turned to see what or who was restraining her.

"Sally?"

"Yes, it's me. Carolyn, you're in your nightie. Let's get you inside."

Sally put an arm around Carolyn's waist to steady her. Now that Carolyn wasn't fighting her, she managed to swivel around and steer her in the direction of her home. Carolyn's legs moved like a wooden puppet on strings.

"Where is he?" Carolyn swayed.

She assumed she meant her husband. "I think he's at work. I'll call him once we've got you indoors," Sally said.

"No! Keep him away from me. He's killing me!"

Sally's front door opened, and Paul stood there. He had his bicycle with him and a small backpack on his back. When he spotted his mom, he looked at her sheepishly.

Sally had asked him so many times not to bring the bicycle through the house, but yet again here he was, ignoring her request. The bicycles were kept in the shed in their backyard, and given their house was in mid-row, Paul had to exit through the yard's back gate, follow the narrow alleyway at the back of the houses, then turn right along another path to reach the road. Which is precisely why Paul took his bicycle through the house, leaving dirty tire marks on the rugs.

"Paul, Carolyn's sick. Call 911 and ask for an ambulance."

Paul hesitated, staring at the scantily dressed woman who was barely able to stand. "Now!" Sally said sharply.

He leaned his bicycle against the wall, then took his phone from his pocket and dialed. "What do I say?" he asked.

"An overdose or poison."

"Shit!"

Paul spoke to the 911 operator as Sally focused on getting Carolyn into her house. The layout of each townhouse was similar, but the décor was different. Carolyn had pale gray stone floors, pale wood furniture, and collages on the walls made of driftwood and shells. The two couches were white leather and

Carolyn collapsed onto the nearest one. "So sleepy," Carolyn said as she lifted her legs and lay down.

"Carolyn, stay awake. Can you tell me what you've taken?" Sally had ruled out alcohol. The woman's breath was stale, even bitter, but it didn't smell of alcohol.

Carolyn waved her floppy hand. "Matt tells me what to take," she blurted. "Killing me."

"What did Matt give you?"

"Don't know. What day is it?"

Paul ran into the room, his phone near his ear. "Mom, they want to know what she's taken."

"I don't know," Sally replied. "Just give them the address and ask them to get here as soon as possible. She's going to sleep."

Paul relayed the message.

Carolyn's eyes were closed. "Oh no!" Sally tugged at Carolyn's arm and pulled her upright, but Carolyn flopped forward like a ragdoll. "Wake up!" she said. "Carolyn!"

"They said they're on their way and to keep her conscious. And it would really help to know if she's taken drugs," Paul said.

Sweat dripped down Sally's hairline with the effort of keeping Carolyn upright. "Go to their bathroom. Open the cabinet. Look in the drawers. Bring all the medication down here."

"I can't snoop like that," Paul protested.

"Paul, you have to. This could be a matter of life or death."

"Oh-kay but I don't like it." Paul ran up the stairs.

Carolyn had fallen asleep. "Carolyn? Wake up?"

She hated doing it, but she gave the woman a couple of pats on the cheek.

Carolyn groaned and half-opened her eyes.

Just then, the sound of footsteps reached Sally and Matt walked in. Taking in the scene before him, he stormed over to where Sally was kneeling beside Carolyn. "What the hell are you doing?" He looked at his wife. "Christ! What have you done?"

"We called an ambulance. What did you give her?"

"Fuck you. Now, get out of my house!"

His aggression stunned Sally for a second.

Paul raced down the stairs with his backpack slung over one arm. "I got all the medication." When he saw Matt, he paused on the stairs. "Oh," he muttered.

"What the hell is going on?" Matt grabbed Paul's bag and ripped it from him. He looked inside, then held out the open backpack for Sally to see. It contained boxes of medication. "How dare you!"

"Hey!" Paul said. "The operator wanted to know what she's taken."

"Get the fuck out of my house. You're both out of your minds."

"I'm not leaving her. We must keep her conscious. Talk to her!" Sally yelled.

SEVEN

Carolyn was rushed away in the ambulance, with her husband at her side. Sally had wanted to go with them, but Matt refused, so she drove to the hospital and waited for news in the busy ER waiting room.

"Please let her be okay," Sally mumbled.

Sally was seated on a plastic chair between a child with a deep cut on his hand and a woman clutching her abdomen. She had chosen a seat facing the two busy receptionists, one of whom was getting a hard time from a man clutching his arm and demanding that he be seen immediately. The receptionist— a woman in her thirties who was doing her best to hide her mounting irritation—asked the man to take a seat because there were several emergencies before him and his broken arm would be seen to as soon as possible.

Sally was going to be late for work, so she called Olivia at the bookstore.

"I'm at the hospital. I may be here awhile. I'm sorry to let you down."

"Take all the time you need and keep me posted," Olivia said.

Sally then used her time to think through everything that had happened.

At the airport, Carolyn had appeared upset but hadn't shown any obvious signs of illness. Last night, Carolyn argued with Matt on the roof terrace. She was lucid. She wanted him to give her space. He had refused to leave. Sally assumed they both spent the night in the house because the RAV4 was still there in the morning. Today, Carolyn was totally different again. She couldn't stay upright without Sally's support. She was also confused and unaware that she was walking into the path of a moving truck. She had lapsed into and out of consciousness. Carolyn's decline had happened so fast. Sally didn't know enough about bipolar disorder to know if her symptoms might be linked to the mental illness. How had she gotten so ill in such a short time?

Sally frowned when she thought about Matt. From what she had overheard of his conversation with Carolyn last night, it sounded as if he thought he could simply brush his infidelity under the carpet and everything would go back to normal. Who was he kidding! Of course, he had denied that he was poisoning her, but today he'd been more concerned about getting Sally and Paul out of the house than keeping his wife conscious.

The more she interacted with Matt, the more she was inclined to believe Carolyn. Matt might not be administering poison, but he might be deliberately overdosing her?

Sally ran her fingers though her hair. Her scalp prickled at the thought that her next-door neighbor might have caused his wife's illness.

Poison was usually administered through drink or food. At least that's how cop shows on TV portrayed it. As she sat pondering this, Sally suddenly realized that if Matt was poisoning her and he wanted her dead, he wouldn't assist the doctors as they tried to fathom what was ailing Carolyn.

Sally went straight to the reception counter. Both receptionists were busy with patients. How long did poison take to kill a person? Sally guessed it all depended on which poison. Sally tapped a foot impatiently. The man nursing a broken arm was shouting at a receptionist and a security guard had been called. The other receptionist was doing her best to communicate with a woman who didn't speak English and was on the phone asking for a Bangladeshi translator.

The security guard was doing his best to move the man away from the receptionist. Sally's patience was gone.

"Excuse me!" Sally called out. "Carolyn Tate. I think she could have been poisoned. Can you let the nurses know?"

"Please wait your turn," the receptionist said.

Sally moved as close as she dared. The aggressive man shoved the security guard.

"She was in an ambulance. I think she's been poisoned. The doctors should know."

At last she had the receptionist's attention. "You family?"

"No, I'm... a friend. She told me her husband was poisoning her."

"Did she say what poison?"

"No, but she thinks the man who is with her did it."

The receptionist screwed up her eyes as if she wasn't sure if she should believe Sally. Sally said, "I used to be a cop. I think Carolyn may be in danger. At least tell the doctor. Please."

"Okay." She pointed at the door leading to ER. "Bed three. Through there. Find a nurse and tell her what you know."

"Thank you."

Through the door were rows and rows of cubicles divided by curtains. In the middle was an oval-shaped nurses station with computers and monitors. It was noisy and hectic. Patients screaming. Beepers sounding. Machines ticking. Nurses and doctors calling out, issuing instructions. The cubicles didn't have obvious numbers to guide her so she approached the third cubicle in from the door she'd been through. The curtain separating the cubicle from the nurses station was drawn back and the bed was empty. Sally's heart missed a beat. Where was Carolyn?

"Can I help you?" a nurse asked.

"Carolyn Tate?"

"I'll have to check." She darted through the gap between the two semicircular counters, tapped a keyboard, then stood up and pointed.

"Are you caring for her?" Sally asked. "I think she may have been poisoned."

"What with?"

"I don't know."

The nurse's beeper went off. A doctor, an Indian woman in a white coat, swept back a cubicle curtain, her beeper also sounding. The nurse dashed out from behind the counter and raced to the cubicle she had been pointing at. The doctor jogged into the next cubicle too. Sally watched as Matt stood helplessly to one side. Two nurses were already in there. Matt attempted to speak to the doctor. She asked him to leave.

Sally felt her legs grow wobbly. She leaned with her back to the nurses station. The machine monitoring Carolyn's heart rate and other signs had flatlined. A nurse cut the top of Carolyn's nightie to gain access to her chest. Sally felt as if she had been punched in the gut. She couldn't get enough breath.

"Please don't die! Don't give up!" Sally said to herself.

A nurse steered Matt out of the cubicle and asked him to let them do their job. He didn't see Sally, who was standing too far behind him to notice, but Sally caught a glimpse of his face. The fierce eyes and the clenched jaw were replaced by the haggard look of a man about to lose everything.

The doctor held up the two pads of an electric cardioversion. "Clear."

Carolyn's heart must have stopped. *Don't give up, Carolyn! Come back to us. Please!*

The doctor placed electric cardioversion pads on Carolyn's bare chest. There was a whine from the machine, then a boom and Carolyn's body bounced. It was so unnatural. So brutal.

It was as if Sally were watching the scene in slow motion. The heart monitor didn't change. No beeping. The lines were flat. The doctor used the electric cardioversion again. Carolyn's whole body jumped higher off the bed. The doctor shook her head.

Matt yelled, "Do something! Save her!"

"Time of death 11:19 a.m." The doctor turned to look at Matt. "I'm so sorry. We did everything we could."

"No! Try again!" Matt shouted.

"She's gone, Mr. Tate. I'm sorry."

Sally couldn't breathe. Carolyn couldn't be dead. She was okay yesterday.

Her lungs ached for oxygen, forcing Sally to part her lips and exhale. She staggered backward. She watched as the machines around Carolyn were switched off. The beeping and humming stopped. Carolyn lay still, unnaturally so, her hair splayed out like a mermaid in water. Matt had Paul's backpack slung over his shoulder. It had contained the medication in their bathroom cabinet.

"Mr. Tate, we can give you some time with her, then she'll be moved to the morgue."

Matt stared at the doctor, then at his wife covered in a white sheet. "I have to get out of here." He turned on his heels and fled, taking the backpack with him.

Sally's stomach roiled. She took a few breaths to try to control the nausea, but it didn't work.

Oh no, I'm going to spew.

She didn't make it to a bathroom in time. Stinging vomit shot up her throat and poured out of her and onto the floor. Her nose stung and her eyes watered. Using a tissue, she wiped her mouth and nose, but the stench of vomit filled her nostrils. Sally glanced at Carolyn's motionless body on the gurney with a solitary nurse with her. She had died at the age of twenty-seven, far from her family in England, believing her husband wanted to kill her. The only person present in her last moments was the very person Carolyn believed had poisoned her. A sob slipped from Sally's lips. If only she had taken Carolyn's fears seriously when they'd met two days ago, might the poor woman be alive?

"Why didn't I try?" Sally said aloud.

"Are you okay?" asked the nurse who had been attending to Carolyn.

Sally nodded. "I'm sorry about the mess. It's just... such a shock."

"I'll see to it. There's a chair over there. Take a seat."

"What happened? Why did Carolyn die?"

"Her heart gave out, but we don't know why. There'll be an autopsy. Do you need to sit down?"

"No," Sally said, partly talking to herself. "I need to know who killed her."

EIGHT

Sally drove into the city on autopilot, impelled by a desire to correct her mistake. To seek justice for Carolyn Tate.

The shock of Carolyn's death had hit Sally like a tidal wave and Sally still felt as if she were underwater, being churned around and around by the wave's force. How she managed to get to Franklin City's police station, where homicide was based, she had no idea. She didn't remember which route she took. The only thing she did remember was to call Paul.

"Is Carolyn okay?" Paul asked.

There was a whoop and a loud splash in the background. Sally had encouraged Paul to continue with his plan to spend the afternoon with Reilly—his parents had a swimming pool. It was good to hear the boys having fun. Their joy helped lift Sally's spirits a little, after Carolyn's death just twenty minutes ago.

"Paul, Carolyn died. They did all they could to save her." More splashing. In the distance, Reilly was asking Paul if he wanted ice cream. Paul was uncharacteristically silent. "Paul? Are you okay?"

"But she can't have. She was talking. Why didn't they do something?"

"It happened so fast. Her heart gave up."

Sally squeezed her lids together for a second, to rid her eyes of the tears welling up. When she opened them, she saw a fire hydrant, pedestrians. Her car jolted as it mounted the sidewalk. The car jumped. She yanked the steering wheel to the left and just managed to avoid colliding with the fire hydrant. *Bump!* The car was back on the road. Her face flushed red, the adrenaline racing through her. She had very nearly crashed her car. She had to concentrate.

"You handled the emergency so well, Paul. I'm so proud of you."

Paul was silent. When he was upset he would either lash out and punch things or he'd become silent. "Do you want me to take you home? It's a big shock for all of us and sometimes we need time to simply absorb what's happened."

"I'll spend the day here messing around." He wanted distraction. *Fair enough*, Sally thought. "Was she poisoned, like you thought?" Paul asked, his voice stronger.

In the background, Reilly yelled, "Chocolate chip or berry swirl?"

"Nothing for me," Paul yelled back.

"We don't know," Sally answered. "There'll be an autopsy, then we'll know. Can you keep the poisoning theory to yourself? Just for now. I'd rather this didn't become public knowledge."

"I already told Reilly."

Sally grimaced. It would be on Reilly's social media by now.

It was lunchtime and she knew where to find Detective Freddie Clarke. Clarke was a man of routine. For the six years that he had been lead detective on the homicide squad, he always bought his breakfast from Julie's Diner and his lunch from Wong's Noodles, which was renowned for its hand-pulled noodles in a variety of delicious sauces. At the end of the day, unless a case interfered with his plans, he would go straight to a gym down the road, where he'd work out for an hour.

Wong's Noodles was located in the subterranean level of Franklin's railway station, which had been built in the 1930s. The station was known for its domed glass roof above the railway tracks and for the tunnels and subterranean archways where you could find diners, cafés, a grocery store, and an old-fashioned shoeshine.

Seated at a side table in Wong's Noodles, Clarke had a napkin tucked into the neck of his perfectly ironed collared shirt. He was using chopsticks to deftly shovel the long and wide strands of noodle, coated in a meaty sauce, into his mouth. He saw Sally approach and raised a blonde eyebrow. She hadn't warned him that she was coming.

Their relationship had grown a little tense after Clarke had stuck his neck out for her and investigated her claims that her ex-husband sexually assaulted Stacy Green. Clarke became deeply unpopular as a result because Scott had always been a well-liked and respected cop. There was an unwritten code at Franklin PD: nobody turned on another cop. And Clarke did exactly that. He had believed Sally when she said there was a diary, and that in it, Stacy had incriminated Scott. The diary, however, was never found, and Clarke had to close the investigation, having alienated himself from many of his colleagues.

Was that why Clarke always ate his lunch alone?

Clarke took a second napkin from a dispenser and wiped some sauce from the side of his mouth. Then he gestured for her to sit opposite him.

"To what do I owe the pleasure, Sally?" Clarke asked, with a hint of sarcasm.

Clarke's head of thick blonde hair and light blue eyes gave him a Scandinavian appearance, but his mother was Dutch.

"I'd like your help with a suspicious death," Sally replied.

"Is it official? The suspicious death, I mean?"

"Not yet. The person has only just passed away. I came straight here."

"Oh-kay. You know I only investigate suspicious deaths. There's a process we work through."

"I know."

"Did you call the police? Is there a crime scene?"

"Um, no and no. But the victim was convinced her husband was poisoning her."

Clarke rolled his eyes. "Do you do this on purpose? Because last time I did you a favor, it backfired on me in a big way."

Where should Sally start? Perhaps now was not the best time to convince Clarke that he should investigate Carolyn's death. Hunting him down to the one place he could get some peace had been a dumb idea. She stood.

"I'm happy to see you at the station."

"Nah, stay. You're here now. You hungry?"

"Not after what I've just witnessed, no. Looks good, though." Sally plonked herself down on the chair.

"The best." Clarke picked up the black plastic bowl and placed it close to his lips. He used the chopsticks to sweep the last of the noodles and meaty sauce into his mouth. When he'd cleared the bowl, he put it down and then, once again, wiped his mouth with a napkin. "Okay, shoot."

"My neighbor just died in ER of heart failure. I think she may have been poisoned or given a drug overdose by her husband, who's a pharmacist."

Clarke took the napkin out of his shirt collar, scrunched it up, and dropped it into the empty bowl. His tie was still tucked inside his shirt. "That's a big accusation, Sally. You want to tell me why you think this man killed his wife?"

Sally's cheeks went as red as the chili sauce bottle on the table. She took a deep breath and told Clarke everything she knew about the events leading up to Carolyn's suspicious death, including Carolyn's conviction that her husband was poisoning her.

"Watching someone you know die is distressing," Clarke said. "It can mess with your head. And you've been through a lot recently." He was referring to Foster's attempt on her life and her inability to prove that Scott was a rapist and a pedophile. "Maybe you're assuming the worst when there could be a simple medical reason for what happened."

"My instinct tells me her death isn't natural or even accidental." A few years ago, she would never have had the courage to back her instincts like this, but having had the mental strength to outwit Foster and send him to jail, Sally was learning to trust herself. "She was afraid. I'll never forget her fear in her eyes. Matt's behavior was suspicious. He didn't want her taken to hospital. He tried to cancel the ambulance. Please, Detective, can you just look at the autopsy report when it's ready?"

Clarke finished his soda.

"Sally, I got a lot of respect for you, you know that. But you haven't given me a good reason to break protocol. Everything you've told me is supposition. Do you have any idea how many homicides I have on my plate? And that doesn't even include the cold cases I don't have time to touch."

"I know you're really busy. All I'm asking is that you take a quick look at the autopsy."

He sighed. "Did Carolyn have any medical conditions that you know of?"

"She was bipolar and taking medication for it."

He nodded. "If she died at the hospital, why do you think the husband killed her and how did he do it?"

"Maybe Matt's problem was that Carolyn knew about his

affair? Until three days ago, Carolyn was a successful brand director, levelheaded and healthy. Okay, she was on bipolar medication, but I mean physically she looked great. This morning, she didn't know me. She walked into the path of a truck. She could barely walk straight or talk."

The more she told him what she knew, the flimsier her theory sounded, even to her own ears.

"Did you witness him administering an overdose or a suspicious substance?"

"No, how could I?"

"Did she have bruises on her body? Any sign that she was held down?"

"I didn't see any."

"Is it possible Carolyn took an overdose and her husband had nothing to do with it?"

"Yes, I suppose so but—"

Clarke held up a hand to stop her. "Trust in the system, Sally. If the autopsy reveals anything to suggest that her death was suspicious, my team will be called in. Until then, it's not my case."

"But if he poisoned her, he'll get rid of the evidence. By the time you're called in, it'll be too late."

"You're underestimating the power of forensic investigation. Plus, I have other priorities. A husband and wife shot dead in their home. A drive-by shooting." Clarke counted off his active cases on his fingers. "A woman found in a park, raped and her throat slit. Do I need to keep going?"

"No." Sally knew Clarke well enough to recognize that she was wasting her time.

He must have noticed her glum expression.

"Sally. If anyone else came to me with such a fanciful story, I'd have told them to get lost." Clarke stood. "Trust in the judicial system."

"How can I? Men like Scott are free to continue assaulting

girls, protected by other cops because cops don't tell on their peers. It's a boys club."

"Not everyone's a member," Clarke shot back. "If you have such little faith in us, why bother to come to me? I've given you my answer."

"I'm not a detective. I can't do this alone."

"You didn't think that when you blundered into Foster's lair. I told you then, as I'm telling you now, don't play detective. Have some patience and trust the process."

Sally tightened her jaw to stop herself saying anything that might alienate the detective. She had already said too much.

"See you around, Sally."

Clarke paid at the counter.

She left the restaurant, took the escalator up to the railway concourse, then out onto the street. Her whole body ached with tension. She had handled Clarke badly and now she had put his back up. She'd been foolish to see the detective so soon after watching Carolyn die. She'd let her emotions drive her words.

As she headed for the parking lot, she thought about the house next door and how Carolyn would never return there.

Sally burst into tears.

NINE

In 1992, when Sally shot a man dead in the line of duty, the police department was rife with gossip about the high-risk shot she took to save a child's life. She had been a beat cop for two years and had discharged her weapon on two separate instances without a fatality, until she and Anders Haugen were called to a home invasion. The intruder, a drug addict, held a revolver to a six-year-old girl's head while the mother was told to find a stash of drugs he clearly believed was in the house. It was an almost impossible shot because the intruder used the girl as a shield, kneeling behind her. Only his forehead and the top of his skull were visible. Haugen told her not to take the shot—it was more likely that she'd kill the child than the man with the knife. But the home invader was off his head on what transpired to be ice and he was counting down to the moment he'd fire his weapon at the child. Sally took the shot and the bullet hit the man between the eyes. After that, Sally was called One Shot by her fellow police officers as a mark of respect.

A year later, Sally left the police and joined the district attorney's office as a victim support advocate and she allowed her gun skills to dwindle. When she handed in her police-issue gun, she had no interest in getting a license to carry her own pistol. Killing the intruder had saved a child's life, but for a long time after Sally had nightmares. She relived the moment the blood splattered on the wall and the girl's face. She saw in graphic detail the huge hole in the back of his head and the fragments of bone and brain on the carpet.

Then, in 2010, Richard Foster and his son, Aiden, began kidnapping, raping, and murdering girls between the ages of eleven and thirteen. When the grandfather of one of their victims contacted Sally in 2015, she was dragged into the unsolved case and became a target—it was the first time the duo had targeted an adult. It had been her somewhat rusty shooting skills that had saved her life. After that, Sally had purchased a Glock 19 and a couple of boxes of ammunition and arranged for a gun safe to be installed in her bedroom. Once a week, she went to the shooting range to hone her skill, then the pistol went back in the gun safe. Never again would she face a killer without a gun. Never again would she allow someone to threaten her son, who had almost died at Aiden's hands. Paul was Sally's world. She loved him more than life itself.

Sally's trip to the shooting range today wasn't about keeping her aim accurate. It was about letting off steam. She had cried for Carolyn until her head ached and her eyes were sore. She had cursed Clarke for his refusal to get involved in the case and cursed herself for tackling their meeting so poorly. Spouting about her lack of faith in the criminal justice system had only served to alienate Clarke. Now what was she supposed to do? The autopsy would take a couple of days. More clear-cut homicides would be prioritized.

Still in her running gear from this morning, Sally drove home, showered, changed into a blouse and pants, took her pistol and a box of ammunition from the gun safe, and then headed over to the indoor shooting range.

"Olivia, it's Sally. I should be with you by two. Is that okay?"

"Of course it is. And if you need the rest of the day off, no problem."

Sally pulled up outside the indoor shooting range. She had already completed the safety agreement form and shown her picture ID, so the manager on the front desk merely greeted her and allocated her to position ten of sixteen public lanes for handgun-caliber firearms up to twenty-five yards.

"You using brass-cased and jacketed ammo?" the manager asked.

"As always. Is it busy?" Sally said.

"Nah, just three guys. Shouldn't be too noisy," the manager said.

She picked up safety glasses and ear protectors, then took the steps down to the basement. The range was solid concrete, with bullet-resistant multilayer dividers between each land and a shelf where shooters could place ammunition.

Positions two and three were taken by two guys in their early twenties who were shooting competitively, boasting about who would get the best score. As Sally walked behind them, she noticed a water bottle. One of the men drank from it, then handed it to the other with a "Cheers!" Naturally, drinking alcohol was prohibited, and anyone suspected of taking drugs or alcohol was not permitted onto the range, but Sally had a hunch there was more than water in the bottle. Position fifteen was taken by a retired guy with a handlebar moustache who Sally recognized and they exchanged nods. Sally was glad he was there. If the two young men got rowdy, she knew the retired guy would keep them in line.

Sally put on her eye and ear protectors and loaded the magazine into her Glock 19. She took up a comfortable shooting stance and tried to shut down her overly busy mind. She thought she heard the whine and then the deafening boom of the electric cardioversion shocking Carolyn's heart, then the silence as everyone held their breath, hoping to see a sign that her heart had started. Sally closed her eyes. *Concentrate on the target.*

She opened her eyes and stared at the paper target's rings. Her hand trembled, which didn't normally happen. One of the reasons she was a good shot was she could hold her body very still. Today was different. Adrenaline was possibly still coursing around her body. And she was holding on to her anger. She was angry at herself for failing to help Carolyn. And angry at her husband for causing Carolyn so much misery and, more importantly, possibly being instrumental in her death. If she was going to hit the target, she needed to channel that anger.

In her peripheral vision she saw that she was being watched. The shorter of the men nudged the other.

"Twenty bucks says she won't even hit the target," he shouted to his friend, loud enough that she could hear him through the ear protection.

The friend looked Sally up and down. What did he see? A middle-aged woman in a feminine blouse with short feathery hair? Did they think she was too old to shoot straight or was it because she was a woman? On previous visits to the range, she had sometimes noticed men shaking their heads when she entered the range. Or a subtle *tut*. But these two guys were clearly goading her.

The taller guy waved his pistol around, using the barrel to point at Sally and the man with the handlebar moustache.

"It's grandma and grandpa day," he snickered.

The rude comment she could ignore, but a person waving a possibly loaded gun around had to be dealt with. Someone might get killed.

"Excuse me, can you keep your pistol unloaded and facing the ground unless you're aiming at a target?"

"Oooh, ain't you a feisty old lady! Maybe you should mind your own business?" He slurred his words.

His short friend laughed. "Watch and learn, Grandma. We know how to shoot."

He reminded her of Scott, who never missed the chance to mock her achievements. His mission had always been to destroy her self-confidence so that she became more and more reliant on him. Scott had fancied himself as a good shot, but Sally was far better and everyone at Franklin PD knew it. That made Scott livid. He worked hard to persuade her to leave policing and become a stay-at-home mom. It was one of the few battles Sally won against Scott.

Sally's roiling anger over Carolyn's death now turned into cold fury at the arrogant and rude men who assumed she was a poor shot. *I'll show you!* It was just what she needed to force her to focus.

Sally settled into her shooting stance once again, raised her Glock and looked down the sight at the target. She relaxed her breathing and just before she softy pulled the trigger, she held her breath.

The tall guy nearest to her snorted. "Went wide."

Sally knew he wouldn't be able to see where it had gone—her target was too far away from him, and he was viewing from an angle. Sally was confident she'd hit her mark, but she'd have to wait until she'd emptied the magazine before she recalled the target to inspect it.

One shot, she said to herself. And blocked their chatter and laughter from her thoughts. She saw only the target, calmed her breath, and then fired until the magazine was empty. Following safety protocols, she then checked the magazine truly was empty, just in case she had miscounted, and then holstered her weapon on her hip. Sally recalled her paper target with the click of a button and a mechanical whir as it followed the ceiling rail until it stopped right in front of Sally.

Every single bullet had hit the bullseye bar one, which had cut the line between the bullseye and the ring around it. Sally took down the paper target and walked over to the men who had belittled her. She turned the target around so they could see the shots.

"Holly crap!" The short guy blinked at it.

"Not bad for a grandma," Sally said curtly. "I guess you owe your friend twenty bucks."

That wiped the smirks off their faces.

Sally continued to practice until her time at the range was up. The men left her alone after that, but they grew noisier and began to mess about more. On the way out she mentioned her concerns to the manager, who took it seriously and sent a member of staff to investigate. Sally headed for the exit, buzzing from her victory over the arrogant young men.

As soon as she sat in her car, she switched her phone off silent mode and she saw a text message from Paul:

He's posted on Facebook.

The image was a screen grab from Matt Tate's Facebook profile. The photo was a head-and-shoulders shot of Carolyn smiling. Matt had written:

I'm brokenhearted to share the news of my beautiful wife's passing. Carolyn Tate passed away today, age twenty-seven, from a heart problem. Love you forever, Carolyn.

"Was it heart problems?" Sally thought aloud. "And did you love her?"

TEN

On her way to work, Sally stopped at the Living Room Café. She needed a take-out coffee and a berry muffin to lift her blood sugar levels. She still had the adrenaline shakes and she didn't want to arrive at the bookstore in need of food. Olivia had already been kind enough to allow her to start late.

Heading for the counter, Sally joined the line of people ordering take-out. As she waited, her eyes wandered around the crowded café. She loved the comfy couches and big armchairs where you could curl up and relax. The coffee was great too. As she looked around, the door opened and three women walked in. Sally instantly recognized them. They were Carolyn's three friends who'd been with her at the airport. Nicole, the mannequin woman, entered Hollywood-style, pausing in the doorway, presumably so everyone could admire her perfect figure. Then she made straight for the two deep couches positioned either side of a low coffee table. Currently a solitary man in his early twenties sat on one of the couches, a tablet in his lap and earbuds in his ears. Nicole sat next to him and spoke. The man removed his earbuds. Sally wasn't able to hear what she said to him, but she wiped away what might have been a tear as she talked. The man didn't stand a chance. He picked up his mug of coffee and his tablet and moved to another part of the café. Nicole's friend joined her and sat down heavily on the sofa, chatting with the tall dark friend as if they didn't have a care in the world.

Sally felt sick. Did these women know their friend had just died? Would they be at a café if they did?

The petite Asian friend was the only one to appear distressed. She covered her face with her hands and her shoulders bobbed as she cried. Her grief appeared heartfelt. Perhaps they did know about Carolyn, after all? The dark-haired woman put an arm around her and tried to comfort her, then she spoke to Nicole, who got up and joined the line to place their order. There were four people in the line between them. Sally tried to catch her attention so she could say how sorry she was for their loss, when the woman's phone rang.

"Oh, Lachie, thank God." Pause. "Yes." Pause. "I don't know, but I wish I hadn't." Pause. "That's all very easy for you to say, but it's not that simple." Nicole looked over her shoulder at her friends. Both friends were watching her. She then turned back to face the café counter. The line moved forward.

Nicole cupped her hand over her phone and said, "Talk to Matt. Invite him round. Please, honey?"

Sally must have been staring because Nicole looked straight at her and glared, as if to say, *Stop watching me.* Sally looked away and waited in line, wondering if she should introduce herself? The coffee line shifted forward, and Sally placed her order: cappuccino with one sugar and a berry muffin.

She then stepped away from the counter and stood in a corner, partly hidden by a bookshelf with books, magazines, and a few potted plants on it. When it was Nicole's turn to order and the barista asked where she was seated, she pointed at the couches which her friends occupied.

"Is Lauren okay?" the barista asked. "She looks kinda upset."

Sally now knew the name of the woman who was crying.

"Our friend just passed away. You knew Carolyn Tate. It's a terrible shock."

The barista's jaw dropped. "What? When? I mean I saw her only yesterday, in here, ordering coffee."

"I know. We can't believe it either." Nicole rested a hand on her chest, like it was a stage performance. "We don't know what to do with ourselves. I guess it's the shock."

Nicole paid for her order and then joined her friends. Sally couldn't help watching them through the shelving of the bookcase. Nicole air-kissed Lauren and the dark-haired friend and then sat opposite them. The shared grief quickly became a quarrel. Nicole's gestures were angry. Lauren's were pleading.

The barista called Sally's name and she collected her takeout. Sally took her time to leave the café, pausing briefly near the couch where Lauren and the dark-haired woman were seated. On the dark-haired woman's scrubs, the badge said PIONEER VET HOSPITAL and underneath was pinned a name tag that said BECCA.

"I can't bear this," Lauren said between tears.

"We all have to stick together," Nicole said. "Stay strong, Lauren. It's all for one and one for all, right?"

"Is it?" Lauren said, bitterly. "It's always about what you two want. She's dead! Don't you see?"

"Keep your voice down," Becca said. "You're making a scene."

"A scene?" Lauren stood. "Carolyn died. And you don't even care."

Lauren ran from the café. Sally followed her. Lauren undid a padlock around a bicycle.

"Excuse me," Sally said behind Lauren. The woman

jumped and turned around. "I'm Sally. I live next door to Matt. You're Carolyn's friend, right?"

Lauren's heart-shaped face was wet with tears. "Yes, sorry, I didn't catch your name."

"Sally Fairburn. Carolyn's neighbor. I just wanted to say how sorry I am for your loss. She was a lovely person, and it's a tragedy she died so young."

"Thank you. I... I have to get back to work."

"Me too, but if you need a shoulder to cry on, you can find me at Olivia's Bookstore or at home. I only knew Carolyn as a neighbor, but she struck me as someone very special."

"She was."

"Do you know what could have caused someone so healthy-seeming to die so suddenly?"

Lauren shook her head, her lips squeezed together in a line. The look Lauren gave her was like the one Sally had seen when she'd escorted victims of crime into the courts to face their abuser.

Fear.

ELEVEN

It was a cool evening as Paul and Sally stood at Zelda's grave. He didn't join her very often and Sally didn't ask him to. Paul had his life ahead of him and she didn't want him dragged down by his sister's death, although it was comforting to have him with her every now and again.

Sally removed the yellow flowers from the vase, emptied the stagnant water in the vase and replaced it with fresh water. Then she put a beautiful bunch of tiger lilies in the vase. Their tall stems came up to the marble girl's shoulder. Sally had removed the anthers so the orange pollen wouldn't mar the white marble.

"Hello, Zelda," Sally said. "Paul's here and he's got a gift for you."

Paul was used to his mother addressing the statue of Zelda this way.

"Hey, sis," Paul said. "I found this shell on Anclote Island beach and made a necklace for you." He held out the swirling shell in yellow, orange, and gray that hung from a leather string. He untied the string, then placed it around the statue's neck and tied it in a knot, then he stepped back. "Looks good. Mom has one, too."

Sally sat cross-legged facing the statue. "Looks great." She peered up at her son. "I'm going to read a chapter of this book," Sally said, holding up a paperback copy of *The Weight of Feathers*. "If you want to wait in the car, I'll give you the keys."

"Nah, I'm good." He lay down on the patchy grass between Zelda's grave and the grave next to it, closing his eyes.

Sally knew he might look complacent. But he was used to being in a cemetery and he found it as cathartic as Sally did. He'd seen a child psychologist for two years after his sister's death, and she had encouraged him to visit Zelda's grave and to tell her what he was feeling. He would lie in the grass, as he was doing now, and chat to her.

Sally read chapter two of the book and when she'd finished, she could hear Paul's soft snores above the sound of the grasshoppers chirping. She smiled. Fortunately for him, he didn't dwell on negative emotions or events anymore. Occasionally an event or a person would remind him of his father, and he'd struggle to keep his anger under control. But mostly, his inner demons were behaving themselves. Sally wished she were more like that.

"It's not been a good day," she said to Zelda's statue. "My neighbor died. I think it might be murder. The police aren't treating it as a homicide and I don't know what to do, other than keep an eye on her husband." Sally spoke for a few minutes about Carolyn's fears that her husband was poisoning her. "I feel so ill-equipped to do anything about it. But I have to do something. I did it again, you see. Like you, Carolyn needed help and I didn't give it. I have to try. Do you agree?"

Sally stared at the statue, wondering what her daughter would say if she were alive. She would almost certainly encourage her to investigate. But how should Sally go about it?

"She agrees, Mom," Paul said, his eyes still closed. "And I do too."

"I'm not sure where to begin, apart from watching Matt whenever I can."

"That's a start, right?" Paul said, opening his eyes and sitting up.

He brushed the grass of his back.

"I guess it is," Sally said.

TWELVE
JULY 15, 2016

The dawn sun was like a yellow globe hiding behind the trees at the edges of Angel Lake. The water reflected the blue and mauve sky and the dark trees, their tips like the jagged points of a crown. Last night had been cool and this morning a wispy mist clung to the lake's surface. By the time the sun had risen above the tree line, the mist would have evaporated.

It was a beautiful view, but Sally's heart was heavy. Carolyn wouldn't see the dawn light ever again.

Sally and Margie ran side by side along the lake's shore. They had been friends since elementary school. Even then, Margie had always taken care to look good and Sally was the scruffy one. Now, as they ran, Sally glanced at her friend's perfect round bob with side-swept bangs, her smooth Jamaican skin, and her color-coordinated running gear, which today was black with flashes of orange. Sally, on the other hand, hadn't bothered to brush her hair, which bounced as she ran. Her baggy T-shirt and running shorts were the first thing she had pulled out of her closet.

A duck waddled across their path and they both deviated to the right to avoid it, then the rhythmic crunch of their running shoes on gravel continued. While Sally didn't need to run so early, her friend did, so Sally made sure she was up and ready at 6 a.m. every weekday morning.

Sally told Margie about Carolyn's death and Clarke's refusal to get involved until there was evidence of foul play. "I didn't know her that well, but her death has floored me. I wish I'd taken her seriously."

"Honey, don't do this to yourself. A woman you hardly know tells you she's being poisoned and she looks like the picture of health? Nobody would take it seriously."

"What if she's right?"

"Then the autopsy will prove it, and the cops will look into it. Clarke's right. Carolyn could have died from any one of hundreds of medical conditions. Or she might have taken an overdose because of her husband's infidelity. You don't even know a crime's been committed. As my dear mom would say, you're jumping at shadows."

"I don't know about that. Matt didn't seem to give a damn about his wife's ill health. He even tried to stop the ambulance. And then there's her friends. What a weird bunch! One of them, Lauren, is afraid of something or someone. None of it makes any sense."

Margie asked. "Has this got anything to do with Zelda's death?"

Sally stared straight ahead. She didn't want Margie to see her eyes grow watery, as they always did when Zelda was mentioned. Her darling girl died six years ago, but it seemed like yesterday.

"I guess it does. I failed to save Zelda and now I've failed Carolyn."

"Listen to me. You didn't fail Zelda. Scott did." She paused to allow the message to sink in. "Since Zelda's passing you've done everything you can to hold Scott accountable. And I understand why you want justice for Carolyn, but should you get involved? I mean, how do you know her death wasn't natural? You could upset a lot of people if you interfere."

Sally blinked away the water in her eyes and sniffed. "You could be right, but her husband doesn't seem to care about her sudden death."

"Are you sure about that? How do you know that her husband isn't grieving? Maybe he's blaming himself. Maybe he knows he made her miserable shortly before she died and he's got to live with that for the rest of his life?"

Sally smiled at Margie. "You always talk sense. And I know I can get carried away sometimes. But I come back to what Carolyn said. She said that her husband was poisoning her. Two days later, she's dead. I think I owe it to her to ensure her death is thoroughly investigated."

Margie shook her head. "Not all cops are bad, Sally. Okay, you married the worst of the bunch. Scott is a sadistic narcissist and a pedophile. But Clarke's a good man. He stuck his neck out when he made Scott a suspect. He did the best job he could. For what it's worth, I think the best action you can take is to wait for the autopsy report and take it from there."

"Maybe Robert can help," Sally pondered.

"Robert?"

"Dr. Lilia, he's an associate medical examiner and a friend. He owes me."

"Tread carefully, my friend."

"I'll just tell him what I know. I won't tread on anyone's shoes."

"I think you already are. Clarke won't like it, one little bit."

Sally was quiet for a while. "I'm thinking of contacting a PI."

"PIs don't come cheap," said Margie. "At least the good ones don't. I took on a PI once when we had an employee stealing our charity funds. The guy we used was Nick Dudgeon. He did his job, but he was slippery *and* expensive."

"How was he slippery?"

"We paid an upfront fee, then after that he kept asking for money to cover additional expenses."

Sally wasn't in a position to pay a PI much at all. She had a small sum set aside for Paul's education. Paul's trip to Tampa had come from her meager pension. The only way to cover a PI's costs would be to sell something. She needed a car, so that wasn't up for grabs. She could sell some of her jewelry. Her engagement ring was hidden in a box in her study. An emerald and two small diamonds on a gold band. If she was lucky, she might get five hundred dollars for it.

They came to a halt at the old wooden jetty, which marked the five-mile point. A fisherman had set up his lines and was seated on a folding stool. They used the time to stretch out their legs and drink water. The sun was above the trees and the mist on the lake was no more. Perhaps the idea of employing a PI was a bit extreme, and to be honest, not something she could afford. But Sally wouldn't let this drop. Sally had to know why Carolyn died. She resolved to contact Dr. Lilia at 9 a.m., when he started work.

Once home, Sally showered, and with a towel wrapped around her, she selected her clothes. She planned to take Paul kayaking, so she donned her swimsuit, a pair of shorts, and a loose-fitting T-shirt. She ran her fingers through her wet hair and ruffled it, which suited the cut, then she went back to the bathroom to smooth on sunscreen. Her phone rang and she answered. The moment she heard the voice she regretted not paying attention to the fact the phone number was restricted. Since Foster had begun pestering her from jail, Sally had made a rule that if the phone number was silent, or not listed in her contacts, she let the call go to voicemail.

"Hello, Sally." The unmistakable baritone, the hint of a London accent softened after many years in Franklin.

Sally sucked in a sharp breath. Just his voice sent a shudder up her spine. The fine hairs on her arms and the back of her neck stood up. Sally moved a finger across her phone to end the call.

"Uh-uh. Don't cut me off," Richard Foster said, as if he could see what she was about to do. "I'm sorry to hear about your neighbor. She was a nice lady."

"How do you..." Sally stopped herself just in time. Had her death been on the news? If it had, he would know the deceased lived in her street.

Don't engage with him.

"I know everything about you, Sally."

Her legs almost gave way. She grabbed the edge of the basin to steady herself. She had to sound strong. He mustn't know how terrified she was.

"Foster, stop calling me. No more flowers. No more notes."

"Don't you want to know how I found your address and cell number?"

She assumed that he had corrupted sources within the police force. Cops who owed him favors? Or prison guards who could be incentivized to do it?

"I don't care."

"What *do* you care about, Sally?"

"You think I would tell you!"

"No need to be like that." His voice was level and unhurried. She was the one getting riled, not him. She was handling him all wrong. "All right, then I'll tell you what you really care about. You think Carolyn's death is suspicious. Am I right?"

It was as if Sally was falling through a black hole. She wasn't aware of the bathroom tiles or the basin or the mirror on the wall. How did he know what she was thinking? Her mind raced to answer the question. Only Paul, Margie, and Clarke knew that she suspected Carolyn had not died of natural causes. They would never, ever communicate with Foster about her.

Did Clarke mention her suspicions to another cop? Was that cop bent? Was that how Foster knew?

"Why do you think that?" Sally said after what felt like an eternity. Sally was lightheaded. She couldn't feel her limbs. Part of her mind told her that she had taken the bait, that she should end the call before it was too late. But she had to know.

A playful note entered his voice. "If I told you, it would spoil all the fun, wouldn't it? If you want to know, come and see me. My diary's looking relatively empty this week."

The thought of seeing Foster again made Sally retch. Bile shot up her throat and into her mouth. Sally did her best to swallow, but the bitter taste remained on her tongue.

"Go to hell!" She listened to silence for a full ten seconds before she concluded that Foster had ended the call and literally left her hanging.

THIRTEEN

It wasn't easy getting Paul out of bed and into the car by 8 a.m., even with the promise of kayaking and a picnic breakfast. It was harder still for Sally to put out of her mind Carolyn's sudden death and Foster's chilling phone call.

She had lain awake most of the night, reliving every moment of her interactions with Matt and Carolyn, even the times when they merely passed each other on their way in or out. Until Sally's meeting with Carolyn in the bookstore, there was nothing to suggest that Matt hated his wife enough to kill her. And there was the friends' weird behavior. And why did Lauren seem so afraid? Only she had appeared genuinely saddened by Carolyn's passing.

Then Foster had caught her in a distracted moment, and she'd taken his call. As Sally packed a picnic breakfast into her waterproof backpack, all manner of questions spun around her head. How did he know that she believed Carolyn's death was suspicious? And what did Foster really want from her? Was this all about revenge? Sally was his nemesis. She was responsible for depriving him of his freedom. Because of her he could no longer continue to rape and murder innocent girls.

Sally had loads of questions and no answers—and no idea how to find those answers. However, she had at least made one decision: she would not tell Paul about Foster's phone call. She saw no point in upsetting him, which it would certainly do. She needed to protect him. Sally could live with what Foster had tried to do to her. But Aiden Foster's attempt on Paul's life was another matter. It was difficult to know how Paul's ordeal would impact him in future.

Paul had been trapped in a panic room in a sealed vault in a safe house when Aiden had turned off the power that controlled the air supply. Paul couldn't flee. He couldn't fight either. He had been trapped. Now, whenever Paul felt the slightest bit threatened, he lashed out—straight into fight mode without a moment's hesitation. Dr. Kaur explained that his heightened survival instinct was kicking in. The psychologist had encouraged Paul to pause, to breathe in for five counts and out for five counts, five times, before he took any action or responded verbally, giving him time to ask himself if hitting out was the best plan. Sometimes it worked. But sometimes, in the heat of the moment, his temper got the better of him.

During their car journey, both Sally and Paul had been quiet, lost in their own thoughts.

By the time they arrived at Angel Lake, there was real heat in the morning sun and the first wave of kayakers were returning their craft to the storage locker. Sally and Paul exchanged greetings with some of them. They were going to use Margie's two kayaks, which were stored there. Before Margie's husband's passing, she and Henry had enjoyed their times together on the lake. These days Margie didn't take her kayak out much. She said that it reminded her of Henry and the pain of missing him was too sharp. However, she was more than happy for Sally and Paul to use them whenever they liked.

Once they had donned life jackets and sunscreen, they carried the two kayaks to the water's edge, then they set off, heading for Hope Island, a state park with a deciduous forest and a mile-long sandy beach on the east side, which is where they were heading. The beach was popular with shellfish harvesters and visitors who liked to follow the trail around the one-hundred-twenty-acre island. Sally had packed ham, potato, and cheese quiches and berry trifle, which she had made last night as she mulled over the sad and disturbing day she had been through. She had also packed peanut butter granola bars and some bananas, as well as soft drinks. Paul was a big eater.

They set off for the island at a leisurely pace. It was cooler on the water and the rhythmic splash as their oars hit the water was soothing. They passed a couple of ring-necked ducks and a blue-winged teal.

"Look! Up there!" Paul looked high in the sky.

A bird with a hooked beak hovered over the island, its wings beating rapidly as it watched its prey.

"American falcon, I think," Sally said. The birds swooped down and vanished behind some trees.

In the distance, a small sailboat floated across the lake.

"Is that a Sunfish?" she asked.

Sunfish was a popular brand of sailing craft for beginners and kids.

"Think so. Optis is better. I won the under-sixteen's Opti race when I was staying with David."

"You didn't tell me. That's amazing. Congratulations!"

"Can we buy our own Opti? I could teach you."

Sally couldn't afford to buy a sailboat, but she didn't want to dent her son's enthusiasm. "We could look into joining a sailing club and use their sailboats. But don't you have enough on your plate, what with school and football?"

"I'll make time, Mom. And I'll teach Reilly so he can come with me." Paul stared wistfully at the sailing boat race.

"I'll look into it, okay? But even joining a club costs money and I don't get paid much at the bookstore. Have you thought about getting a weekend job?"

"Maybe I could work at the sailing club. Clean the boats. Book people in. Something. Then maybe I can take a sailboat out when nobody's using it?"

"Worth a try. We could drop by the club later today and inquire, but I have to be at work by ten."

"I'll go later. Me, Ben, Reilly, and Andy are going trail biking. I'll talk to the manager on my way home."

"Good idea."

The water was choppier the farther out into the lake they went, and the tide was working against them. "Shall we pick up the pace? The sooner we get there, the sooner we can eat."

Their paddles sliced the water a little faster and Paul sped ahead.

When they were close enough to the island's shore, they hopped out of their kayaks and waded through the shallow water. Another kayaker had the same idea and was already seated under a tree, eating a picnic. Farther down the beach, a dinghy had been pulled ashore and two middle-aged men were bent over spades as they searched for clams, which they threw into buckets. A great blue heron investigated some of the other holes the men had dug, probably searching for any clams they had missed.

Sally and Paul pulled their kayaks a few feet up the beach then headed for a shaded rocky area, where they ate their breakfast picnic. When it was time to leave Hope Island, the journey back was much easier because the tide was with them. On the way home, Sally left a voicemail for Dr. Lilia:

"Hi, Rob, this is Sally Fairburn. Could you please call me? I need your help regarding the Carolyn Tate autopsy. I think foul play was involved."

Sally planned to share the photo of the medication from Carolyn's bathroom cabinet when she had spoken to Lilia. Of course, he was under no obligation to talk to her about the autopsy. She wasn't a cop and she had no right to intervene. But she hoped that, given the many years they had known each other, he would at least hear her out.

Sally made a quick stop at a florist, where she bought a bouquet of white lilies and white roses and a condolence card. Showering quickly, she dressed, cleaned out her backpack, and then said goodbye to Paul, who was in the midst of a video game. Then she knocked on Matt's house door. His car was in the street and, given his loss, it was to be expected that he wouldn't be at work today.

He opened the door and when he saw Sally, he pulled his head back in surprise.

"I'm so sorry for your loss," Sally said. She held out the flowers and card. "If there is anything I can do, please, just ask."

"Thank you." He rubbed his forehead, as if trying to remember something. "I... er... I've been meaning to thank you. For what you did for Carolyn."

He was a good-looking man, but today his skin was gray and he looked wrung out.

"I just wish we could have saved her," Sally said.

"I... I can't believe she's gone."

"If I can help with any arrangements—the funeral, the after-party, flowers, anything—please just ask."

"I haven't gotten around to that."

"Will the funeral be local, or in England?"

"Oh, here. Her parents are flying out tonight, arrive tomorrow."

They must be beside themselves with grief, Sally thought. It's bad enough to lose a daughter, but to lose a daughter when she is overseas is worse.

A vehicle honked a couple of times. Matt looked into the street and waved. Sally turned to find a metallic gray Mercedes SUV had stopped outside Matt's house and a woman waved at him through the open window. It was Nicole.

"Mattie! Help me unload the boxes, will you? There's nowhere to park."

"Sure!" Matt shouted out. Then to Sally, "Excuse me."

This was the friendliest Matt had ever been with her and Sally wanted to return the favor. "I'm on my way out. Your friend can have my parking space."

"Thanks!"

Matt jogged over to where Nicole's shiny Mercedes was blocking the road. Sally reversed out of her parking bay. Matt was already unloading flat-packed boxes from the trunk of Nicole's car. Sally couldn't help but wonder what it was that Matt would be packing up. She was tempted to ask, but she was late for work so she drove away.

FOURTEEN

It was easy for Sally to track down Matt's lover, Daisy Sheene, twenty-one, singer in Matt's band, Quills and Spines. Matt was the lead guitarist and songwriter. Daisy's distinctive blonde hair with the last three inches dyed pink was distinctive enough to enable Sally to find information on the band. The local media had run a few stories praising Daisy's vocals, predicting that with her as lead singer, they had a chance to hit the big time. A newspaper article helpfully revealed that Daisy worked at Walmart in Lincoln when she wasn't performing or rehearsing.

On her lunch break, Sally drove to Walmart, on the off chance that Daisy was working. This store was the largest in the area, positioned on the outskirts of town where other super-stores were located. Sally picked up a shopping basket, keen to look as innocuous as possible, then walked through the store methodically, starting with the checkout counters and then up and down the aisles. Daisy was stocking shelves in the babies' aisle. In the obligatory Walmart navy shirt and black pants and her hair tied in a ponytail, she looked more approachable than her glamorous media shots portrayed.

"Excuse me?" Sally said to the young woman. "Are you Daisy, the singer in Quills and Spines?"

Daisy put the pack of diapers down on the floor and smiled. "I am. Did you come to our gig?"

"No, but I've heard you have a great voice."

"Thanks," Daisy said, her smile widening.

Sally looked down, finding it difficult to broach the subject of Carolyn's death. She decided to focus on Matt and his loss. "I live on the same street as Matt." Sally wanted to distance herself from him so that Daisy might open up to her. "He must be so devastated at Carolyn's sudden passing."

Daisy's smile faltered. "Yeah, he's pretty shook up by it all. We're doing what we can to help him. Be there for him."

"I guess there are no more performances for a while?"

"There sure are! The band is what he needs right now. It makes him happy."

"Do you know what happened to Carolyn? I mean, why did she die?"

"I'm guessing it's got something to do with all those drugs she took to stop her flipping out." There was a mean sneer on her face.

"Flipping out?" Sally asked.

"She took pills to stop her going crazy hyper or mega depressed. When she was depressed, poor Mattie couldn't even get her out of bed. It was a nightmare for him."

Daisy wasn't sympathetic about Carolyn's illness and she showed no remorse for sleeping with the dead woman's husband. "Matt and Carolyn were different people," Sally said. "I always wondered about that. But opposites sometimes attract, right?"

Daisy looked one way and then the other, then gave Sally a conspiratorial look. "Can you keep a secret?"

"Sure."

"She tricked him into marrying her."

"Really? How?"

"She told him she was pregnant. They got married, then she mysteriously lost the baby. Matt thinks she was never pregnant, and so do I."

Ouch! The talons were out.

"I do hope he doesn't leave Pioneer Heights. That happens, doesn't it?" Sally said, keeping the dialogue light and chatty. "When people lose a spouse or partner, they often move to a new area so they can leave the pain of their loss behind."

"He won't hang around for long. We have plans... the band, I mean. We're ready to hit the big time. There's a talent scout coming to our gig next week. You should come. We're playing at the Bald Rock Hotel."

Daisy was clearly ambitious, and Matt was integral to the success of the band. Was her hold over Matt pervasive enough to convince him to kill Carolyn, who might have been a hindrance? Was now the time for Sally to throw a hand grenade and see how Daisy reacted?

"Have you heard the rumor?" Sally asked. "There's talk that Matt killed her."

"You shouldn't say shit like that. He'd never do that. He's too nice." Daisy tossed her head.

"But he had an affair with you, right?" Another hand grenade.

"Excuse me? Who the hell are you?" Her eyes narrowed. "Are you a reporter?"

"Just a neighbor."

"Then fuck off or I'll call security."

It was time to make a hasty exit. As soon as Sally was through the Walmart doors, she sat on a street bench waiting for her heart rate to calm. Daisy was an ambitious young woman. And she seemed happy that Carolyn was out of the way. Maybe Matt wasn't a killer. But would Daisy kill to have Matt all to herself?

FIFTEEN

The bookstore had been busy all afternoon and Sally hadn't had time to think about either Carolyn or Foster. At 5:30 p.m. Dr. Robert Lilia returned her call.

"Sally! I apologize. Been meaning to call you. It's been back-to-back autopsies. We're down one forensic pathologist."

"I totally understand. And I know my timing sucks, but could I come by now and explain why I'd dearly love your help?"

"Your timing's good. I was about to take a break. Remind me of the deceased's name."

"Carolyn Tate."

"Give me a moment and I'll take a look at who did the autopsy. Ah, yes, it was Rachel Donoghue. Very thorough, but new. Are you saying you want a second opinion?"

Robert Lilia had been a forensic pathologist for twenty-seven years. "Yes, I'd like that very much."

"I take it this isn't an official request?"

"No, it's not. I knew Carolyn and I believe she was murdered."

"This will need to be managed carefully."

"I understand."

"Can you be here in an hour?" Lilia asked.

"See you then."

Olivia was happy to lock up the shop, and Sally completed the four-mile trip to the Forensic Pathology Unit at Pioneer Valley Hospital by 6:30 p.m.

It was a cream brick four-story hospital with various extensions added over the years. She left her car and walked around the outside of the main building, to the rear entrance where the Japanese garden was available to patients convalescing. There was a mini waterfall made of boulders and two cherry trees near a bench, as well as bushes and flowers in pinks and whites. Through a set of double doors, she turned left and at the end of the corridor a sign announced the Forensic Pathology Unit. She pressed the buzzer and Lilia answered.

"I'm outside your unit," Sally said into the intercom.

"Give me a minute. I'll come out," Lilia said.

Sally stared out of the window and watched the waterfall splash into a narrow pond that then recycled the water back into the waterfall. She wished she could remove her shoes and dunk her feet in the cool water.

Lilia came through the door followed by a burst of Bob Marley singing "Trenchtown Rock." Lilia liked to work with rock music playing in the background. He meant no disrespect by it, but he found it made dissecting bodies easier to do. Over his blue scrubs he wore a white lab coat with his name and position embroidered onto the right chest area. He was a big man with a bald head and a trimmed white beard and blue eyes that glinted with amusement from behind his bifocals. In his hand was a manila folder.

"Sally, good to see you. Shall we sit in the garden? We can talk privately there."

Sally followed Lilia to the Japanese garden, where they sat on the wooden bench.

"What is your interest in Carolyn Tate?" he asked.

"On Tuesday she told me her husband was poisoning her. On Thursday she died suddenly. I found her outside her house wearing just a nightie, confused and disoriented and barely able to stand up. Her relationship with her husband was not good. He was having an affair."

Lilia nodded. "I listened to your message only this afternoon. I have a rule that cell phones must be switched off here. As a result, the autopsy was done without the benefit of your perspective." He peered at her over his bifocals. "You know I cannot share the result with you or anyone other than the next of kin, the hospital, and the police."

"I know this puts you in a difficult position. But I feel I owe it to Carolyn to discover the truth about her death. Could you at least tell me if there was evidence of foul play?"

He scratched his beard. "All right. You helped us out with Martin, so I guess I owe you. But this has to stay strictly between us."

"Goes without saying. How is Martin doing these days?"

"Doing well. At college. Wants to be a doctor. A heart surgeon, so he tells me. Not a forensic pathologist, sadly. There's a real shortage of forensic pathologists these days. The youth of today isn't interested in working with dead people. I don't see it that way. I see it as helping the living to understand a loved one's death."

A decade ago, Lilia's sixteen-year-old son, Martin, was arrested for breaking and entering. Martin had become addicted to ice and this was his first break-in, hoping to steal goods that he'd sell to pay for his addiction. Lilia and his wife had done their best to help their son, but the boy had checked himself out of rehab. Sally regarded him as a victim who needed support, not jail time, and worked with the boy's lawyer to persuade the court that he should have a noncustodial sentence, providing Martin returned to rehab, which he did.

"So, as I say, Rachel Donoghue did the autopsy." Lilia opened the folder holding the report. Sally could see it from where she sat. Pathologists assigned a code by which they identified the body, rather than referring to them by name. They did this to distance themselves. It was best not to see them as people so they could remain emotionally detached. Carolyn was cadaver PVH-2015-28. The initials of the hospital were first, the year of the autopsy, and then the case number after that.

Sally couldn't help but feel sad that a young woman with a great life before her was now nothing more than a series of letters and numbers.

"It says here that the case"—he meant Carolyn—"was on lithium for two years for bipolar disorder. This in itself isn't dangerous unless she took too high a dose and failed to hydrate herself adequately. However, there were no signs of excessive lithium in her system or of her being dehydrated. She died from a heart attack, but what triggered it isn't clear. The autopsy result is inconclusive."

"There has to be a reason for the heart attack. Could poison have caused it?" Sally asked.

"Rachel has done a standard poisons test, which came back negative."

"What does standard mean in this instance?"

"Household poisons and well-known poisons such as arsenic and ethylene glycol."

"Is there such a thing as an advanced poisons test?"

"As a matter of fact, there is, but we only use it if the police have identified a death as suspicious. In this instance the police are not involved, and it was Carolyn's death in ER that created the need for an autopsy—any death at a hospital requires an autopsy. The fact Carolyn's report says inconclusive is enough for us to release her body for burial."

"What does the advanced test entail?"

"It looks for fifty different poisons, including some very rare ones. We don't do these tests here. They have to be sent away, which means delaying the release of her body for another twenty-four hours."

"Let me get this straight: Carolyn could have been given a lesser-known poison, right? And we wouldn't know about it from the tests already done?"

"It's possible. But I have no good reason to order the advanced test."

"Here are a few reasons." Sally counted them off on her fingers. "One, the victim believed she was being poisoned. Two, she went from a healthy woman able to handle a high-powered job to someone sick and terrified. Three, her husband wanted me to cancel the ambulance when his wife was barely conscious. Four, and I know this is a long shot, but the husband is a pharmacist. He has to know which drugs can kill, surely? And five, he had motive. He was having an affair. Perhaps Carolyn refused to divorce him or there were financial reasons why he couldn't afford to divorce her, so he, and perhaps his lover, saw to it that Carolyn conveniently died."

Lilia removed his bifocals and rubbed his eyes. "Everything you said suggests her death might have been murder, but where is the proof?"

"If I had proof, the cops would be all over this. Please, Rob, do the advanced poisons test. That's all I ask."

"I have to tell you that the body has been made available for collection. The undertakers will take her away tomorrow."

"Please, Rob, do this one favor for me."

Sally felt bad for Carolyn's parents, but it was just twenty-four hours and then Sally could rest knowing she'd done all she could to discover the truth.

"I'll talk to Rachel. As long as she's okay with doing the additional test, I'll approve it."

Sally smiled. "Thank you, my friend."

SIXTEEN

Paul had gone to the movies with his buddies, which meant Sally could get some chores done and then, she hoped, have a quiet night in. She emptied the washing machine, grabbed the bag of pegs, and began hanging out the washing, starting with the jeans. Only there was something off in the air. Smoke. It wasn't a barbecue's smoke—there was no hint of lighter fluid, charcoal, or of cooking fat.

She gave up hanging her washing on the line and used the tumble dryer instead. Wafts of gray smoke continued to blow over the rear fence, coming from Matt's backyard. The townhouse yards were small and Sally's had just about enough space for a small tool shed, her washing line, a wooden bench, and a small table. She used the bench to peer over the fence between her property and his. His yard was paved. There was a fishpond in one corner with golden and orange fish darting about. The potted plants were in need of watering: the leaves and flowers were wilting. At its center was a steel circular firepit and the embers were smoldering. The ash was thick and items were still burning. Had Matt and Nicole boxed up some of Carolyn's belongings and burned others? Why so fast?

Sally thought of Carolyn's family in England on their way to attend their daughter's funeral. Would they want to take some of her personal possessions home with them?

Sally coughed and her eyes stung. She was about to step down when the setting sun's light bounced off something pinkish-purple in the fishpond. The sun seemed to be reflecting off a painted metal object among the dull greens and browns of the pond weed.

Sally stepped off the bench and ducked inside, shutting the back door. Even away from the smoke, her eyes stung. Had something intended for the firepit ended up in the pond by mistake? Sally knew she shouldn't take a look, but she couldn't resist. As long as Matt wasn't home, Sally could nip into Matt's backyard and look at the shiny pink object. Their yard gate wasn't locked.

When Sally had checked the street for the RAV4 and Nicole's Mercedes, and saw neither, she rang Matt's doorbell. There was no answer.

Why would Matt leave a burning firepit unsupervised on a hot summer's evening? Embers could easily blow in the wind and cause a fire.

Sally hopped back into her house, shut the door, and donned a baseball cap, tucking her hair inside it, then she grabbed her tongs from the kitchen drawer. If she were caught, Matt had every right to be furious. Sally vacillated for a few seconds. *Have I become the neighbor from hell?* A voice in her head egged her on. *Just a quick look, that's all.*

A narrow path ran between two rows of townhouses, hers and those on a parallel street. The overgrown laneway was mainly used as a place for people to store their garbage bins. Once Sally was sure that nobody else was about, she poked her head into Matt's backyard. The heat from the firepit hit her in the face like a furnace. She glanced at the fishpond and felt sorry for the goldfish; they must be suffering from the hot weather *and* the heat from the fire. Sally looked through the glass door and into Matt's house: there was no movement inside.

Sally quickly shot a couple of photos of the firepit. It wasn't just sheets of paper that were smoldering. Photos too. Just the edges remained, although some faces and bodies were just visible. With the tongs, she removed what was left of a sheet of paper and some corners of printed photos and put them on the paving stones to cool off.

Now she turned her attention to the pond. She kneeled at the edge and put her face near the water. The pinkish-purple rectangle among the pond weed was a cell phone. Sally thought back to her meeting with Carolyn at the bookstore. Carolyn had an iPhone with her, cased in a purple and pink plastic cover.

The sun was lower now and the rays flickered through three pencil pines in a neighbor's yard, and this made it harder to see the bottom of the murky pond. Sliding her hand carefully into the water, trying not to disturb the leaflitter and pond weed, the tips of her fingers touched the flat smooth surface of the phone. The fish darted away, some churning the leaves and dirt with their tails, then hid under the weed, their bulbous eyes watching her hand.

Pausing to allow the murky water to settle, Sally then clenched her fingers around the edges of the phone and pulled it out of the water. Would the tough plastic cover have protected the phone from water damage?

And why was a phone in a pond in the first place?

Sally inspected it. It looked like the one she had—an iPhone 6.

If Matt and Nicole had gone to the trouble of burning items in a firepit on a stifling-hot day, why not burn the phone too? Perhaps water damage was an easier option—chuck it in the pond and everything on it would be destroyed. Perhaps burning a phone was more difficult to do successfully?

Sally knew that an iPhone 6 wasn't waterproof, just water

resistant. She needed to dry off the phone as fast as possible and hope it hadn't been in the pond for too long.

Picking up the remains of photos, the page that looked to be a bank statement, and the soggy phone, Sally headed for the gate. As she shut it, movement at an upstairs window of Matt's house caught her eye. The slatted white blinds were down but the slats were open to allow light in. Two of the slats were held apart by a hand. Sally saw the flash of a face, then the slats fell into place and the figure behind them couldn't be seen.

Someone was watching her. Flushing with embarrassment and fear, Sally made a quick exit from the yard.

In her kitchen, she laid the wet phone on the kitchen counter, as well as the burned remains of photos and a document, then she grabbed a towel and gently patted the phone dry. The screen displayed a flower as a screen saver and the time and date. That had to be a good sign.

All the while she expected there to be an angry knock on her door. Matt—or whoever she'd seen at the window—had every right to demand to know what she was doing.

Sally whipped off the baseball cap, which left a sweaty hairline. That firepit sure did emanate a lot of heat.

"What possessed you?" Sally said to herself.

It was too late now. She had done it and she'd have to bear the consequences.

She quickly searched on the internet for advice on how to save an iPhone 6 from water damage. The site she found instructed her to switch off the phone, which she did. It told her to dry not just the exterior surface but all the ports too. To do this Sally had to find a way to remove the protective cover. After a bit of fiddling and a broken fingernail, the cover came off. The phone inside appeared to be dry, but the SIM card port, the buttons, and the camera had not been covered by the plastic, so she used a soft cloth to wipe away water from the card port and then dried the SIM. The trick, the article said, was to leave the phone to dry, with ports open, for ideally twenty-four hours. One of the last tips was about using a home damp-reduction product known as DampRid to suck up excess moisture. Sally had a tub of it in the cupboard under the laundry sink. She placed the phone, SIM, and tub of DampRid in a large plastic bag and sealed the bag and left the phone to dry out.

When Sally had done all she could to save the phone, she moved on to the other items she had rescued from the firepit.

Sally sat on a barstool at the kitchen counter and laid out the five blackened photographs and piece of paper. The document was a bank statement, but the top had been burned away so the account name wasn't visible. She could see some dates and transactions. The bank account was in the red. She would look at it more thoroughly later—the photos looked more interesting.

Sally's first thought was, why destroy photos? And wouldn't Matt have more important things to do after his wife's passing, such as notify friends and relatives? Even though Carolyn's body was being held for another twenty-four hours, a funeral director had to be appointed, a church or other place of worship contacted about availability for a service, a burial or cremation site decided upon, and arrangements made for Carolyn's family when they arrived in Franklin from England.

Her next thought was that people didn't generally print photos these days, unless they were very special or if they intended to frame them.

She examined each of the five pieces of photo in turn.

One was a corner and all she could see was a pair of legs. Slim legs, bare. Female. It told Sally nothing.

The second one was a piece of night sky and red light, possibly lasers. Not helpful.

The third was the close-up of an electric guitar and a hand. Hairy, had to be male. Were these photos of Matt's band?

The fourth was backlit by a candle; wineglasses, Matt's

face, and a woman behind him. She was in shadow, but her stare was more like a glare.

The fifth one was the least burned. Again candlelit. The backs of a man and woman heading through an arch and beyond that arch was blackness. Sally couldn't be sure, but from the woman's blonde hair and the man's build, she hazarded a guess that the couple was Matt and Carolyn.

Why would Matt want to destroy a photo of him with his wife?

Or was there a woman in the house who wanted all trace of Carolyn gone?

SEVENTEEN

JULY 16, 2016

Sally squinted at the time on her digital alarm clock and groaned. It was 5:04 a.m. on Saturday and she'd had another restless night. She had dreamed that she was floating on a raft and she was trying to call for help using a pinkish-purple phone identical to the one in the pond, but there was no signal, so she threw it away. Then a giant whale burst out of the sea and swallowed her.

She closed her eyes and told herself to get another hour's sleep, but she couldn't stop thinking about the mysterious iPhone drying out downstairs. She gave up on her efforts to sleep and crept downstairs so as not to wake Paul. In the kitchen, she scooped some coarse coffee grounds from an airtight container and dropped a measured amount into her coffee plunger. Then she boiled the kettle and poured the water into the coffee plunger to brew. She'd wait four minutes, then lower the plunger to the bottom of the glass pitcher, and pour a lovely cup of coffee.

With an hour to kill before she went on her morning run, she decided to check out the phone. She was meant to leave it to dry for twenty-four hours, but she just couldn't wait. Her curiosity got the better of her. Was this Carolyn's phone as she suspected?

She took the phone and SIM card out of the plastic bag and left the pot of DampRid in the bag. Once the SIM was in the phone, she pressed the "on" button and waited.

"Please work."

The screen stayed blank, and her excitement turned to disappointment. Pouring herself a coffee, she took another look at the phone. There had been a delay, but the screen was lit up now, with the date and time displayed. *So far so good*, Sally thought. If she were asked for a passcode, however, she would not get any further. But there was no request for a passcode. She opened settings and, right at the top, the name *Carolyn Tate* appeared.

"Yes!" She punched the air.

Sally knew she might be tampering with evidence, but she needed proof that Matt had killed his wife and the phone might give it to her. Until she had proof, Clarke wasn't going to investigate.

Next, Sally tried to open Carolyn's Facebook app. But the phone wouldn't connect to the internet, which impacted Google, other apps, and social media. Sally tried to view the contacts list, but it wouldn't open.

"Damn!"

She opened up the photos file. It worked and she chose the most recent photo, which was of Carolyn and Lauren, taken the day before Sally met with Carolyn at the bookstore. It was a selfie. They were possibly at a bar. Both smiling. Carolyn looked the picture of health.

What about Carolyn's emails?

Without the internet connection, Sally couldn't access new emails, but she could view older emails that Carolyn had already viewed on her phone.

Flicking through a few, she found most were work related,

so she selected emails from friends or from Matt. An email from Lauren Duthie, dated a week ago, was interesting:

Hi Carolyn,

Don't let Becca and Nicole upset you. They don't mean any harm by it. I know they were insensitive. I felt it too. They shouldn't tease you about that silly girl. She's just someone in his band. Matt's always been a bit of a flirt, but he adores you. If you ever want to chat, just call me, okay?

Big love, Lauren

Sally sat back and thought about its contents. A week ago, Lauren was trying to convince Carolyn her husband wasn't being unfaithful, yet a few days later she was at the airport with Carolyn, who was about to catch Matt meeting his lover at the airport—if the two Laurens were the same, and surely they were, how had Carolyn's theory become a certainty?

Sally liked the kindness of Lauren's email. Perhaps Lauren might be a good person to talk to?

Carolyn replied to the email that day:

Hi Lauren,

Thank you for your lovely email. I'm sure Nicole and Becca were only joking, but I really am worried that Matt has lost interest in me. And he was the one desperate to get married when I wanted to wait a bit. And he's always in a bad mood, even though his business worries are over. The only reason I can think of for his change is Daisy. Ever since she joined his band, Matt is different. I watch you and James together and I so wish Matt was as attentive as James is to you. But please don't tell Becca or Nicole or anyone I told you this—espe-

cially not Matt! I so need a friend to open up to right now. I
hope you don't mind me dumping this stuff on you.

Why don't you come around for coffee one Saturday
afternoon? Matt is at band practice then, so we will be alone.
Just you and me, right?

Carolyn x

Carolyn came across as lonely and Sally wished she had
reached out to her and been more friendly. The comment about
Matt's business worries sparked Sally's interest. This was news
to Sally. If he was in financial difficulty, that would put their
relationship under pressure. But Carolyn had been a brand
director and Sally guessed she would have been paid well. Sally
didn't think it was a motivator to kill his wife, so she kept
searching through the emails. She would focus on the first year
of their relationship.

Sally found an email from Becca Watts, who had to be the
tall woman with the long dark hair. It was sent Wednesday
morning, before Carolyn met Matt at the airport.

Hi Carolyn,

I've been trying to get hold of you. Please call me. It's about
Matt.

Becca

Sally found it interesting that Carolyn hadn't responded to
Becca's calls. Was Becca the source of the distressing phone call
on Wednesday morning when Carolyn was about to leave for
work?

All of Becca's emails were brief and to the point, mostly
about social arrangements.

Next, Sally came across emails from Matt. Mostly about reminders of get-togethers and when his band was doing a gig or about a practice session. His sign-off was from Tate & Slavik Pharmacy. A quick flick through some emails and Sally worked out that the "Slavik" was Nicole and Lachlan's surname. Matt and Lachlan owned two pharmacies together, one in Pioneer Heights and the other in Lincoln, a working-class suburb about three miles away.

Sally yawned. There were hundreds more emails to go through, which would take hours. She had twenty-five minutes before she was due to meet Margie for their run. She switched back to Carolyn's photo and video albums.

One video file caught Sally's eye because the thumbnail was of a woman with blonde and pink hair.

The video clip was shot at a strange angle: side-on. It was dark and the alleyway was lit by a light over a fire exit door. Daisy was pacing, a cigarette in her hand. Music was a rumble in the background. She had on rose-tinted glasses and a pink vest that showed off the tattoos on both her arms. Her tight black leather skirt and knee-high black boots finished off the rock-chick look. Sally guessed they were outside the rear of a venue where they were performing.

"She knows," Daisy says, flicking ash on the ground.

"She doesn't. I promise, babe," Matt says, in black leather pants, black waistcoat, no shirt underneath, messed-up hair.

"What are we gonna do? You promised me."

"I'll deal with it," Matt says.

Daisy stabs Matt in the chest with a finger. "Deal with her, or I'm gone."

EIGHTEEN

Saturday was the busiest day of the week at the bookstore and Sally had to be in by 9 a.m. That still left plenty of time for her morning run beforehand.

She left her house feeling nervous about bumping into Matt after she had sneaked into his backyard yesterday. Carolyn's cell phone was in her purse, tucked inside a sunglasses pouch for safe keeping, and her purse was in the bedroom. On her lunch break she might have time to explore more of Carolyn's emails so she planned to take the phone to work with her. The fragments of the burned photos and the remains of a bank statement were stored safely in a desk drawer in her study.

Keen to get moving, Sally waited for a car to pass by, then headed across the street, and followed the sidewalk to the park where she'd hook up with Margie.

Straight ahead, a bearded man in a black baseball cap sat in a silver Hyundai Sonata. For a split second he looked straight at her, then he turned his head. In that moment his stare was so intense that Sally felt a stab of something deeply uncomfortable. Neither the man nor the car were familiar, and at 6 a.m. it was unusual to have someone loitering in their car with the engine running. Except perhaps for an Uber driver waiting for a passenger?

The driver switched on the engine and hurriedly drove off.

She was probably being paranoid, and she dismissed it from her thoughts. Setting off at a leisurely pace, she met up with Margie in the park. Their ten-mile run gave Sally a chance to talk about Carolyn's phone and the burned photos, her meeting with Dr. Lilia, and Foster's phone call.

"I feel a whole lot better when I talk things through with you," Sally said. "A burden shared is a burden halved, as Mom always says."

"I know what you mean. You were a tower of strength when I lost Henry," Margie said. "I don't know what I would have done without you. Our morning chats were like therapy, helping me find some happiness when I was lost in grief." She smiled at Sally.

"You did the same for me when Scott walked out. That's what friends are for." They turned onto a forest trail. The first part would be tough because it was uphill, but most of the trail leveled out and then did a loop, taking them downhill on their return.

"You've become quite a detective," Margie commented. "The poisons test is a great result." She gave Sally as scrutinizing look. "What happens if it comes back negative? Will you accept her death was natural?"

"You're worried about me. No need."

"You took a big risk fishing the phone out of the pond. Promise me you won't do something that risky again?"

"I can't promise because I might. If the poisons test comes back positive, then I'll hand over the phone to Detective Clarke. There's a video on there that suggests Matt and Daisy wanted Carolyn out of the way."

Margie tutted. "How do you intend to explain to Clarke how you got hold of the phone, huh?"

"I don't know."

"If you tell him the truth, he's well within his rights to charge you with trespassing."

"I'll think of something."

At the end of the run, they stretched out under a shady tree in Pioneer Park. Margie talked about the mental health speech she was giving at the library later that day. Then she suddenly changed tack.

"Have you heard anything more from Foster?"

"Yes, he called me on a cell phone, and I mistakenly answered."

Margie screwed up her eyes as she looked at Sally. "You spoke to him, didn't you?"

"*He* spoke to me. He knew about Carolyn's death and that I thought it suspicious."

"How would he know that?" Margie asked.

"I've no idea. He wants me to go see him."

"Please tell me you're not going to?" Margie said. "He's toying with you."

"No way am I seeing him," she replied too fast, as if trying to convince herself. "I just wish he'd leave me alone."

"You heard anything back from the prison warden?" Margie asked.

"Only that they're looking into the flowers and phone calls. All it takes is a corrupt prison guard or a visitor willing to organize the flowers. I don't have much faith that they'll find out who did it."

"Maybe you should get a new cell number so Foster can't reach you?"

"He knows my address, so he can still reach me."

"Stay strong, my friend. Don't let him unsettle you," Margie said.

Having said goodbye to her friend, she slowed to a jog as she entered her street. She said good morning to a neighbor walking his French bulldog, then she crossed the road, taking the gap between her Honda Civic and Matt's RAV4. Sally's car was a 2008 model, but she took care to have it serviced regularly and the only damage to the exterior was a small indentation on the rear bumper. Which is why the wavy line etched along the side caught her eye. She stopped and looked closer, then ran a finger over it. The scratch was deep. Her car had been keyed.

"Damn it!"

She could try touching it up with paint and a small paint-brush. Fixing it properly would mean spray-painting both doors and while her car insurance might cover some of the cost, she would lose her no-claim bonus.

The neighborhood had a low crime rate, and she hadn't heard about cars being vandalized. And anyway, why would somebody vandalize her old-model Civic when there were plenty of luxurious cars to scratch? Wasn't keying meant to be about car envy?

She had forgotten about the man in the Hyundai Sonata who had given her a penetrating look. Sally looked all around but she couldn't see a Sonata. Perhaps she was jumping to conclusions, which she was prone to do. Maybe she was unlucky and it was done by kids.

Sally leaned down to inspect Matt's RAV4—there were no scratches. Parked to the left of her car was a blue Honda Accord. She inspected its paintwork—again no scratches. Hers had been specifically targeted.

"Don't sweat the small stuff," she said, collecting her mail from the mailbox, then, opening her house door and stepping inside.

She would call her insurer and ask if she should report car vandalism to the police.

She had one letter, her name and address printed on the envelope, but there was no postmark or stamp. It must have been hand-delivered. Her first thought was that it was a note from Matt, telling her how angry he was about her entering his backyard without permission. Or might it be a simple thank-you for the flowers she gave him?

She used her finger to slit open the envelope and took out the piece of notepaper. Unfolding it, she read the typed message:

I'M WATCHING YOU.

That was it.

In capital letters.

Three simple words, loaded with menace.

The note slipped from her fingers and floated to the floor. A jolt of fear had her staggering backward. She had been hot and sweaty from her run. She now felt a cold sense of dread.

Her first thought was that it was from Foster. Yet another way of messing with her head. Then she considered Matt. Did he know about her taking Carolyn's phone and the burned photos? Was he warning her off? But he could have told her to her face. Why leave a note when he lived next door? Then, once again, she thought about the bearded man in the Sonata who had looked straight at her. He was most definitely watching Sally's house.

Sally peeked out of the living room window. She couldn't see the stalker's car. Everything looked normal. But this note told her it wasn't. Someone wanted to scare her and it was working.

Sally quickly drew the living room drapes.

The menacing note and the damage to her car had to be connected.

They were a warning.

They knew where Sally lived.

They knew which car she drove.

But who was the threat from, and why?

NINETEEN

The bookstore hadn't been as busy as normal, so Olivia took the opportunity to change their window display while Sally served the customers. The highlight of the morning had been the retirement village book club. Three men and five women ranging from their mid-sixties to their eighties met once a month to discuss the selected novel. They were good for business because they always ordered their books from Olivia and usually treated themselves to slices of home-baked cakes too.

Sally stayed behind the counter at the front of the store, seated on a wooden stool, stroking the cat purring on the counter. The book club members were positioned around the largest table in the store. Teacups clanked on saucers and the debate about the selected novel grew louder, until Denis, a retired dentist, leaned back and called out.

"Sally, can you spare a minute? We need you to settle an argument."

"Sure." Sally wandered over to the seated group.

On the table were eight copies of *The Girl on the Train* by Paula Hawkins. Sally hadn't read it.

Denis said, "Do you think it's possible that an alcoholic, nursing a hangover, could spot a murder from a moving train? I think the notion is absurd, but Sylvia thinks it's entirely credible."

Sylvia nodded confidently.

"I don't know. I suppose alcoholics can function despite their addiction and many can behave normally. I would have thought the greater issue is the speeding train."

"It wasn't speeding," Sylvia piped up. "It had slowed on the line. You're misleading Sally."

"I thought it was moving," Denis said.

"It had stopped, hadn't it?" another lady said.

"Oh, never mind," said Denis. "Another question for Sally. You've faced a killer. None of us, thank the Lord, have. My question is, would you pursue a killer again?"

"What's that got to do with the book?" said Sylvia.

Denis shrugged. "I'm interested. It's not often you get the chance to talk to someone who's vanquished a serial killer."

"Denis, leave her alone," Sylvia said protectively.

Sally felt she owed them an answer. "I don't think so. The horror of it haunts me. If you'll excuse me, I should get on with the orders." Sally didn't wish to get roped into talking about Richard Foster.

Pajamas slapped the countertop with her tail, clearly happy at her return. Sally tried to focus on ordering in stock. But her thoughts were now hot-wired to Foster and whether he truly did have evidence against Scott.

"Sally?" Olivia said, sticking a poster on the wall for the sixty-sixth Ruth Rendell mystery, *Dark Corners*. "Some guy has walked past the shop three times already, like he wants to come in but can't bring himself to do it. Do you have an admirer you haven't told me about?"

Admirer—no. Freaks who scare me—plenty.

"No admirers," Sally said. "What does he look like?"

"Oh, beard, cap, jacket, fortyish."

Sally's hand slid from the keyboard. *It's him! The man in the Sonata!* "Is he there now?"

"Can't see him." Olivia turned to face Sally. "What's wrong? Do you know who he is?"

Sally didn't want to move. "Liv, can you see a Hyundai Sonata in the street? Gray-silver."

"One second." Olivia pursed her lips with concentration as she fiddled with the positioning of a book, then she looked across the street. "Nope, can't see it."

She then joined Sally at the counter. "I guess he's not someone you want to see, am I right?"

Sally nodded. "If you see him again, please tell me."

"I can tell he's freaking you out. I'll call the cops."

"I saw him outside my house earlier."

Olivia picked up the store's landline. "I'll get rid of him."

"No, it's okay. It's probably nothing. If he comes back, I'll talk to him."

Sally didn't mention the menacing note or the keying of her car. If she had, nothing Sally could say would stop Olivia from making the call.

———

Lunchtime came and went, and the bearded man didn't show. The book club caught the retirement village's bus home and after the lunchtime rush, the bookstore settled into a more leisurely rhythm. Sally took a late lunch break and, fearful of meeting the bearded man in the street, she ate her packed lunch in the back room. Paul dropped by with Reilly and a buddy from the football team called Ben, who played cornerback. Liv was clearly delighted to see the boys and treated them to cakes and soft drinks on the house. Then they left for the ten-pin bowling alley. Sally's phone rang. She hoped it was Dr. Lilia, but she didn't recognize the cell number. She hesitated. Foster used the prison's landline to call her, so it probably wasn't him.

Sally answered with a simple, "Hello."

"Why haven't you come to see me, Sally?"

She was wrong. It was Foster.

Sally didn't want his voice poisoning her ear. She held the phone only just near enough so that Foster would hear her. "Stop calling me."

Olivia saw the horrified look on her face. "Sally?"

"Whose phone is this?" Sally demanded.

"It wasn't easy to come by. I have information for you."

"I don't want it. Go away!"

"I'm worried about you," Foster said.

"Ha!" Sally's laugh was rich with derision. "You don't feel emotion, Foster. Not even for your own son."

"Ouch, that's nasty, and there was me trying my best to be nice. You should visit me. There's something you need to know."

"I will never visit you."

"You might want to reconsider that statement. Have you noticed a man following you?"

Sally stepped back into a bookcase with a thud and she hit the back of her skull on the shelf's edge. Books wobbled. "You sent him?"

"I did not, but I know who he is."

Liar! How else could you possibly know about the man watching me?

"Is this payback because I didn't come running? You sent someone to spook me? Well, it's not going to work."

This was all about Foster finding her most vulnerable spot and then poking it until she gave in and did as he wanted.

"Listen to me, Sally. I did not send anyone to watch you. I know who he is," Foster said. "There's a seven thirty visitor's slot tonight. I've taken the liberty of booking you in. You know where I am."

TWENTY

After work, Sally took Paul and Reilly for a late afternoon swim in Angel Lake. The boys splashed about while Sally swam laps, but every so often she stopped to look up and down the shoreline to check on them. Was the bearded man lurking somewhere, watching them?

Sally was rattled. Not just because she was convinced she was being watched but because Foster had confirmed it. How did he know?

What's more, he claimed he knew who was watching her. The only way he could possibly know was if he had sent the bearded man, surely? He was trying to rattle her so that she would run to him for answers.

Sometimes, when she needed to calm down, Sally would dive under the water. It was quiet beneath the surface, and she felt cocooned from the people and events that troubled her. For a few seconds she was able shut them out. Sally took a deep breath and dived. Sunlight lit up the stones and plants on the lake's floor. The water was so clear that she could see a school of small silvery fish zipping in one direction and then turning en masse in the other direction as if they were one being. It fascinated her that fish and birds could move in such a large group with such synchronicity.

When she could hold her breath no longer, she surfaced and blinked the water from her eyes. The boys were headed for the shore and Sally decided to do the same. She wanted to keep a close eye on them.

The lake's sandy beach was narrow and littered with driftwood in shades of silver and had a gently sloping bank that led up to a grassy strip. Beyond was forest. Sally had set up a spot in the shade of a big pine. She dried her face with a towel and rubbed her hair.

"I have drinks and snacks." She opened the zipper of a cooler bag.

The boys helped themselves to cans of Coke and Sprite, muffins, and muesli bars. All the time, Sally kept watch, her shoulders tense.

———

After dropping Reilly home, it was close to 6:30 p.m. by the time Sally and Paul reached Pioneer Drive. Sally unclipped her seatbelt and swiveled to look at her son. "What would you like for dinner. Salmon or beefsteak?"

As she turned, Sally caught a glimpse of the silver Hyundai Sonata—bearded man in the driver's seat—through the passenger window.

"Oh, crap."

"What's up, Mom?" Paul followed her line of sight. "Who is he?"

"Don't stare."

Paul swiveled his head to look at Sally. "Why? You look scared."

She forced a smile. "Not at all. Probably visiting someone who lives here."

"You tell me not to keep things from you. It goes both ways, Mom."

"Okay." Sally sighed, weighing up just how honest she should be. "When I went for my run this morning, that man was in his car and stared at me. He drove away. Then Liv said she saw a bearded man in a cap walking past the bookstore several times. And there he is again. Parked in the same spot he was in this morning."

"That's totally weird." Paul peered at the man in the Sonata, who was looking at his phone. Then the bearded man looked up, saw them watching him, and looked back down to continue to stare at the phone. "If he's creeping you out, call the cops."

Sally struggled to decide if she should tell Paul about Foster's phone call. So far, she had tried to keep the details of the calls from Paul, who should be enjoying his summer vacation, not worrying about her possible stalker. But Paul wasn't stupid and he knew when she was on edge, so she quickly filled him in on the calls.

Paul's face darkened. "Son of a bitch! Foster sent this guy to stalk us?"

"Foster denied it, but he says he knows who the man is."

"He's lying. That's what psychopaths do, Mom. Everyone knows that! I'm telling this guy to fuck off!" Paul released his seatbelt.

"No, don't!" Sally took his arm. "Leave it to me. I'll deal with him."

"He can't do this!" Paul was seething. "We have rights. He can't stalk people!"

"Don't do anything hasty, okay. I'm calling the cops."

Once Paul's temper was up, there was no telling what he would do. And the last thing she wanted was her son to pick a fight with the man watching them. Who knew why he was there or if he carried a weapon.

Sally dialed the number for Franklin PD. This wasn't an emergency situation, so there was no need to use 911.

Dot, the PD officer taking phone calls, recognized Sally straight away. Dot had been a cop for thirty years and showed no interest in packing it in. The police department was her family. Sally explained the nature of her call.

"We've noticed a man watching our house. He's here now, parked over the road. I think he followed me to work today. Can you send a patrol car to talk to him?"

Sally gave Dot her address, the car's make and model, and the license plate, as well as a facial description of the man watching them.

"I'll send over a patrol car," Dot said. "It's a busy afternoon, Sally. The sun must have turned people crazy. I'll get one to you as soon as possible."

Sally hung up.

"They on their way?" Paul asked.

"May take a while."

"He could be gone by then," Paul moaned. "What do we do until they get here?"

"Go in the house and wait."

Perhaps they had been sitting in their car for too long and the bearded man was spooked because just then his car's engine growled into life.

"Told you. The dirtbag's leaving." Paul threw open the door.

"No!" Sally said.

Paul was out of the car before she could stop him.

Her heart leaped into her mouth. In the few seconds it took for her to open the car door and get out, Paul had already reached the Sonata and was knocking on the driver's window in loud and aggressive thuds.

"Hey, there! What are you doing here?" Paul yelled.

There was a moment when the bearded guy looked straight

at Paul, then her view of the man was blocked by Paul's upper body.

The car engine revved, and the Sonata sped away, forcing Paul to jump out of the way.

"And don't come back!" Paul yelled after the receding vehicle.

Paul jogged back to where Sally stood.

"Jerk!" he said.

She took him in a hug, her heart pounding. He was shaking, like he was freezing cold. "Why did you do that? What if he had a gun? I can't lose you, Paul."

"It's all cool, okay?"

"He could have run you down. Shot you. Please, promise me you won't do that again."

"You can stop worrying, Mom. Look, I'm in one piece."

She was trembling as she carried the cooler bag and her purse inside. Paul shut the door and deadbolted it. Paul had never done that before. There had been times when she came home to an empty house to find the back door unlocked or ground-floor windows wide open because house security didn't register on her son's mind.

"What's the matter?" Sally asked.

"Nothing." He was pale. Very pale.

He walked away. In the kitchen he opened the refrigerator.

"Did that man say anything to you?" Sally asked.

"Not really." Paul looked down. "I'm going to have a shower."

Paul never usually bothered to shower after being in the lake.

"Tell me what happened. Did he threaten you?"

"He was just trying to scare me. But I don't scare easy." He stood tall and puffed out his chest, but she could tell from the shudder in his voice that he was afraid.

"Paul? Just tell me."

"Okay, he ran his fingers across his throat like this." Paul demonstrated.

Sally felt the floor move, or so it seemed. "He threatened to cut your throat?"

"I guess so. He's just a jerk."

The cops came and went. Paul told them about the man's silent threat. They said they would try to locate him through his car license plate. When the cops were gone, Sally changed her clothes into a loose linen blouse and sweatpants, then she cooked steak, fries, and peas and they ate ice cream in front of the TV.

To hell with healthy, Sally thought.

Paul selected an episode of *Brooklyn Nine-Nine* to watch. It was good to hear Paul laugh and she hoped their relaxed evening at home might help him forget their stalker.

On Sally's hip, tucked under her shirt, was her Glock 19. Fully loaded. If the bearded man ever tried to hurt her son, she would be ready.

TWENTY-ONE

Sally and Paul were relaxing in front of the TV when the doorbell rang. She whipped her head around, on edge since their stalker had threatened Paul. The outside light wasn't on because they weren't expecting visitors, but through the glass panels of the door she could make out one, possibly two people outside.

"Ring again," the woman said. "They're home."

The drapes were closed, but the blaring TV probably gave their presence away.

Paul lay across the sofa, a cushion propping up his head. He didn't react to the doorbell ringing, so glued was he to the TV program, all thoughts of the stranger's threat seemingly forgotten. Sally wished that she could move on from such a terrifying encounter so easily. Sally briefly toyed with the idea of ignoring her visitors, then changed her mind. Sally rose from the armchair and slid her hand beneath her loose blouse. The solidity of her Glock 19 in a pouch on her belt was comforting.

"Who is it?" Sally called out, keeping a solid wall between her and the new arrivals.

"Nicole and Lauren." The voice was cultured, and forceful.

It had to be Nicole, who Sally had seen with Matt yesterday. "Can we have a quick word?"

"It's late," Sally called out. "What is it about?"

"Mattie."

Sally flicked a look at Paul, who had continued watching TV, oblivious to Sally or the people at the door. Sally's first thought was that they were going to complain about her entering Matt's backyard yesterday. Perhaps they'd demand she return the things she took? She stared down the hallway. The photo and bank statement were in a desk drawer in her study, as was the SIM. Sally had no intention of giving them to the women, although explaining why she took them might be difficult to explain. A second thought lessened her worry on this matter. If the person who had seen Sally in Matt's yard had told Matt what she did, he wasn't the kind of man to ask someone else to deal with his issue—he would have hammered on her door the second he heard.

"One moment!" Sally called out. Then she went around the sofa and stood between Paul and the TV.

"Mom!" he complained.

"We have visitors. We can finish this episode later, I promise. Would you go upstairs? I think after what happened today, I'd rather you weren't involved."

Paul sat up, a crease down the cheek he had been lying on. "Who are they?"

"Friends of..." Should she say Carolyn or Matt? "...Carolyn."

Paul stood, stretching out his arms as he yawned and then shuffled across the polished floor in his socks and went upstairs. When he was gone from view, Sally opened the front door. The women were bathed in the orange glow of the streetlight.

Nicole extended a hand and Sally shook it, glimpsing the French manicure of Nicole's perfect nails. "Come in."

Nicole walked in, hurriedly followed by Lauren, who

smiled apologetically. Sally shut the door to find Nicole eyeing the living room in a way that made Sally feel as if she were being judged. Lauren stood awkwardly, trying to avoid eye contact.

"Please sit. Can I get you a drink?"

Both women said thank you, but no. Nicole took the armchair, Lauren the sofa. Sally sat next to Lauren. "I'm so sorry for your loss. Carolyn was a lovely neighbor and I'll really miss her. How can I help?"

"We're worried about Mattie," Nicole said. She looked straight at Lauren, whose hands were clasped together in her lap, her shoulders up near her ears. There was no doubt that Lauren was tense. Nicole, however, seemed calm and controlled. She continued, "And we want to ask for your help."

"Help?" Sally said, astonished.

"We know you're a former cop *and* you defeated those dreadful murderers..." Her voice trailed away. "What were they called?"

Lauren finally spoke, but in a small voice, "Richard and Aiden Foster."

"That's right. Dreadful people." Nicole shook her head and her ponytail swung from side to side. She was dressed for the gym. Perhaps she had just come from there. But, as previously, not a hair was out of place and there was not a hint of sweat. "It's been one hell of a day! So, we—that is Becca, Lauren, and I —want to do something about Daisy."

"Matt's lover?" Sally said.

Nicole looked put out. "Oh, you know about her. Who told you?"

"Carolyn."

Nicole stared at Sally for a second or two. "Right, okay. Sorry, when did she tell you?"

"A few days before she died." Nicole frowned. Lauren's knuckles had turned white, she was clenching them so tightly.

And her eyes were watery, just like the other day. This conversation was clearly upsetting her. Less so Nicole. "Didn't she tell you?" Sally very deliberately asked.

On the morning before Carolyn met her husband at the airport, Sally overheard part of a phone conversation in which somebody had tipped Carolyn off about Matt's early return from the convention and his plan to meet Daisy.

"Well, of course she did. We're her best friends." Nicole straightened her back. *Are you her best friend, or just pretending to be?* Sally wondered. "She told us the morning of that ghastly scene at the airport."

Someone had tipped off Carolyn, and Sally would bet it was either Nicole, Lauren, or Becca. Why was Nicole pretending otherwise?

"I was at the airport, meeting my son," Sally said. "It was obvious something was wrong. I watched Matt and Lachlan arrive. I hope you don't mind me asking, but why did you slap your husband?"

"I don't see how that's any of your business."

"You came here for my help." Sally left the implication hanging in the air.

Nicole flicked her ponytail over her shoulder and didn't look happy that Sally had given her no wiggle room.

"Because the toad lied to me. He told me that Matt was staying for the whole week and he'd come back early to manage the pharmacies. He failed to mention that Matt was also leaving the convention early so he could be with his little whore."

"What does it matter now if Matt sees Daisy?" Sally asked.

"Because we care about Matt. Daisy is a selfish little bitch. She wants Matt to invest in the band. He's her meal ticket to what she thinks is her chance to be a star. She's got talent, but not that much talent. And the business is in trouble. Matt needs to invest in the business, not squander his inheritance on her."

Money, Sally thought, *was often a motive for murder.*

"When you say inheritance, do you mean that Carolyn left a will bequeathing her money to Matt?"

"That's right. And she was a wealthy woman. Not that he married her for that reason, he obviously loved her," Nicole hastily added. "Daisy has her eye on Matt's inheritance, which gives her motive for murder, right? We want you to prove that Daisy killed Carolyn."

Sally frowned. Carolyn had been convinced that Matt was trying to kill her. Now Nicole seemed sure that Daisy had done it. Either way, Carolyn's wealth could be a motive—for one or both of them. Matt needed money for the business. Daisy wanted to use Matt's inheritance to help make her a star.

"Does Matt know you're here?" Sally asked.

"No and don't tell him. He's besotted with the girl. This is just between us."

"Is Becca in on this?"

"Yes. She couldn't join us tonight because she's on night duty at the vet hospital." Nicole had a stretchy belt around her waist that doubled as pouch for her cards, keys, and phone. "We'll pay you, naturally. I was thinking five hundred dollars up front. Cash." She took out a small wallet. "Or I can do a direct deposit now, if you give me your bank details."

Sally was about to say no to the task, then she changed her mind. With Lauren's and Nicole's help she would have a better chance at solving the mystery behind Carolyn's death. But she didn't want to be paid. She just wanted to do right by Carolyn.

"I'll do what I can, but I don't want payment."

"Really? Oh, thank you!" Lauren said, coming to life for the first time.

"Suit yourself," Nicole said, putting her wallet away. "Now what do you need from us?"

"What do you know about the autopsy?" Sally asked.

Sally knew that the advanced poisons test might take twenty-four hours. She wanted to find out what *they* knew.

Nicole replied, "They're doing more tests apparently."

"How do you think Daisy killed Carolyn?" Sally asked.

Lauren cringed, as if a giant spider had run into her lap.

Nicole noticed. "Lauren, if this is too much for you, take my car keys and have a rest."

Lauren nodded, took Nicole's keys, and let herself out of Sally's house.

"She was very close to Carolyn."

"Do you have any thoughts on how Carolyn died?" Sally asked once again.

"No, I hope you'll find that out." She handed Sally a business card. "Call me anytime."

The business card included a website for online kids clothing, the kind of business that a busy mom could do from home.

When Nicole had left, Paul came down the stairs.

"Proud of you, Mom. You've got your first private case!"

TWENTY-TWO

JULY 17, 2016

It was Sunday morning and Sally wasn't working today. It was also the one day that she didn't go running. She liked to sleep in and then cook a special breakfast. Paul more often than not spent the day with his friends, but sometimes they'd go for a hike or explore a location they hadn't been to before.

This Sunday morning, Paul glowered at his mother across the breakfast table.

"I'm not going," he said.

Sally hadn't slept a wink last night. She hadn't been able to stop thinking about the man who had threatened her son's life. It was possible that he only intended to scare Paul away. But what if the man actually intended to slit Paul's throat? And on top of the threat, there had been the warning note and the vandalism of her car.

"He threatened you, Paul. I can't have you at risk. Please, just a few days. George and Ellen would love to see you."

Her parents lived in North Bend, a country town about an hour's drive from Pioneer Heights.

"Grandad hates me and it's *so* boring. Why can't I stay with my friends?"

"Because they live too near us. I want you out of harm's way. And your granddad doesn't hate you. He can be critical, that's true, but he loves you."

Sally thought about her upbringing and how her father had always put her down, just as he did Sally's mom, Ellen. Even when Sally had joined the police and graduated from police academy, he scorned her choice of career and told her that she would never last. He had been right, sadly. But not because she couldn't do the job. She'd loved it and she was good at it, but Scott had already scooped her up and captured her in his web of lies by then. Plus, once they were married, he'd piled on the pressure to become a stay-at-home mom. She hadn't completely caved, although the victim advocate role she moved on to was a more nine-to-five role.

"Critical?" Paul stared at her openmouthed. "He's a bully. Like Dad. Grandad won't stop telling me what to do and we'll argue, like we did the last time we saw him."

That was last Christmas. It had been a disaster and they had left her parent's house as soon as they could.

Paul folded his arms across his chest, his pancakes only half-eaten. "And what about you, Mom? Who's watching your back?"

Her heart melted. His desire to protect her made her feel so proud of him but also scared for him. She was his mom and it was her job to protect him, although protecting a headstrong teenager with the strength of a grown man wasn't easy.

"My darling, I love you more than life itself. I love the way you look out for me. But I know how to look after myself and I'm not the one who was threatened by that man. We don't know who he is or why he's watching me. Watching *us*," she corrected herself, because perhaps now he was watching Paul too.

"I'll be careful, Mom. I can stay with Reilly. I promise if I see that dickhead anywhere near me, I'll tell you."

Sally thought about Paul's proposal. Would he be safe enough?

Did *"I'M WATCHING YOU"* include Paul? Or was it about her? Was Carolyn's killer letting Sally know that he or she was watching her investigations? Was it a way of making her stop?

Sally was loath to stop for a number of reasons. Top of the list was for the guilt she felt at failing to heed Carolyn's plea for help. Then there was last night's visit from Nicole and Lauren. They believed that Daisy was the killer and they too asked for her help. Also, it struck Sally that if somebody wanted to stop her investigations, it was because she was onto something. But what was she onto? Was it on Carolyn's phone perhaps? And, on top of which, like Paul, she hated giving in to bullies. Sally had vowed that after Scott was out of their lives, she would not be bullied ever again.

The bearded man in the Hyundai Sonata had, to the best of her knowledge, begun watching her yesterday morning. The day before, she had sneaked into Matt's yard and rescued Carolyn's phone and the burned fragments from the firepit. That day, she had also spoken to the forensic pathologist, Dr. Lilia, who had agreed to conduct an advanced poisons test. The bearded man's appearance and her actions yesterday must be connected somehow.

The question was who had told the bearded man to watch her?

Was it Matt? Or perhaps it was his lover, Daisy? Private investigators didn't come cheap, and unless Daisy, who looked to be twenty-or-so years old, had wealthy parents, Sally doubted she would be able to afford to pay a PI. On the other hand, Matt owned two pharmacies. He would be more likely to be able to afford a PI. But how many PIs threaten people in the way the bearded man had threatened her son?

Then there was the question of how Richard Foster knew

that she was being watched. Was it possible that he was behind the bearded man's appearance, the note, and the vandalism of her car? Had he arranged it out of spite because Sally wouldn't see him? He was certainly the kind of man to use intimidation to get what he wanted.

"Mom?" Paul said.

Sally must have been lost in her thoughts too long.

"I have an idea," Sally said. "I'm happy to call Reilly's parents and ask them if you can stay for a few days." Paul whooped. "Please hear me out. We should know the result of the advanced poisons test today. At that point, it will either become a homicide case for Detective Clarke or the question of her sudden death will be put to rest and we can all get on with our lives."

"What about your promise to Nicole and Lauren?"

She thought about that for a minute.

"If Clarke takes on the case, I'll contact Nicole and suggest that she deals with the detective."

"Okay," Paul said. "But I think you should keep looking, even if Clarke takes the case. You're good at it."

Sally smiled at him. "I'll call Grace now." Grace Doyle was Reilly's mom.

Sally dropped Paul at Reilly's house shortly after her call with Grace. Both boys were happy with the arrangement and disappeared into Reilly's den. Sally had a cup of coffee with Grace and told her about the bearded man watching her house and his threat to Paul, also that the police were trying to track the man in the Hyundai Sonata. Grace was understandably concerned and promised to keep an eye out for the man with the beard and black cap.

Sunday and Monday were Sally's days off. Olivia kept the

bookstore open seven days a week, and when Sally was off, a college student studying for a bachelor of arts in American literature worked the other two days in Sally's place.

Driving home, Sally felt a little lonely. Paul was so much a part of her life that when he wasn't with her, there was a gaping hole. Sally could spend the day doing chores around the house, but that was a terrible waste of a beautiful summer day. She was determined to clear up Paul's messy smelly room, wash clothes, and vacuum, but then she'd like to enjoy the company of a friend. On the spur of the moment, she rang a woman who she hadn't seen for years and asked if she was free to meet for lunch. Hannah Sanchez sounded pleased to hear from Sally, but she wasn't available for lunch. They did, however, agree on a date and time to meet up when Hannah was back from a business trip. Hannah was one of the many friends Scott had succeeded in alienating to the point that they stopped seeing Sally at all. Only recently did Sally have enough confidence to contact them and explain how Scott gaslighted her, that he was out of her life, and she dearly wanted to rejuvenate their friendship.

There was no sign of the stalker when she pulled into Pioneer Drive. The tension in her shoulders relaxed as she entered her home and shut the door behind her. Dumping her purse on the lounge room coffee table, she switched on the radio to fill the house with music, then opened the closet under the stairs where she kept the vacuum cleaner and other household stuff. She carried the vacuum cleaner up to the landing, where she left it outside Paul's room. Opening his bedroom door, she found clothes on the floor as well as draped over every possible surface, including a pile of dirty washing in a corner where he kept his dumbbells. The room stank of teenage testosterone, sweat, and dank socks. Sally opened the windows and got to work.

With a pile of washing in her arms, Sally went downstairs and filled the washing machine. Once that was running, she headed back to the stairs' closet and grabbed the duster and household cleaning spray. Passing her study, she remembered the bank statement she had taken from the firepit and left in her desk drawer. Once she had cleaned Paul's room, she would take a look at it.

In her peripheral vision, she noticed her study wasn't quite as she had left it. She took a couple of steps back and stood in the doorway. The study was snug, with just a desk, chair, and filing cabinet, on top of which was a printer. On the wall were some framed photographs. A young Sally, in police academy uniform, smiling proudly, her shiny brown hair tied back in a tight bun. Next to it was a group shot, taken on the first day at the district attorney's office. On the desk was a recent framed photo of Sally and Paul, seated in kayaks on Angel Lake.

Her eyes wandered to the desk. The top desk drawer was open. She froze.

Sally didn't leave drawers open and Paul wouldn't have needed anything from it, surely?

The pens and notepad and other stationery she kept there were as she had left them. But the burned remains of the photos and the partial bank statement were gone.

Sally turned suddenly. Somebody had taken them. Somebody had been in her house. The panic hit her like a car crash. What if the thief was still here? A cold sense of dread racing through her veins had her creeping out of the room. She had to grab her purse and run. She looked toward the back door and gasped, hands clapping to her mouth. It was ajar.

Sally ran into the living room, picked up her purse, threw the front door open, and bolted. Only when she had the car doors locked with her safely inside did she dial 911 and ask for the police.

TWENTY-THREE

The car was hot, but Sally wouldn't leave it until the police arrived. Someone had broken into her house and might still be there.

Sally turned the ignition, then switched the air conditioning to the coldest temperature. Two minutes had passed since she made the 911 call, enough time for the intruder to exit via the back door, take the laneway, and run away.

The rush of adrenaline that had propelled her from the house was now subsiding, leaving her feeling shaky.

"Please hurry!" she murmured.

Sally stared at her front door, then her eyes drifted to Matt's house. His RAV4 wasn't in the street and the house was shut up. The house on the other side of Sally's home had been empty for a while. An investor owned it and used an agency to rent it out. The previous tenants had moved out last week and there was a FOR RENT sign outside. It dawned on her how isolated that left her.

Her phone rang and her heart lifted.

"Dr. Lilia!"

"Sally. We've got the results back from the advanced

poisons test. I've already sent the report to Detective Clarke. You were correct. Carolyn Tate was poisoned."

"Oh my God! Really?"

"It's an odd choice of poison. *Nerium oleander*."

"I have no idea what *Nerium oleander* is."

"A poisonous shrub. Any part of it can be deadly. Often grown in people's gardens. Pretty pink flowers. Can trigger a heart attack if taken in large enough quantities."

"How large?"

"A handful of the flowers and leaves would be enough."

"You mean Carolyn must have ingested it?"

"Correct. Possibly it was hidden inside something she ate or drank. We're checking her stomach contents again. In the meantime, Clarke has been notified that this is a suspicious death."

"Thank you so much for doing this. I'm relieved to know my hunch was right, but sad that someone would murder such a lovely woman in the prime of her life."

"Thank you for the tip-off, Sally. Oh, and just to be clear, I haven't mentioned your intervention to anyone. Not to my team nor to Clarke."

"I understand and thank you once again."

A patrol car and an unmarked police Suburban arrived ten minutes later. The two plainclothes detectives came over to where Sally sat in her car. She switched off her engine and exited her vehicle.

"Detectives?" Sally had expected the patrol car, but not homicide detectives.

Detective Clarke was accompanied by Detective Esme Lin, the youngest and newest member of the homicide squad. Sally had a soft spot for her—she had saved Paul from Aiden Foster, and Sally would always be grateful to the Chinese American detective.

"You have an intruder?" Clarke said, giving nothing away about why he was here. Robbery wasn't his bag.

"I think he's been and gone. I got home, found some photos and a document was missing from my study, then saw the back door was open. And before you ask, I always lock the back and front doors."

"Did you see the intruder?"

"No."

"We'll take a look. House keys, please."

She handed them to Clarke, who called over the patrol officers and gave them the keys. The uniforms let themselves in. Lin finished her call and came over. "Stolen car, reported missing two nights ago."

"Why assume you have an intruder?" Clarke asked. "Maybe your son left the back door open?"

"No, I checked before we went out. Yesterday there was a menacing note put under my door. My car was keyed. Then I noticed a man watching me. He threatened to slice Paul's throat."

Clarke and Lin exchanged glances. "What man?" Clarke asked, his frown deepening so much that his protruding brow hid his eyelids.

Sally filled them in on the bearded man watching her yesterday in the Hyundai Sonata who had gestured to Paul that he would cut his throat. "I gave his car number plate to the patrol officers yesterday."

"Check on that, Lin," Clarke said. Lin walked away and made a phone call. "See if they've identified the owner."

"Is this connected to Carolyn Tate?" Clarke asked.

"I think so. I think it's because I've been..." She knew that Clarke wouldn't be happy. "Yesterday, I took some things from Matt Tate's backyard. He was trying to destroy them and that made me suspicious. Carolyn's phone and the burned remains of some photos and a bank statement."

"When you say 'took,' you mean what exactly?" Clarke said.

Sally shifted her feet. She had technically broken the law.

"When Matt was out, I let myself into his backyard and fished the phone out of the pond, then the photos and document from the firepit. Matt wasn't home but someone was. They watched me from an upstairs window."

Clarke rolled his eyes. "You trespassed? Jesus! I thought I told you to leave this alone."

A few years ago, when Scott had influence over her, she would have apologized and gone away with her tail between her legs. Not these days. She respected Clarke, but Sally was gradually learning to trust her instincts, and her instincts told her that Carolyn's death hadn't been due to natural causes. She waited for him to speak.

He continued, "I'm guessing the irony isn't lost on you? You reported an intruder today and yesterday you entered a neighbor's property without his permission."

"It was worth the risk. I have Carolyn's phone. It was in the fishpond."

"Fishpond?" Lin said.

"Yes. There's a video of Matt and his lover in the video file. They seem really keen to get rid of Carolyn."

Sally opened her purse and offered Clarke the velvet pouch. "In there."

Clarke nodded at Lin, who took the pouch from her. "Esme, find out what's happening in the house, will you?"

Lin nodded and left.

"Listen to me, Sally," Clarke said. "I'm saying this for your own good. You've told me that you entered Matt Tate's backyard because you smelled smoke and you thought Matt was in danger. That's right, isn't it?"

He was giving her just cause for her illegal entry. She took the hint, although the words stuck in her throat. She was a terrible liar. "Yes, that's what happened."

"Did you call the fire service?" Clarke asked.

"No," she replied, playing along, "there was no need. I discovered it was a smoldering firepit."

"I see. And you said that you fished the phone out of the pond because you assumed someone had dropped it there by mistake?" Sally nodded confirmation, but she blushed at the lie.

"Good," he said. "I'm glad we've cleared that up. Now, follow me." He led her to his Suburban. We'll talk in here." He got in the driver's seat, switched on the engine and the air conditioning. She sat in the back. He swiveled in his seat so he could look at her. "Tell me everything you know about Carolyn Tate."

This had to mean that Clarke had seen Dr. Lilia's amended autopsy report. But she couldn't let on to Clarke that she already knew.

"The autopsy concluded it was a suspicious death?" Sally asked.

"It did. Poison. I don't want any 'I told you so' from you, okay?" Clarke gave her a half-smile.

"I wouldn't dream of it. I just want you to find her killer."

TWENTY-FOUR

Sally's intruder was long gone. The forensics team arrived and dusted her back door, study door, desk drawers, and other surfaces the thief might have touched. The only items taken from her home were the five burned remains of printed photos and a bank statement, which Sally wished now that she had paid more attention to. Clarke had insisted she check her gun safe. The safe was locked and her Glock 19 and the ammunition were where she had left them.

Detectives Clarke and Lin were next door speaking to Matt. Sally wondered how he was taking the news that his wife had been murdered. The spouse or partner was always a prime suspect in such murders and Matt would probably realize that.

Sally found it impossible to settle with people in her house. They walked around her in blue coveralls and masks as if she had a contagious disease. She had been told not to touch any hard surfaces such as doors, windows, or the refrigerator door, in case the intruder had touched them.

But how did the intruder get in? There was no sign of forced entry. Only Sally, Paul, and Margie had keys to the house. The theft must have taken place when Sally and Paul were with the Doyles. But before she had left home, Sally had checked that the back door was locked as well as the front. The only way the thief could have known the house was empty was if they were watching the house.

Sally shuddered.

The bearded stalker was back. It had to be him. Sally sat on the bed afraid to go out, at least until the locks were changed. She lay back on the bed and stared at the ceiling. The fan was circling, creating enough air movement to cool the bedroom. All this was happening because Sally wanted justice for Carolyn. Was it time for her to walk away? Clarke was on the case. Sally suddenly sat up. What if the man watching her assumed she had brought Clarke in to investigate? He had warned her not to interfere and this appeared to be an escalation.

The thought made her nervous.

There was a pile of unopened mail on the coffee table, and she went through it, just to give herself something to do. There was a power bill and a newsletter from the city council about Fourth of July celebrations and the ensuing road closures. Among the unsolicited mail was a postcard from Abbott's Locksmiths. There were testimonials from satisfied customers and the guy who ran the company, Craig Abbott, was local. She called the number.

Craig answered after a couple of rings. He was cheerful and helpful and went through her options for new locks as well as suggesting she get a house alarm.

Sally asked about the cost of a house alarm.

"Depends on which system," Craig said. He detailed some options and costs.

But even the most basic house alarm was more than Sally could afford.

"I'll stick with door and window locks for now."

They agreed on a time and Sally hung up.

She stood wearily and headed for the stairs. Her phone

rang. She recognized the cell number. It was the one that Richard Foster had used to contact her before.

"Go away!" she muttered, letting it ring.

It stopped ringing. A few seconds later her phone pinged: she had a phone message. Sally would not listen to it.

"To hell with it."

There were two marked police cars and the unmarked Suburban in the street. Nobody was going to enter her house with them there. Sally needed to get out and go for a walk and clear her head. As she scooped up her purse, she saw she had a text message. Thinking it might have been from Paul, she opened the message:

> *I have the name of the man who's following you. It'll be weeks before the Shar-Pei and his stupid pups work it out.*
>
> *I've booked you a visitor's slot at 2:30 p.m. Don't be shy. Richard.*

Shar-Pei was Foster's derisory name for Clarke because the detective had loose skin on his face that created a rolling effect on his forehead and jowly cheeks.

"Urrrrr!" she groaned through gritted teeth. His arrogance was infuriating.

The pressure over the last few days must have really gotten to Sally. She was like a pressure cooker about to blow. She shoved the phone in her bag, grabbed her sunglasses and keys, and threw open the front door. On her doorstep was Clarke, who stepped back, startled by her sudden appearance.

"Going somewhere?" he asked.

"Yes, I need some air. Do you want to speak to me?"

Sally stood in the doorway, unwilling to let Clarke in. She really had to get away before she screamed.

"Thought you should know that the Hyundai Sonata was stolen two days ago."

"And the owner? Could he be lying?"

"*She* is a woman in her sixties."

"Right, so she's not my stalker." Sally told Clarke that she believed the man was still watching her because he knew that she and Paul were out that morning.

"We have an APB out on the vehicle and we've distributed your stalker's description."

"Could he have switched cars?" Sally asked.

"Very possible. You've seen his car, so he'll probably dump it and steal another. We'll keep searching."

Sally thought about Foster's text message, the words already etched on her brain. How did a maximum-security prisoner know that Clarke would have difficulties identifying her stalker? Sally parted her lips, about to tell Clarke about Foster's claim.

"Yes?" Clarke said, tilting his head.

"Nothing. Can I go now?"

"Sure." Clarke watched her get into her car.

If he knew where she was going, he'd think her raving mad.

Perhaps she was...

TWENTY-FIVE

Cops incarcerated at the Walla Walla State Penitentiary didn't tend to live long. Often they met with a mysterious accident of some description. Sometimes they took their own lives, rather than wait for the inevitable. From the moment Richard Foster walked through the prison gates to serve his life sentence, he had a target on his back as large as DC's Capitol Rotunda. Not only had Foster arrested some of the prison's worst offenders—now determined to wreak their revenge on him—but he was also a child killer, and child killers were fair game for the prison population.

The odds of Foster surviving long in Walla Walla were extremely low, even if he was kept in a separate wing from the general prison population, where the child murderers and pedophiles were locked up for twenty-three hours a day and took their shower and walk alone. But Sally knew Foster to be clever, ruthless, and manipulative. He would be able to buy, blackmail, or intimidate his enemies into submission. Sally was already regretting her decision to visit him. A year and two months ago he had imprisoned her, then tried to kill her. He was going to bury her body in the forest behind his house, where he had also buried the young girls he'd murdered.

Sally was escorted by a white prison guard with a mustache into a room that stank of unwashed bodies and bleach.

"He don't get visitors," the guard said. "He's real excited."

Sally's stomach heaved. The thought of giving Foster any kind of pleasure made her sick to the stomach. She glanced at the guard. He walked in a breezy way as if they were going to a picnic.

"How long do I get?" Sally asked.

"Meant to be fifteen minutes. But if you want more, you can have it." He winked at her.

Bars slid electronically closed behind her and Sally almost fainted. So much adrenaline was coursing around her body, she couldn't stop her hands and legs shaking.

"I've changed my mind. I want to leave."

"Not a problem. I'll escort you out."

He turned full circle, but Sally stayed put. She had some questions.

"You said he doesn't have visitors?"

"That's right. His lawyer used to come. Not anymore."

On the drive to the prison, Sally had considered how Foster used a cell phone to call her and how he managed to keep tabs on her stalker. She'd guessed that he had someone on the outside doing his bidding. Perhaps another bent cop like Foster. Though the only way Foster would have use of a cell phone was if he used one that belonged to a guard, or one was smuggled in for him. Either way, the guards had to look the other way.

"Has Foster got a cell phone?"

"No, ma'am. Not permitted."

"He called me from a cell phone."

"We'll check his cell. Ma'am, if you want to leave, we go now. I got other visitors to escort."

Sally looked back the way she had come: a long corridor

with two sets of electronic barred gates and a guard at each gate. The guard at the nearest gate was watching them, probably wondering why they had stopped. "Glenn, what's up?" he called.

Sally saw his name badge on the guard's breast pocket.

"Nothing to worry about," Glenn called back. "The lady's leaving."

Sally stared in the opposite direction. A solid steel door, with a square Perspex panel at the top. Beyond that door was the room where Sally would sit on one side of a wall and talk to Foster on the other side. He couldn't touch her or hurt her, but he could see and speak to her.

"It's okay. I'll see him."

Glenn set off immediately, leaving Sally to catch up. He opened the steel door and gestured to the only object in the room, an orange plastic chair. "Sit there. Panic button's on the wall. Don't go near the Perspex. He can't break through, but they sometimes like to spit through them holes."

Holes had been drilled into the Perspex to enable sound to travel. Glenn paused, waiting for her to sit.

She wanted to run, but it was too late for that. Foster already knew she was there. It was his victory.

The chair seat was sticky; she didn't want to imagine why. The barrier between her and the next room was concrete blocks three feet high and then it was Perspex to the ceiling. The walls were a depressing beige. On the other side of the Perspex was an identical plastic chair, which was empty. Glenn closed the door behind her with a clank.

She had to grit her jaw to stop from screaming at the guard to come back. Memories of the hideous basement room where Foster imprisoned her touched her like cobwebs clinging to her skin. The room was full of toys, make-up, and jewelry for girls as young as eleven and as old as thirteen. Those girls were Foster's playthings.

Sally took a deep breath and held it, then exhaled a long slow breath, hoping to calm her terror.

The solid steel door in the opposite room creaked open and Foster, in an orange boiler suit and handcuffs, entered. Sally peed a few drops, unable to control her bladder. She had faced him in court over a year ago, but she hadn't been alone with him since he held her captive in his basement. Now, despite the solid barrier between them, she felt vulnerable and exposed.

Foster had lost the paunch. His hair was grayer, as was his skin—prisoners didn't get much access to sunshine. He looked older than his sixty-one years, although he walked with the confidence of a man who knew his power and reveled in it. He might be a lifer, but Foster had connections outside the jail walls. Rumor had it that powerful people owed him.

The prison guard nodded at Sally and the relief at his familiar face was just what she needed. She knew some of the prison guards from her time as a victim's advocate and Tank was one of them, a huge Black guy who dwarfed Foster. Tank walked away and positioned himself by the door, his eyes on Foster.

"I knew you'd come," Foster said, leaning back into the chair.

Be strong, she told herself. *Find out what he knows and get out.*

"I'm here for information," Sally said. "You said you know the man who's following me."

"Not so fast. What's the rush? You're looking well." His eyes dropped to her tanned arms. "Ah, summer. Not that you'd know it was summer in here. Billy and I used to walk for miles, then we'd watch the sun go down. How is Billy?"

He was talking about his black Labrador. Sally had to be careful about how much she told him. The retired couple who had adopted Billy had stipulated that their identities must be kept a secret.

"He's with a good family. Being looked after well."

"Glad to hear it. He's a good dog. Isn't it funny how dogs love you, no matter what you do?"

Foster stared down at the floor with a whimsical smile. Billy was Foster's soft spot, if a psychopath had such a thing. Foster would kill without a moment's hesitation, but he had treated his dog like a prince. *Psychopaths can imitate emotion, be careful*, she told herself.

"That's true. Dogs are forgiving," Sally said.

"Have you forgiven me, Sally?"

She wanted to yell at him that she despised him. But she kept her face neutral. "No. Are you sorry for what you did to those girls?"

Foster looked up and chuckled. "No. Surely you must know me by now? I don't regret what I did. I only regret getting caught. And most of all I regret Aiden's death." His sunken eyes narrowed. "Which you were responsible for."

Sally felt as if a cold hand had run up the length of her spine. "He tried to kill me, Richard. It was him or me, you know that."

He stared at her for a moment, his eyes boring into hers. "Wish I'd remembered you were such a good shot. Anyway, probably for the best. I wouldn't have wanted this existence for my boy." Foster looked around the spartan room. "How is your boy doing? Paul, right?"

Sally's skin prickled and a flush spread up her chest to her neck. "Paul's off limits." She changed topic fast. "Tell me what you know about the man following me."

He crossed his legs. "Nothing comes easy in life, Sally. If you want what I know, you have to do something for me in return."

Sally's mouth was so dry, her tongue felt leathery. She was negotiating with the devil. Every instinct told her to run and never come back. But she was afraid for her son. She wanted the stalker who threatened him to be caught. "And what might that be?"

"Patience. We'll get to that." Sally was desperately trying to take control of their meeting, but Foster kept wrenching it from her. After all, he had what she wanted, and he knew it. "Heard from your husband recently?"

"Ex-husband. And no."

If Sally were a voodoo doll, Foster was sticking every painful pin possible into her. Foster had been a Franklin PD detective when Scott was a beat cop.

"I never liked Scott."

It was such an unexpected statement that Sally stared at Foster.

"I thought he was Mr. Popular," Sally said.

"He liked to think so. He was an arrogant prick most of the time, and a shit cop too. Lord knows how many times he applied to be a detective and got knocked back every time."

"I didn't know that."

"Yeah, well, you wouldn't. He was one of the best liars I've ever met."

"That I do know."

Foster laughed. "He used to call me limey behind my back. Had no respect. I called him turd-face behind his back, so I guess we were all square." Foster had left the UK's Metropolitan Police and joined Franklin PD in 1981, then worked his way up the ranks to homicide detective. His accent remained East London. "He's a wannabe and I hate wannabes."

"Wannabe what? Detective?"

His eyes glinted with a sick glee that almost caused Sally's heart to stop. "You know what I mean," he said. "Don't pretend to be naïve."

Sally's head was buzzing. How much did Foster know about Scott's assault of Stacy Green? Is that what he meant by wannabe? Was that poor girl Scott's only victim and Foster looked down on him because of it?

Sally's stomach roiled and a bitter taste entered her mouth. She had to clear her throat.

Her biggest issue right now was her stalker. But how could she get Foster to tell her what he claimed he knew about him?

Foster wasn't only a psychopath. He was a narcissist, sadist, and had Machiavellian tendencies. He was also a very clever detective. She decided to massage his ego and see what that might do to loosen his tongue.

"I used to admire you," Sally said. "When I was a cop, I wanted to be a detective like you."

"Flattery, huh?" He chuckled. "I *was* good, wasn't I?"

"You still are. You know who my mystery stalker is, and the police don't have a clue."

"By police you mean Clarke?"

Sally nodded.

"What a total twat he is! He couldn't even work out that I was the Poster Killer when I was right under his nose."

"If you're better than him," Sally said, "prove it. Tell me the name of my stalker."

He wagged a disapproving finger. "Not so fast. I haven't told you what I want."

There was a lump in her throat. What hellish request was he about to put to her. "Okay, tell me."

"I'm shut in a maximum-security cell for twenty-three hours of every day. It's the boredom that gets me. You want my help, you visit me every day. And each day I'll tell you a bit more."

Sally blinked a few times. She had anticipated far worse. She would gladly be his distraction from boredom if it got her the identity of her stalker.

"You haven't given me anything yet. I'll visit you once a week, only if you tell me something useful right now."

"Every day."

"No can do. Once a week."

"Shit! You've changed. You used to be so malleable."

"Those days are over."

Foster scratched his stubbly chin. "Okay. He's a former cop."

"His name?"

"That's tomorrow's visit."

Sally dug her fingernails into her palms. "You can't be serious. I just want his name."

"I told you, you have to earn it."

"Stop playing games!"

"As you wish." He stood slowly. Over his shoulder, he told the guard that their meeting was done.

"Wait!" Sally stood, her chair scraping on the floor.

Her plea fell on deaf ears.

TWENTY-SIX

Sally sat in her car in the prison parking lot waiting for her pulse to slow. She had embarrassing sweat marks on her blouse and her face was still flushed from her encounter with Richard Foster. He knew how to press all the right buttons and Sally felt as if she had been turned inside out. And all that she had gleaned from him was that her stalker was an ex-cop. Sally shook her head. If he were telling the truth, and that was a big *if*, this was yet another reason for Sally to doubt the integrity of Franklin's police force.

Although Clarke and Lin had proved to be good apples in a barrel of rotten fruit.

Should she simply pass on the information to Clarke and make that her last visit to Foster? She squirmed in her seat as she imagined Clarke's look of incredulity when she told him that serial killer Foster was the source. Clarke would laugh her out of his office. However, he might take Nicole's information about Daisy Sheene seriously.

Sally drank from her water bottle, then she picked up her phone and called Clarke. It went to voicemail. She didn't leave a message. Instead, she tried Detective Esme Lin.

"Hey, Sally. Everything okay?" Lin said.

"So far, so good. Haven't seen my stalker today. Maybe you scared him away." She dearly hoped that was the case. "That's not why I called. I have some information about the Carolyn Tate investigation."

"Go on."

"Have you seen Carolyn's will?" Sally asked.

Lin hesitated a beat. "You know I can't tell you its contents if I had."

"I know, and what I'm about to say may just be gossip, but I've been told that Carolyn was wealthy and that Matt is to inherit."

"If that were true," Lin said carefully, "are you saying Matt killed his wife for her money?"

"Maybe. Although, I also think his lover, Daisy Sheene, has motive. Don't you?"

"Tell me why you think that."

"She's an ambitious singer in Matt's band. I've spoken to her, and I got the feeling that she sees Matt as her ticket to stardom. She wants Matt to put his money into the band. I don't know for sure, but perhaps Carolyn put her foot down and didn't want to use her savings that way. What if Daisy saw Carolyn as an obstacle to her ambitions?"

"Does the boss know you're talking to suspects? Because I think he'll be real mad."

"My chat with Daisy was before homicide took the case. I just thought you should know."

"Thanks for that, Sally. Stay safe."

Stay safe! Sally's eyes bulged: she had forgotten that the locksmith was coming around. "Will do."

The dashboard clock told her she had just enough time to reach home before the locksmith arrived. Sally set off and as she searched for a parking bay near her house, she noticed a van for Abbott's Locksmiths was parked out front and a blonde man in dark blue shorts and shirt was on her doorstep checking his watch.

Sally called out through her open car window. "Hello! Are you Craig?"

The man turned toward her, saw her, and smiled. "Sally Fairburn?"

"That's me. I'll just park. Sorry for keeping you waiting."

She found an empty parking bay a little farther along the street and then jogged along the sidewalk.

"Thanks for coming on a Sunday."

"It's a seven-days-a-week service, ma'am," Craig said cheerily.

Sally opened the front door and led Craig inside. He was a lanky guy in his fifties with thick fair hair and glasses. Sally left her purse on the kitchen counter and offered him a soft drink. He declined.

"If you'll excuse me, I should get started. I'm back-to-back with appointments." Craig examined the front door lock. "You sure you want this changed? It looks new."

Sally appreciated his honesty. "I had a break-in this morning. There was no forced entry, so I think the intruder had a key. I'd like both door locks changed and the window locks on the ground floor too."

"You got it!"

Craig checked the back door lock and the windows, gave her a price, and then when she'd okayed it, got started.

Sally felt grimy after her prison visit. She wanted to shower and change into fresh clothes, but she'd have to wait until Craig was gone. The whine of the locksmith's drill set off a headache and she went upstairs to the bathroom to find some painkillers. When she descended the stairs, the drilling had stopped. The front door was wide open, so Sally guessed that he was getting the new locks from his van. Taking out a jug of ice-cold water from the refrigerator, she swallowed two painkillers. There was still no sign of Craig. She stood on the front doorstep and saw the van doors were shut. Perhaps he was working on the back door?

"Craig?"

"In here," he called out from her office. She found him installing key-operated window locks. "One key fits all the window locks," he said, holding up a small key. "Keeps things simple. I'll give you spares."

"Have you done the door locks already?" she asked.

"Not yet."

It seemed strange that he'd started on the front door and then installed a window lock instead of completing the first job, but maybe he'd gotten distracted. She watched him work for a few seconds.

"Do I know you?" Sally asked. "Your face is kind of familiar."

"Been working this neighborhood for thirty years. You've probably seen me around."

It was a déjà vu moment, but she couldn't recall where she had seen him. Perhaps it was at the school? "Do you have kids?"

"Two, all grown up."

She shrugged it off and took her laptop to the living room and did some research on *Nerium oleander*.

It was a poisonous plant, and if ingested in large amounts, could impact the gastrointestinal system, the heart, and the central nervous system of an adult. While Carolyn hadn't complained to her about the gastrointestinal effects of nausea and vomiting, Sally had witnessed the cardiac reaction— Carolyn was pale and cold due to her heart not functioning properly. Most of all Carolyn had been drowsy, her limbs shook, and she went into a coma just before she died—symptoms of the oleander impacting her central nervous system.

Sally sat back and thought about how Carolyn might have ingested the plant without knowing. The articles she had read said that the leaves tasted sweet. Sally thought back to her conversation with Carolyn in the bookstore. Sally had a coffee and Carolyn had tea in a teapot. Did Carolyn drink tea regularly? If so, perhaps the poison was in some loose-leaf tea and administered over a long period?

Craig's drill went off. He was working on the back door and Sally stepped out the front door so she could make a phone call to Olivia and hear what she said.

"Liv, do you remember when Carolyn and I met up? I drank coffee and Carolyn had tea. Can you remember what kind of tea it was?"

"Easy. Rooibos loose-leaf tea in my polka-dot teapot. I remember because I love rooibos but not many people ask for it."

"I've not tasted it," Sally said. "Does it taste sweet?"

"A little. And smoky. A little woody maybe. Why do you ask?"

Sally thought it best not to go into the why. "Just wondering."

"Hmmm, are you doing your investigator thing?"

"Just thinking about Carolyn." Sally changed subject, reluctant to talk about what she was really doing. "Everything going all right at the store?"

"All good."

"See you Tuesday."

Sally thought about rooibos tea. If Matt didn't drink it, then adding oleander to it would only poison Carolyn. Suddenly she remembered Nicole arriving at Matt's house with flat-packed boxes, the same day that Matt lit the fire in the firepit. Had he destroyed the source of the poison in the fire, or had it been hidden away in boxes?

Dialing Nicole, she left a message for her to call her.

Where were the boxes now? Sally wondered.

TWENTY-SEVEN

The graphic design company where Lauren Duthie worked was housed in a hip business park where the tenants were mostly artists, fashion designers, architects, and boutique home builders. Stage one of the development was complete. Stage two was underway, and the eastern side of the Fernside Corporate Park was a noisy building site dominated by a tall crane.

Nicole had been slow to return Sally's phone call. When she did, all she said was that Matt had wanted Carolyn's possessions gone from the house and they were now stored in Lauren's home garage. Sally left Lauren a message asking if she could see her after work. She'd received no response. Sally didn't know where Lauren lived, but she did know where she worked.

Sally parked in one of the visitor parking bays outside a metal-and-glass three-story building and on entering the air-conditioned office, she studied the list of businesses housed there. Jay Graphic Design was on the top floor. She took the stairs and found the entrance at the end of a long corridor. The logo of the company was a Steller's jay, a bird with black feathers on its head that stuck up, with a dark blue body. Through the glass panel next to the entrance door, she could see straight into the design studio. There were perhaps fourteen desks, with people working on large screens. There didn't appear to be a receptionist, which meant Sally would have to ask the person nearest the door if she could see Lauren.

Sally hesitated. Should she wait in her car until Lauren left the building? Earlier, Nicole mentioned that Lauren cycled to work, and she usually left around 6 p.m. Sally liked to think she was a patient person, but she was keen to look inside the boxes in Lauren's garage as soon as possible, although would Matt be dumb enough to hide the poisoned tea in a storage box? Perhaps the tea was already gone, burned in the firepit and dropped in a dumpster. But when she was a cop, she'd learned time and time again that when offenders are under pressure, they do stupid things that ultimately give themselves away.

Sally made her decision and entered the design company's office. A young woman with nose and eyebrow piercings looked up and gave Sally a warm smile, then asked if she could help her.

"Can I see Lauren Duthie, please? I'm Sally Fairburn."

"Is she expecting you?"

"It's a personal matter."

The woman raised a pencil-thin black brow and then headed for a desk in the far corner by the window. Sally hovered near the door, shuffling from one foot to the other and feeling very self-conscious. Lauren wore her hair tied in one long braid, just as she had when Sally saw her at the café the other day. The young woman spoke to Lauren who shook her head and stared intently at her screen.

Seriously, was Lauren saying no? Lauren had asked her to prove that Daisy murdered Carolyn. At least, Nicole had asked her, and Lauren had been with her. The work colleague looked pissed, said something more to Lauren who then came over to Sally.

"Sorry, Sally. I can't talk now. I'm on deadline."

"No problem," Sally said. "Can I drop around tonight? I want to look inside the boxes in your garage."

"Boxes?"

"Matt's boxes. The ones Nicole packed up."

Lauren fiddled with the end of her braid. "The garage is a mess. Can you do it another time?"

"You asked me to look into Carolyn's death and I think the boxes may be important."

"Why... do you think that?"

Lauren wasn't making this easy...

"It's a theory I have. Please. It could really help."

Lauren literally wrung her hands. Sally almost felt sorry for her.

"I don't know. Ask Nicole. She may not want them touched."

Lauren was clearly shy, and Sally wondered if she had gotten used to deferring to Nicole and Becca. From the few emails that Sally had read on Carolyn's phone, Sally had the impression that Carolyn and Lauren were on the outer circle and Becca and Nicole were on the inner, and the latter dominated the group.

"I spoke to Nicole. She directed me to you."

Lauren clenched her eyes and grimaced as if she'd been stung by a bee. What was wrong with her? "Okay. What time?" she said, opening her eyes.

Lauren and Sally agreed on 7 p.m. and Lauren gave Sally her home address. Then Sally was ushered out of the door as fast as possible without being rude.

"Carolyn mentioned you," Sally said, on the way out.

"Really?" Lauren looked flattered.

"I believe she was very fond of you."

"And I was fond of her. We were alike. Newly married, a bit shy. The quiet ones."

"I'm sure she appreciated your friendship."

Lauren's eyes and mouth drooped. "I wasn't a good friend in the end. None of us were."

———

Lauren's home was a 1950s renovated house located on a street-to-street lot with a garage that took three cars. Above the garage was a guest room. The front of the house faced six lanes of traffic that thundered past.

"It was the only way we could afford a big block of land so close to the city."

James, her husband, wasn't home when Sally arrived. Lauren was marinating chicken legs in a delicious-smelling spicy sauce. She seemed to have calmed down a little since their last chat, but she was still on edge.

"Does your husband work in the city?"

"What? Oh. Yes. The Office of Housing. Why do you ask?"

"Just getting to know you. I'm on your side, remember," Sally said.

Lauren led Sally out of the back door toward the garage, across a cracked concrete patio and a lawn that was so patchy it was mostly dry mud. She opened the roller door with a remote control. There was one vacant space for a car. The rest of the garage was filled with furniture, tools, a wheelbarrow, and plastic and cardboard storage boxes, all of which had a coating of dust on them. Lauren pointed to the fresh-looking boxes on the far right.

"I don't know what's in them. Nicole helped Matt pack them, not me."

It was as if Lauren wanted to negate responsibility for their contents.

Sally inspected the outside of the first box. There was nothing on the side to tell her what was stored inside. "Why the urgency to pack up Carolyn's things?" Sally asked, ripping off the tape and opening the top of the box.

"Matt said they broke his heart every time he saw them."

The clothes inside had been roughly folded. Underneath them were shoes and purses. "Where are these boxes going?"

"The clothes are going to a thrift store. I haven't had time to take them there."

Sally picked up a silk blouse and inhaled the perfume that smelled like lilies. Carolyn must have worn it recently.

"Do you know Carolyn's parents?"

"No, but she talked about them. They're on their way here. It must be terrible for them." Lauren's voice was brittle and when Sally looked around, Lauren had covered her face. Sally stopped what she was doing and went over to give Lauren a hug. The girl burst into tears.

Sally waited for the tears to subside. Then she said, "If it's upsetting you to watch, I'll be just fine on my own."

Lauren shook her head. "Don't mind me. You go ahead."

"If you're sure."

Sally closed the first box and opened the second. More of Carolyn's clothes, including some lacy underwear. Sally felt like a voyeur and shut the box quickly.

In the third box she found paperback books, photo albums, some mugs with a floral design, keyboard, mouse, a desk lamp, cuddly toys that looked very old and very loved, some framed photos of Matt and Carolyn and also of a couple in their sixties. She held up the framed photo. "Are these Carolyn's parents?"

Lauren was wiping her nose with a crumpled tissue. "Yes."

"What happened to her laptop or did she use a tablet?"

"I don't know. You'd have to ask Matt."

The fourth box was full of her winter clothes, boots and woolly hats and scarves. The fifth box contained a throw for the bed, a framed painting, some cookbooks, a jewelry box. Sally lifted the engraved wooden box out and lay it on the concrete floor of the garage. She opened the lid. There were earrings and necklaces inside including pearl earrings that looked real.

"Her parents might like to keep these," Sally said.

Lauren edged closer and peered over Sally's shoulder. "I'll keep the jewelry box aside. When they arrive, I'll ask them."

Sally opened the top of the sixth box, hoping to find packaged food and drink. She looked down at Carolyn's wedding dress and satin shoes. It was a beautiful dress with lace and little pearls on the bodice. Only nine months ago, Carolyn got married. Sally felt a rush of anger. How could he discard her wedding dress the day after she died? Beneath it was a wedding album, and a box of wedding memorabilia.

Six boxes. None contained tea. "Are these all the boxes?"

"I... I think so. Umm, I need to get dinner ready. James will be home soon." Lauren made to leave.

"Just one more question." Lauren turned to face her. "Were there any pantry items taken from the house?"

"I... don't know." Lauren looked away.

Sally could tell Lauren knew more than she was saying.

"Lauren, if someone took anything from Carolyn's pantry, I need to know."

Lauren backed away. "So what if they did?"

"They? Who, Lauren? Whatever they took might contain the poison used to kill Carolyn."

Lauren gawped at Sally as if a flash camera had blinded her for a moment.

"Lauren? Are you okay?" Sally asked.

"Please, just go."

Lauren was keeping a secret and she was afraid.

But who was she afraid of?

TWENTY-EIGHT

All the way home, Sally tried to work out who or what Lauren was scared of. Was it Matt? Or perhaps Daisy? Or was Lauren implicated in Carolyn's death herself? She couldn't believe that Lauren was the murdering kind, but Sally had never ceased to be amazed at the seemingly nice people who had committed murder.

Of Carolyn's three female friends, she was definitely closest to Lauren, who came across as sensitive and therefore might be the most likely to tell Sally what was really going on. Sally wondered how much of what she had learned that day was of use to the homicide investigation, and should she pass it on to Clarke? It was all circumstantial or else incomplete.

In her head, she went through what she knew. Her stalker was an ex-cop, but she didn't have a name. Sally had failed to find any pantry items in the boxes that Nicole and Matt had packed up so her theory that the oleander had been in Carolyn's tea remained just a theory.

Then Sally had a light bulb moment. What if there were more boxes than the ones stored in Lauren's garage?

She made a call.

"Nicole, how many boxes did you pack?"

In the background, two young kids were squabbling. "Boys! Stop fighting!" Nicole sounded harried. "I can't remember. Seven, maybe. Why is it important?"

There had been six boxes in Lauren's garage.

"Did you clear out any pantry items, or wine?"

"Not that I recall." Nicole yelled at her kids to be quiet.

Sally stifled a sigh. If seven boxes had been packed up and one was gone, it was possible that it contained the evidence Sally was searching for. Nicole and Matt had packed the boxes before Clarke took on the murder case, so the poisoned product could have already been disposed of. She made a mental note to call Detective Lin and talk about her theory that Carolyn's love of loose-leaf tea might have been her undoing.

"It's important, Nicole. Please try to remember. Any food and drink that only Carolyn consumed?"

"Perhaps a few things. Check the boxes."

"One box is missing."

"I must have miscounted."

"Tell me about your friendship group," Sally said. "How did you first meet?"

"Now's not a good time. My twins are trying to kill each other."

"I'm happy to wait." Sally sat on the line while Nicole separated her boys, ordering one to his room and the other to the kitchen. Nicole picked up her phone again.

"How does our friendship help you find the killer?" Nicole asked. There were a few seconds of silence. "Oh, I see. You think one of us did it?"

"It's background research, that's all. How did you meet Matt and Carolyn?"

"Through my husband. Lachie, Matt, Becca, and I were at

college together. Matt and Lachie studied pharmacology. Becca was doing veterinary science and I was studying medicine. We were close. Still are."

"Medicine? Are you a doctor?"

"Was for two years, then the twins arrived, and our lives got too hectic. I gave up work. The boys are starting elementary school this fall and I plan to go back to work as soon as I find the right position."

"And Lauren?"

"She worked on the logo and website for the pharmacy when she was just starting out as a graphic designer. Over time she became a friend."

But not part of the inner sanctum, Sally thought.

"And Carolyn? How did she meet Matt?"

"At a winetasting. We were all surprised that he chose her. She was far too... wholesome and conservative. He's always liked wild girls."

"Is Daisy a wild girl?"

"She's a manipulative bitch. I told you already, she's after his money." Nicole *really* didn't like her.

"Were you surprised Matt had an affair?"

"To be honest, no. Mattie's always been a ladies' man. He seemed to be totally into Carolyn when they first met, then when they married, it's like a switch was flipped, and he seemed to lose interest in her. Daisy latched on to him at an opportune moment."

"Thanks, Nicole, that's been helpful."

"What are you doing about Daisy?"

"The police have her on their radar. I'm doing what I can behind the scenes. I can't interfere in a police investigation."

"So the detectives suspect Daisy?"

"She's one of many suspects."

"Okay, well, call me if you have any news."

When Sally reached home, lights were on in Matt's house. Now was her chance to speak to him. Earlier that day, she had prepared two sheet pans of honey-mustard chicken with potatoes and broccoli. One was for their dinner tonight. The other was for Matt. They were in the refrigerator and ready for roasting. Sally ducked into her house, took one roasting pan from the refrigerator, and then knocked on Matt's door.

It took a while for him to open it. He looked haggard with dark bags under his eyes. The white coat that he wore in his pharmacy was undone, as if he couldn't bother to take it off.

"Sally!"

"Hi, I made this dish for you. Just needs a little oil on top, then roasting in the oven for forty minutes."

"Thank you. Looks great." Matt took the pan from her. "I haven't thought about food. What did you say I needed to do?"

"Shall I come in? I can prepare it and get it in the oven for you."

"Er, yes. Thanks. Come in."

Sally followed him to their open-plan kitchen and switched the electric oven on. "You look exhausted. Why don't you sit down? I've got this under control."

Matt pulled off the white coat, dumped it on a kitchen stool, took a beer from the refrigerator, and offered her one. She refused and asked where the pantry was. The layout of his kitchen was different to hers. He pointed to a set of double doors and she moved over to them, ostensibly searching for the canola oil.

"How are you holding up?" Sally asked, her head in the pantry.

"Not so good."

"Is your family nearby? Can they help?"

"It's just Dad and he's not someone I want to have around. My sister's in San Francisco."

The pantry's floor-to-ceiling shelves were wide, deep, and almost empty. There were no spices, no oils except one unopened bottle of vegetable oil. No teas, no coffee. No opened bottles of cordial. No sauces. No flour.

"You don't have much in here. Did the police take it away?"

"Yeah, they took almost everything. I told them, I didn't kill her. I never would. But they took it all anyway."

Sally found some tea canisters in there with cute English village scenes on them. Sally opened each canister and found them empty.

"Looks like you're low on tea and coffee. Do you want me to get you some tomorrow when I do my grocery shop?"

"No, that's okay. I'll get some coffee tomorrow. Carolyn drank the tea, not me. Nicole took some of it."

How could Nicole forget that she took the tea?

Sally opened the only bottle of oil and brushed it over the chicken and vegetables, then she popped the dish in the oven. To the right of the pantry was a wine rack. It was also empty.

"Did forensics take your wine too?" Sally asked.

"Yes. I mean, no. I gave some to Nicole. I don't drink white, and Carolyn isn't going to—" He gulped, looked down. "She won't be needing them, so Nicole took them."

That was interesting. "Did Nicole ask for them, or did you offer them to her?"

"What? I don't know. Maybe she asked if she could have them."

"I have to get going. If there's anything you need, just knock on my door, okay?"

Matt cleared his throat "I want to apologize again. I was rude, and you were only trying to help Carolyn."

"No need to apologize. I just wish she had pulled through."

Sally left Matt's house, touched by Matt's apology. Tonight

she had glimpsed his grief and remorse. Perhaps he wasn't a cold-blooded killer, after all. She left his house, thinking about the missing tea and white wine, both of which had gone to Nicole.

Why hadn't Nicole told her this?

TWENTY-NINE

JULY 18, 2016

It was Monday morning and Sally watched Foster shuffle into the room on the other side of the brick and Perspex wall. His steps were slow and his back stooped. Tank, the prison guard, waited until Foster was seated on the orange chair before he took up position by the locked door.

"You don't look so good," Sally said.

Foster waved his hand about dismissively. "I'm good. Stop your fussing."

Tank shook his head. Sally noticed a cut on Foster's lower lip and she addressed her next question to Tank. "Did someone attack him?"

"Yeah," said Tank, his voice as deep and resonant as a well. "Guy in the next cell. Shouldn't have happened. Foster's cell should have been locked before the other guy came out."

Sally had to remind herself that beating, stabbing, and rape were part of everyday life at the correctional facility. Foster was a murdering psychopath, and many would thank the man who eventually killed him. It didn't make it right, though. To Sally's thinking, murder was murder, no matter who the victim was.

"It won't happen again," said Foster. "He had an unfortunate accident."

"Accident?" Sally felt queasy.

"Yeah. Somehow his head collided with the wall. Brains everywhere," Foster said calmly as if he were talking about something mundane. "Of course, I had nothing to do with it. I was in the hospital."

Behind Foster's back, Tank rolled his eyes. Sally was lost for words. Foster had arranged his attacker's death. His inside man had to be a guard. Nobody else could have entered the other man's cell. This confirmed what Sally suspected—Foster had a guard or two doing his bidding. She studied Tank for a moment, then returned to the reason she was there.

"We have an agreement," Sally said. "And I'm honoring it. I want you to do the same. Who is the man following me?"

Until her stalker was in custody, Sally couldn't risk Paul coming home. They had chatted on the phone last night, but a phone call wasn't the same as having him with her. Sally knew that one day her son would go to college, then fly the nest. Until then, just knowing he regarded her house as his home staved off the sense of loneliness that she now felt.

"I put some feelers out last night," Foster said. "You didn't give me much to go by, but I think I was right about the identity of your stalker. The guy I'm thinking of is part enforcer, part PI. His clientele are people who want results and don't care about what he has to do to secure it."

Sally's feet and hands had turned icy cold despite the warm stale air in the room.

"How violent is he?"

"Beats people who owe money, smashes kneecaps, handy with a knife."

Sally swallowed a lump in her throat. "His name?"

Foster ran his palm across the stubble on his chin. "He's a bit of a chameleon. Hard to pin down."

His taunts had her blood boiling. *Keep calm. Don't let him get to you.* "I'll take that on board. What's his name?"

"Tell me, has the Shar-Pei come up with any leads?"

"If you mean Clarke, I don't know. He wouldn't tell me if he had."

He leaned forward a touch. "You and I should work together, Sally. Solve the Carolyn Tate case. Clarke has no idea what he's doing. You want it solved, don't you?"

Was Foster actually suggesting they team up? Jesus! A year and two months ago he tried to murder her. What insane planet was he on? It took every ounce of her concentration to stop her face from revealing her loathing for him.

"Clarke's got that under control. All I care about is putting a stop to the immediate threat. My stalker."

Foster tutted. "You're approaching this all wrong. Think like a detective, Sally. The stalker and Carolyn's murder are linked."

How could Foster have discovered that? And if he did know, then he could simply tell her. But that would be too easy, and Foster wouldn't be able to have his fun with her. He wanted her dangling at the end of his fishing line, struggling to be free as he lured her in. Knowing this didn't make it any easier, though. She had to persevere with him, should he truly know the stalker's identity. "I am thinking like a detective, Richard. You say you know my stalker, so I'm asking you to tell me."

"I'm trying to help you. You can solve the Carolyn Tate murder yourself. With my help, naturally."

Foster was doing her head in. She rubbed her temples and then noticed his satisfied smug. She dropped her hands to her lap. He mustn't know he had rattled her. "The name please, Richard."

She was beginning to sound like a parrot.

"Think about my proposal. We'd make a great team. I work

in the background, use my contacts and experience to help you. You follow up on the leads. You get to find Carolyn's killer *and* your stalker."

"What do you get out of it?" Sally asked.

"The satisfaction of showing up Clarke for the dumbass he is. With any luck he'll get demoted. Maybe even put back on the beat."

"You really don't like Clarke, do you?" Sally said.

"He pissed me off one too many times."

Sally shuddered at the thought that one day she might become Foster's target again. For now, he found her entertaining.

"Let's start with the stalker's name," Sally said.

"Will you think about my suggestion?"

"Okay, I'll think about it." She had no choice but to play along.

"Good. Tell me everything you know about the victim. I'll mull it over tonight and we'll chat tomorrow."

"No, Richard. I'm not saying anything until you name my stalker." The power had shifted between them and she sensed it. Foster wanted information from her. Now he would have to earn it. There was a warm glow of satisfaction in her gut. Perhaps, finally, she had worked out how to play his game.

Foster smiled, revealing gray teeth. "You learn fast. I'll make a detective of you yet." Sally stayed quiet. She would stay like that for as long as it took. Just as detectives did when they waited for a confession. "His name's Chester Lee. Former cop. Got caught stealing heroin from the evidence locker and selling it on the street. Spent time in jail for it. As a matter of fact, he was an inmate at this fine establishment not so long ago."

"Thank you for this. I'll pass on the lead to Clarke."

Foster guffawed and then he hunched over, clutching his ribs. His injuries were clearly troubling him. She waited for him to recover. "Don't be ridiculous! If you tell him the lead came from me, he won't do a damn thing about it. Or worse, the idiot will bother me here, asking inane questions."

"Why do you rate Clarke so poorly?"

"One day, maybe I'll tell you. Not now. Here's how you should play it. Chester was a cop when you were a rookie. Tell Clarke your stalker looks like a cop you once knew when you were a PD rookie. Chester was a beat cop then, so your paths would have crossed. If you tell him this way, he's more likely to take it seriously."

His advice made sense. However, she didn't like the idea of lying to Clarke. "What do you suggest I do if Chester keeps following me?"

"Do not approach him. The word is, he assaulted an addict who wouldn't pay up. Cut up his face with a flick knife. If Chester comes near you, lock the doors and..." He smirked. "I can't believe I'm saying this, but call the cops." He leaned back in his chair. "Now, tell me everything you know about the Carolyn Tate murder. Start with how she died."

Before she knew it, she answered, "Poison. I can't say anymore."

"Which poison?" Foster asked.

"Oleander. Perhaps in her tea. That's all I'm saying." She stood.

"I can be patient, Sally. But you *will* tell me."

Sally left the room quickly.

THIRTY

Sally drove through the prison's vast parking lot toward the exit. She was on the phone with Detective Clarke.

"I popped into Matt's house last night," Sally said. "I see you've cleared out most of his pantry. Is this about the oleander?"

"That's not something I'm prepared to discuss," Clarke said.

"I thought you might like to ask Matt where the tea and white wine went."

"I'm guessing you know who took it?"

Sally was silent. Nicole had come to her for help. If she told him that Nicole had taken the white wine and tea from the Tates' house, Clarke would naturally question Nicole. Sally reminded herself that Nicole and Lauren's visit could be a way of deflecting Sally away from the real killer. If Nicole was involved in Carolyn's death, telling Sally that Daisy did it was a great way to keep Sally, and the police, looking in the wrong place.

Clarke sighed. "If you know anything that could help us nail the killer, you have to tell me."

"Okay. Nicole took the white wine and the teas from the house the day after Carolyn died. Carolyn was the only one who drank Chardonnay, and she also had a thing about rooibos tea. Loose-leaf tea especially. Again, from what I can make out, only Carolyn drank it."

"You think the oleander was in the Chardonnay or the rooibos tea?"

"It makes sense, if Carolyn's the only person who drinks both."

"I'll look into it." He paused. "Anything else you want to tell me?"

"In Lauren Duthie's parking garage there are six boxes of Carolyn's belongings. You might want to look through them."

Sally had reached the boom gate at the exit. She waited for the guard to open it.

"I won't even ask how you know this."

She heard his chuckle. She was relieved that he wasn't angry.

"And I think one box is missing. Matt said that Nicole took some of the white wine and tea for herself. What if she removed evidence to protect herself or the killer?"

"Do you have any other reason to suspect Nicole?"

"I guess not."

"Seen anything more of the stalker?" Clarke asked.

"I think I know who he is. He was a cop when I was a rookie. I knew I'd seen his face before."

The lie was too easy.

"Does he have a name?" Clarke asked.

"Chester Lee," Sally said.

A moment's silence, then Clarke spoke. "He's a nasty piece of work. I've wanted to get him back behind bars since he was last released. Thanks for the tip and avoid going places where he can approach you alone."

"Will do, and thanks for looking into this."

After the call, there was a fluttering in her chest—she loathed lying and the thought that she was in cahoots with Foster, by lying to Clarke, had her breaking out in goose bumps. Her mom would describe what she had just done as the slippery slope to oblivion. She'd have to make sure that wasn't the case.

"I won't see Foster again," she told herself, as she drove home.

She regretted telling him what she knew about the Carolyn Tate murder. She should have said no when he had asked about it. Somehow, Foster seemed to get his way.

The road she was on was never busy because it only led to and from the prison. In her rearview mirror she saw a golden-beige Lincoln Town Car with a bald man in sunglasses behind the steering wheel. Her father used to have a car just like it, which he sold the year the manufacturer stopped making them. She assumed the driver was a prison visitor, like her, leaving after a visit.

At the traffic lights she turned left, as did the Town Car. The driver kept his distance. He didn't have a beard or the black cap that her stalker wore. Yet, this felt very much like she was being tailed. Coming up to a crossroads, Sally would normally go straight ahead and then onto the freeway. But she took a right —she had started to feel uneasy. The Town Car took the right turn too. What were the odds that a person leaving the prison would go the exact same route as her?

The road was lined with drive-through fast-food places, a gas station, and sad-looking stores with dirty windows and faded signage. Her phone rang. She ignored it. At the last second, Sally turned into the KFC, but instead of taking the drive-through, she parked at the front of the restaurant and waited, the hood facing the road. The Town Car slowed, then kept going. She watched as it turned into the Pizza Hut next door.

The driver didn't get out or take the drive-through.

Was this coincidence or was another guy now following her? She waited for the Town Car to move or for the driver to get out. Neither happened. There were any number of reasons why the Lincoln driver had parked and stayed in his vehicle. They had to send an email or a text? They needed a break from driving? They were meeting someone there and they were early? She was probably being paranoid because Chester *had* been following her.

She came to the decision that if the Town Car followed her all the way home, she would call the cops.

Her phone beeped. She played the voicemail:

"Oh, hi. Um, Sally. Um, can you call me back? Oh, I haven't said who I am. Silly me. Lauren. Lauren Duthie. Please call me."

Sally was intrigued. Yesterday, Lauren couldn't wait to get Sally out of her garage. Sally turned the ignition and pulled out of the parking spot, then she drove past the Pizza Hut. The Town Car stayed put.

Relieved, she tapped the "call back" button.

"This is Sally Fairburn, you left a message just now. It's good to hear from you."

"Oh, wow! You called me! Right, okay. Um, I think we should meet. I don't know what to do."

"Talk to me. I'll see what I can do to help," Sally said.

"I don't want to talk about it now. Maybe I shouldn't, I can't decide." Lauren was quiet for a moment. "I could meet you this afternoon, if... if you can make it?"

"Sure. How about I come to your house?"

"No!" Lauren shrieked, and then toned down the volume. "No. Do you know the library on East Street? They have meeting rooms upstairs. I'll book one. How does three o'clock sound?"

"Perfect. I'll see you there at three."

"Um, Sally... Don't tell anyone, okay? Especially Nicole and Becca."

"I promise."

Sally felt a flutter of excitement. Was Lauren about to reveal who killed Carolyn Tate?

THIRTY-ONE

The Lincoln Town Car didn't follow her home. It was a false alarm and Sally silently admonished herself for jumping at shadows. Chester Lee was the problem and knowing that Clarke was looking for him made her feel a little more secure. On top of that she had new door and window locks in the house. Everything was going to be okay.

She phoned Paul to see how he was doing at Reilly's house.

"Good. But..."

"But what?"

"I need my football gear. The coach is running a training camp and Reilly and me, we want to go."

"When is it?"

"Today."

"Today! How long have you known about this?" Paul often omitted to tell her about places he'd promised to be until the last moment, which inevitably resulted in a mad scramble to get there on time.

A beat or two passed before he answered. "A while."

Sally sighed. "What time does it start?"

"Eleven thirty. Can you drop my gear over?" It was 10:34 a.m. now.

"Luckily Monday's my day off. I can meet you at school at eleven?"

"Thanks, Mom. You're the best! What's happening with the crazy stalker guy?"

"We have a name: Chester Lee. He's a violent criminal. The police are trying to locate him."

"Can I come home?"

"He's still out there. I'd like to keep you out of harm's way."

"I'm not a kid."

"How about we discuss it after your football practice?" Sally suggested.

"Oh-kay."

Sally rushed to gather Paul's football kit, then she set off for Ronald Reagan High. Finding a parking spot wasn't easy and she had to take a bay in a residential side street. It was 11 a.m. She grabbed the sports bag and then jogged to the school's main entrance, where Paul, Reilly, and his mom, Grace, were waiting. Paul and Reilly headed into the school so they could get changed. Grace and Sally made their way to the sports fields and sat on the viewing platform.

"I hope Paul hasn't been any trouble."

"Not at all. He's a sweet boy. Reilly could learn a thing or two about manners and respect from your son."

Grace put her purse on the floor. Sally looked down and realized that in her rush to hand over Paul's sports gear, she had left her purse and her phone in the car.

"Sorry, Grace, I have to go back to the car. I won't be long." Sally stood. "Keep an eye on Paul for me, will you?"

"Of course."

Leaving the school through the main gate on Cecily Street, Sally walked quickly to her car. The side street had large trees on either side, providing much-needed shade from the fierce sun. Sally was a few cars away from her own when she saw that her driver's door was wide open and beside the door, a dark shadow moved across the sidewalk.

What the hell? Sally stood stock still. In her haste to reach the school, had she left the door open? No, she thought, she distinctly remembered locking it.

Sally approached her car cautiously. A dark shape shifted position on the sidewalk. A few steps and Sally saw legs and shoes poking out. Someone had broken into her car and her purse and phone were in there.

"Hey! Stop that!" she shouted.

The man stood. He had a collared shirt on. The collar was up. On his head was a cream baseball cap and sunglasses covered his eyes. He looked her way for a brief moment, then ran. It all happened so fast, Sally couldn't tell if the man had her purse or not.

"I'm calling the cops," she yelled, but she didn't have her phone. It was a bluff and if he had checked the contents of her purse, the thief would know.

Okay, Sally thought, *let's see how fast you are.*

Sally sprinted after him. She wished she had worn her running shoes. Her thin-soled sandals slowed her down. The man she was chasing ran in a lumbering way, which told Sally that he wasn't fit. She was confident she could catch up with him. All she wanted was her purse back.

Farther down the street, a man in a dress shirt and smart pants was heading toward them. The sidewalk was narrow, so one of the men would have to shift out of the way.

"Stop him!" Sally yelled. "Thief!"

The young guy stopped, stared at Sally, then the man who was about to pass him.

"Grab him!" Sally shouted.

The smartly dressed man stepped aside to let the thief past.

Thanks a bunch! Sally thought, speeding up.

"Call the police!" she said as she ran past him.

The thief crossed the road. He dodged a slow-moving car. Coming the other direction was a concrete truck. With a blast of a horn and a hiss of compression brakes, the truck narrowly missed the man she was chasing.

Sally didn't dare to make the same reckless move across the busy traffic. By the time she managed to reach the other side of the road, the thief had disappeared.

"Damn!" She exhaled, bending down to catch her breath.

Her hairline was damp with perspiration and her feet were sore from running on such thin leather soles. Disappointed at her failure, she walked back to her car.

The car door stood open. She looked in but didn't touch anything. Her purse was lying on the passenger seat. When she checked inside the purse, she found her phone and credit card were still there. So if theft wasn't the reason to break into her car, what was?

Sally took a step back. What if Chester was behind this? Although the glimpses she saw of the man didn't look like Chester. If he had tampered with her car, was it safe to drive? Without touching the door or the frame, Sally sat in the driver's seat, slid the key into the ignition and turned it.

A whine and then nothing, not even a growl.

He had immobilized her car. Why? Was this about demonstrating that she was being watched, as the note clearly stated?

She got out carefully, nervous at what else he might have done to her car, and called Clarke.

"Somebody's broken into my car and immobilized it. I chased him but lost him."

"Was it Chester Lee?"

"I don't think so. But I didn't get a good look."

"Where are you?" She gave the details. "Okay, don't touch anything. I'll get a patrol car to you as soon as possible."

THIRTY-TWO

Paul was fascinated by the equipment in the auto repair workshop, especially the hydraulic hoists. There were three hoists in total and Sally's Honda Civic was raised up on the one nearest Chase Feinstein's office. The workshop was busy—two other mechanics worked on cars and the yard was full of other vehicles waiting to be serviced or repaired. Paul was in his sweats and held a flashlight that pointed into the footwell of her car. Paul didn't seem the least bit intimidated by Chase's similarity to a Hell's Angel—plenty of violent tattoos, unnerving stare, chunky rings on his oily hands, and when he wasn't working in his overalls, he liked to wear a leather vest and ride a Harley. But Chase was a good guy, even though he and Sally had come into conflict a while ago.

Sally was surprised that Chase had agreed to look at her car. Sally's attempts to find the Poster Killer had led her to unearth details of Chase's relationship with a college student called Sophie Blake, the sister of one of Richard Foster's victims. Sally at one point believed that Chase might be the Poster Killer. She also, wrongly, believed that they started a sexual relationship when Sophie was not yet sixteen. She had apologized. But Chase was understandably angry at being wrongly accused.

"Down at the fuse box," Chase said, and Paul shifted the position of the flashlight. "Yup, just as I thought. The fuse for the ignition has been removed."

"Why would anyone do that?" Sally mused.

"To stop you going places," Paul suggested.

"Yes, but why? If Chester is doing the killer's bidding, then wouldn't he be more worried about the police investigation?"

"Maybe you know something that they don't," Paul suggested.

Sally smiled at her son. He had such faith in her. It was good to have his company again, although she was foolish to draw him back into possible danger. "I don't think I do."

"I want to come home, Mom. You've got new locks and everything now, so what's the problem?"

"Can I think about that? I just need to make a call."

He glared at her but didn't argue.

Sally wandered outside and sat on an upturned milk crate. Detective Lin picked up straight away.

"A fuse was removed and the car disabled. It's deliberate," Sally told the detective.

"And you think it was Chester Lee?"

"Who else? Although I didn't see his face, I can't think of anyone else who would do this." Sally hesitated, then went ahead. "I think I was followed this morning by someone else. It was a Lincoln Town Car, a 2010 model or thereabouts. Dad used to have one just like it. This one was golden-beige."

"Chester could've switched cars. Not many cars that model and color about. He probably stole it, so I'll check car thefts in the area."

"It wasn't Chester," Sally said. "The driver had a shaved head. No beard."

"Noted," Lin said. "Where did you first notice the Lincoln?"

Her answer was not going to go down well. "In the Walla Walla parking lot."

"Who were you visiting?"

At least Lin was pretending that she hadn't already guessed. "Richard Foster."

"Jeez, Sally. That's such a bad idea. Whatever possessed you?"

"Okay, I'll come clean. Foster contacted me and said he knew who my stalker was. He identified Chester Lee from my description."

"That's not what you told the boss."

"I'm sorry, I didn't think Clarke would believe Foster."

"You should have told us this straight away. When was this?"

"Yesterday."

"And you visited him this morning?"

"And yesterday too."

Lin must think she had lost her mind.

"Have you considered that Foster sent Chester to watch you?" Lin sounded irritated. "Chester may have nothing to do with the Tate murder and it could be about Foster ensuring that you become his pawn. Has he asked you to do anything for him?"

Sally hated the idea that she was becoming Foster's pawn and she was upset with Lin for suggesting it. "He gives me information. It's a quid pro quo. I'm nobody's pawn."

"I hear you, but does he ask you to do things for him?"

"To visit him. He finds me entertaining."

"Thanks for your honesty, Sally. Don't trust Foster for a second. If he's giving you information, he will want something from you."

"I'm okay. I know what I'm doing." At least, she hoped she did. "What about the Lincoln?"

"We'll make sure cops in the area watch out for it."

After the call, Sally stared at the city towers in the distance. Above the music coming from Chase's radio and the rumble of traffic passing by, there were occasional voices from the business next door and cigarette smoke wafted across the yard from a smoker taking a break.

It was time to mend bridges. Sally went into the workshop and found Chase and her son under her car staring up at the chassis. The car was raised up on a hydraulic hoist. Chase was showing Paul where the brake lines were.

"They're real easy to cut," Chase said. "Sally's lucky the guy didn't sabotage the brakes."

"Chase?" Both Chase and Paul looked at her. "I'm sorry about what happened with you and Sophie. I was wrong to doubt you."

"You almost ruined our lives."

"I know, and I'm really sorry."

Sophie had confirmed that she had been sixteen when they first had sexual relations and therefore Chase had not committed a crime.

Chase nodded and turned his attention back to the car.

"Can you replace the fuse?" Sally asked, happy to move on.

"Already done it. I looked over the rest of the car. It's all good."

"Paul, are you happy to go to Reilly's house this afternoon?" Sally said. "There's someone I have to meet. Then after that, I'll take you home."

"Can I stay with Chase?"

"That's up to Chase," Sally said.

"Sure. Good to have another pair of hands."

Paul looked as if Christmas had come early.

THIRTY-THREE

Lauren wasn't a city person.

Unlike Nicole and Becca, she grew up in Osmandson, a small country town one hundred and fifty miles from Franklin where the pace was slow and where the inhabitants didn't want expensive coffee shops or fancy clothes stores. Her Thai mother was a seamstress and her father ran the only laundry and dry-cleaning business in Osmandson. It had taken her parents a few years to establish themselves in the close-knit community, but once her mom joined the school's parents committee and her dad did some handyman work at the school when he could, they, and Lauren, made some good friends. After graduating from Franklin University with a graphic design degree, she was offered a job at a successful boutique design company in the city, but the pull to go back to her hometown was strong. If she hadn't met James, her husband, at a science-fiction writers festival—she was a huge fan of the genre—she might have returned to her hometown. It was because of James that she started a new life in Franklin, despite feeling like a fish out of water in the noisy bustling city.

Cycling kept her grounded. She could see the sky, the birds, the trees lining the streets. She liked to feel the breeze on her face and she enjoyed the slower pace of travel. She'd discovered a forest trail that took her part of the three miles to work. Lauren's bicycle was old-fashioned, in that it had a woven basket at the front, a mudguard at the back—so often missing from the trendy new bicycles—and the handlebars sat up high. The fastest route to the library where she was due to meet Sally was a busy main road. She hated busy roads, so Lauren went through a residential area. The journey took twice as long, but it was so much more peaceful.

As she pedaled, Lauren dithered about whether meeting Sally was a good idea. What kind of trouble would it land her in? Would Sally be as sympathetic as Lauren hoped? Sally seemed to be a nice person who wanted justice for Carolyn. But how trustworthy was she? Would she go running straight to the police?

That morning, Lauren had watched James smear a thick layer of butter on his toast, then a layer of strawberry jam, his favorite accompaniment to his morning coffee. Consumed with love for him, she had almost told him the truth. What would he think if he knew what she had done? James was the best thing that had ever happened to her and what if she lost him? James was a kind man, but this would test his love.

As for Becca and Nicole, she shoved all thoughts of them aside. If she allowed their demands that she keep quiet to fill her head, she would turn around and lock herself in the house. Why had she ever imagined that those evil women were her friends? And Lachlan was as bad as Matt. Both were smug, selfish men who did whatever the hell they liked, regardless of the pain they caused. And they caused a lot of pain. Matt had been cruel to Carolyn, making out he adored her so she would marry him, when all along he only wanted her for her money. What a mean, callous thing to do.

Perhaps that was what gave Lauren the courage to call Sally

and request a meeting. Nine months ago, on the night of the winetasting when Matt had made a beeline for Carolyn, they had all looked on in surprise at Matt's apparent infatuation. Lauren had been foolish enough to hope that Matt had moved on from his recklessness and womanizing. But no. Not only was he unfaithful to Carolyn, but his pharmacy business was also in trouble and it needed an injection of capital.

Poor Carolyn. Everybody knew Matt had married her for her money, except Carolyn.

Lauren should have been brave and tipped her off, but she had been afraid to lose the only friends she had. So, she was ashamed to admit, she kept quiet and hoped that Carolyn would see through Matt's pretense by herself.

Lauren wanted to make amends for her lack of bravery, which was why she kept pedaling. Her heart pounded, not because she was unfit, but because she was more afraid than she had ever been in her life.

Lauren turned onto Cedar Street. It was a pleasant street with tree-lined sidewalks, neat lawns, and large houses. Lauren would like to move here someday. The busy road they lived on was always noisy; traffic passed by all day and night and Lauren had taken to wearing earplugs to sleep. She glanced at the house she would love to buy, if she and James could one day afford it. Unlike the open lawns fronting many of the houses, tall flowering shrubs with pretty pink flowers screened this house from the road, which gave the occupiers their privacy. On the lawn of the next house, three kids played with a hose, spurting water at each other. Their screams of joy made Lauren smile.

She pedaled faster. She was doing the right thing. Sally would know what to do next.

There was a rumble of a car engine behind her. She flicked a look over her shoulder. It was about ten yards away, matching her speed. Perhaps they were searching for a particular house? They had plenty of room to overtake her. She ignored them.

Ahead was the intersection with Valley Road, one of the main roads into the heart of the city. Lauren liked to dismount at this point and use the pedestrian crosswalk.

The car's engine growled. It was a powerful car. She just wanted the driver to move on. It came up beside her. Tinted windows. Why didn't the driver overtake? A rush of panic had Lauren break out in a sweat. Another thrumming rev of the engine and the wheels turned her way. Tires shrieked. Lauren saw the front bumper, the shiny hood, and the windshield coming at her, just before it plowed right into her side. A searing pain in her knee and a snap of her femur, then the tearing of metal as the bicycle buckled. Lauren was shunted sideways, pain numbing her thoughts. She fell to the ground, the bicycle on top of her. The side of her head slammed into the sidewalk.

THIRTY-FOUR

Sally collected her thoughts as she waited for Lauren in the library's second-floor meeting room. Why disable her car's ignition? Was it about scaring her? Preventing her from meeting Lauren? But how would Chester have known about their meeting?

Her foot jiggled up and down under the table. She was nervous, not just because of the threats leveled at her, but also for Lauren, who was clearly scared. Sally had made a point of phoning Margie to tell her where she was going. A silly precaution perhaps, but it made her feel better.

Through the glass wall separating the meeting room from the rows of nonfiction books on shelves, Sally tried to calm her nerves by watching the people in the library. But every few minutes she checked her watch. From 3 p.m., Sally stared at the stairs, waiting for Lauren to walk up them.

By 3:10 p.m., Sally began to think that Lauren had backed out of their arrangement. Or worse, someone had stopped her. An ambulance, siren wailing, sped past the library, the piercing noise penetrating the walls and causing Sally to leap up and race to the nearest window.

Was she jumping to conclusions, or could that ambulance be on its way to Lauren?

Her hand shook as she tried calling her. It went to voicemail, and she left a message:

"Hi, Lauren, are you on your way? If something's come up, please just let me know." Sally sounded breathy and ill at ease.

Sally paced the room and tugged at her shirt's collar. 3:20 p.m. An ambulance, possibly the same one, wailed as it raced past the library, heading in the direction it had come from. Sally's heart felt as if it had spasmed. Her imagination went on overdrive.

"Don't presume the worst. She might be held up," she said aloud.

She checked her phone for messages and paced some more. At 3:25 p.m. Sally called Lauren again. No answer.

Throwing open the room door, Sally ran down the stairs and went up to the librarian on duty, who was working at a large computer monitor.

"Excuse me, has Lauren Duthie come into the library? She booked a room for a meeting, but she hasn't shown."

To Sally's relief the librarian knew who Lauren was. "No, I haven't seen her. Perhaps she forgot." The woman frowned. "Something wrong?"

"I hope not."

Sally raced from the building and stared in the direction the ambulance had gone. She didn't know whether to go and pick up Paul or wait a little longer. She sat on a shady bench outside the library. Every nerve jangled. Something was wrong.

Her phone rang—a landline number she didn't recognize. Perhaps it was Lauren?

"Hello, I'm a nurse at St. Helen's. We're trying to trace a young woman's next of kin and you were the last person to leave her a message."

Sally's throat constricted. "Do you mean Lauren Duthie?"

"Yes, who is her next of kin?"

"Her husband, James, I think..." In the shock of the moment Sally struggled to recall the name, then it came to her. "...James Duthie. Check her phone's contacts. He should be in there. What happened?"

"Are you a friend or relative?"

"Friend, we were supposed to meet."

"Hit by a car. Knocked off her bike. The police are on their way. The witness who called 911 says the driver swerved to hit her deliberately."

THIRTY-FIVE

"Can I see Lauren Duthie? She was brought in by ambulance."

The ER receptionist checked her computer screen.

"I'll have to check with her husband. Can you take a seat?"

Sally had driven to the hospital as fast as she could and arrived frantic. On the way, she had arranged for Margie to collect Paul from the auto repair shop and take him to the Doyles' house. He would be safe there.

The layout of the waiting room was all too familiar. Only a few days ago, Carolyn had raced to the same hospital. Yet another woman at death's door.

The orange seats were for those being seen by the triage nurse. The blue seats were for the patients and companions waiting to be invited through to the ER area. Sally sat at the end of a row of blue seats near the water cooler.

She closed her eyes. *Please don't die,* Sally said in her head.

Next to her, a man in dusty coveralls grimaced in pain. He was nursing a broken wrist that was so bad a fragment of bone stuck through his skin. Sally gripped her hands together and stared at the floor. She had to be patient. Lauren was in good hands.

"Sally!" She looked up to see Detective Lin standing in front of her. "Come with me."

Sally followed her. "Somebody tried to kill her, right?" Sally said. Why else would a homicide detective be at the hospital?

Lin nodded. "Two witnesses say a dark SUV steered into her, hitting her side-on, and sped away. Neither witness thought to take a note of the plates."

"How bad is she?"

"Broken hip, her ankle is badly bruised, possibly broken. It's her head injury that's the most concerning. She's having an MRI."

It made Sally nauseous just thinking about how much pain Lauren must be in.

"Did Lauren say anything?" Sally asked, dodging a gurney that an orderly was pushing.

"No, she was unconscious. You want to tell me why you were meeting her?" Sally glanced at Lin. The detective must have checked Lauren's text messages.

"She asked to meet up. I think she wanted to tell me something about Carolyn's death. She was afraid. She didn't want anyone to know about our meeting. She specifically mentioned Becca and Nicole."

"Becca Watts and Nicole Slavik?"

"That's right."

They left ER and took the elevator up to level five.

"Two days ago," Sally began, "Nicole and Lauren came to my house and claimed that Daisy Sheene killed Carolyn because when Matt inherits Carolyn's money, she wants him to use it to make her a music star. Well, to be exact, Nicole was convinced that she was the killer. Lauren didn't say much at all, but she was with Nicole, so I assume that she agreed with her."

They followed the signs for the MRI room. As they arrived, Lauren's gurney was about to be wheeled in and a man with messy hair and kind eyes held Lauren's hand. Lauren's neck was in a brace and there was blood on her scalp. One side of her face looked like it had been dragged over gravel.

"I'm right here, honey," James Duthie said. "You'll be okay."

Lauren's eyes were shut, and she didn't respond.

Her leg looked bad too. The skin around the knee and the ankle were bruised and swollen.

The doors to the MRI room closed behind Lauren, leaving James, Sally, and Lin alone in a corridor. James stared blankly at the door for a beat and then turned to Lin.

"Find who did this," he said. "Promise me."

"We'll do all we can. James, I need to have a word with Sally and then, if you're up to it, I'd like to ask you some questions."

James nodded. He slumped into a corridor chair, his face pale. He seemed shellshocked. Lin steered Sally in the opposite direction.

"There'll be a police officer outside Lauren's door twenty-four-seven. It's possible that the driver assumed Lauren was dead. When they discover she's still alive, they may try to finish the job," Lin said.

"Lauren has to know the killer's identity," Sally said.

"Which makes her our key witness. We're searching her house, taking her computer and anything that could help us with the investigation."

"Do you think Nicole was right about Daisy?"

"We'll pull Matt and Daisy in for questioning. Have forensics look over their cars." Lin glanced at James then back to Sally. "I must get on."

"Just quickly, did you find the seventh box?"

"No. Not at Nicole's house or Lauren's."

"I get the feeling that Nicole would do almost anything to protect Matt."

"Even destroying the murder weapon?" Lin asked.

"Very possibly."

THIRTY-SIX

Sally hadn't been looking forward to spending the night home alone. She was relieved when Margie offered to join her.

"We'll make it a girl's night in," Margie said cheerfully. "Watch a romantic movie, eat popcorn, and share a bottle of wine. What could be better!"

Margie brought the wine and the popcorn. Sally made the salads and then grilled some salmon in foil on the barbeque, and they ate on the roof terrace.

"How's Paul doing?" Margie asked.

"He seems to be doing okay. I worry this stalker business will unsettle him."

"Have you spoken to Dr. Kaur, Paul's psychologist?"

"Not yet. You think I should?"

"Does no harm to ask her advice."

Sally stared into the distance, allowing her thoughts to settle. "For now, my priority is keeping him out of harm's way. Someone tailed me today. Followed me from the prison. First Chester Lee and now this guy. It's freaking me out."

"All the more reason to leave it to the police, honey," Margie said. She rested her hand on Sally's. "You going to tell me who you saw at the jail?"

"You won't like it if I tell you," Sally replied.

"You saw Foster?" Margie shook her head. "Jesus! I'm beginning to think you're suffering from Stockholm syndrome. Why would you see that monster?"

"Margie, I know how evil he is. Believe me. But he's been helpful. *He* identified the stalker, and he wants to help solve the Carolyn Tate case."

Her friend put her wineglass on the coffee table and gave Sally her serious look. "Have you asked yourself why he's helping you? What does he want in return? He sure as hell isn't doing it from the goodness of his own heart. He doesn't have one!"

"I know why. He wants to embarrass Clarke for failing to solve Carolyn's murder."

"And you want to help him do this? Clarke's a good guy, remember."

"Yes, I mean, no, I'm not going to embarrass Clarke. Any clues I get from Foster, I'll give to Clarke."

"You're playing a dangerous game," Margie said.

The movie, *Pretty Woman*, was fun to watch, and a welcome distraction from the unnerving events of the day. Margie bade her goodnight and settled into the guest room on the top floor adjoining the roof terrace. Sally climbed into bed and fell asleep immediately. She dreamed that she was in prison and Foster was visiting her. Sally kept asking him why she was in jail, but Foster never gave her an answer. All he said was that she deserved it. His laughter had her slapping her hands against the Perspex wall.

Sally woke with a start.

She had kicked her sheet off the bed and her nightie was bunched around her legs. The vague memory of her dream left her agitated. Sitting up, she leaned over to her nightstand and switched on the lamp. Her digital clock said 11:57 p.m. She wasn't going back to sleep after her nightmare, so she switched on the landing light and headed downstairs. In the kitchen, she opened the refrigerator and took out a carton of milk to make a hot chocolate.

Bang!

Sally jumped and the carton almost slipped through her fingers.

It was the sound of a screen door or unlatched window banging in the wind, too light to be a solid house door. Sally froze, the milk carton suspended in space. Last night, she had taken special care to check that all exterior doors were locked and the downstairs window locks were on. It had to be the screen door at the back and the banging was so loud it would wake her neighbors.

Bang!

Except she had made sure the screen was closed before she had locked the back door.

Sally's breath caught in her throat. Leaving the milk on the kitchen counter, Sally pulled a knife from the knife block; her gun was in the vault upstairs and it would take too long to reach it. She spun around and stared down the dark hallway. The rear of the house was pitch-black. She had no idea who might be in her study or the laundry. Was someone in the house?

Bang!

This time she saw a glint of light hit the screen door at the back. Had the wind loosened the latch on the screen? Sally didn't want to risk unlocking the back door, simply to close the screen. She glanced through the kitchen window. A tree's branches swayed in the wind. It was certainly gusty enough to make the screen slam.

Sally switched on the hall light, then crept along the corridor, the chef's knife held out in front of her. When she passed her study door, she stared warily into the dark interior. She felt the wall for the light and then flicked it on. Darting around the door, her heart thudding, she found no intruder and nothing had been moved. Next, she must pass the laundry and she flicked the light on there to find the space empty once again, apart from the washing machine and dryer. The screen door was clearly visible now, moving back and forth in the wind.

Sally tried the deadlock. It was locked as she had thought.

She toyed with the idea of unlocking it and slamming the screen shut, but that would be foolish given that she had a stalker. Convinced it was only the wind causing the noise, Sally lowered the knife and exhaled a long-held breath.

Just as she began to relax, a ghostly face in a mask appeared at the glass panel of the door, right in front of her. Sally yelped. Dropped the knife. A hand slapped onto the glass, then the next moment he was gone.

The mask was of the Joker, with the long red slit of a mouth and the green hair. Sally ran along the hallway, up the stairs, and diving at her cell phone, she dialed 911.

By the time a police car arrived, there was no sign of the intruder.

THIRTY-SEVEN

JULY 19, 2016

At six in the morning the forest air, normally so cool and fresh, was unusually sticky and cloying. The last thing Sally had wanted to do was go running after her terrifying night. The police had stayed more than an hour, and by the time Sally and Margie returned to their beds, it must have been four in the morning. She was tired, but Margie had insisted they go.

"You'll feel a whole lot better after," Margie said. "And besides, we're not going to give in to a freak in a party mask."

The Falls Trail was a ten-mile loop that took them to the famous waterfall Thunder Falls. It started and ended at Pioneer Park. They had done the hardest part—the uphill run. The trail was level for the next few miles and then it was downhill after that. There were other routes they could take if they wished that would elongate or shorten their time on the mountain, but they liked to stick to the ten-mile trail. Sally was glad Margie had persuaded her to do it. The surrounding pine and fir trees cracked and popped, and occasionally purred as the wind moved the branches.

"I need a drink," Sally gasped. "Can we take a breather?"

"Good idea," said Margie, her skin glistening with perspiration.

Sally took a small water bottle from a pouch around her waist and drank. Margie drank too, then looked up at the hazy blue sky through the narrow gap in the trees lining the path.

"We sure need some rain." Margie then looked at Sally. "Ready? Almost done."

They set off again. The track was uneven in some places and Sally kept an eye out for holes and protruding tree roots.

"It might be a good idea for you and Paul to leave town," Margie said.

"I was thinking the same thing. I don't feel safe in my own house. But it makes me so mad that he's scared me."

"Honey, that's nothing to be ashamed of."

"I was thinking about visiting Mom and Dad, although Paul finds Dad overbearing."

"Maybe that's because he *is* overbearing. I never liked the way he treated you. Or your mom."

The trail narrowed, which forced them to run in single file.

A man in his late twenties ran toward them, his limbs moving with a relaxed but powerful rhythm, not even breaking a sweat. He ran around them, stepping onto the undergrowth, his eyes forward. Perhaps it was because Sally had her hair tucked under a baseball cap, but Matt Tate hadn't recognized her.

"Hi, Matt!" Sally called out.

He slowed and glanced behind him. "Hey, Sally!" He waved and kept going.

He was at a fork in the trail. He could take the way Sally and Margie had come, or the Scenic Trail that included a spectacular lookout over the whole city. It ended two miles west of Pioneer Heights, so Sally and Margie seldom took it. Matt took the Scenic Trail.

"Good-looking guy," Margie said, once he was out of earshot.

"Yeah, too good-looking. That's the guy I told you about, Matt Tate, Carolyn's husband."

"Jeez." Margie glanced behind her again. "Why are the good-looking guys always such bastards?"

"Because they're good-looking, they get away with it. Matt's still on my suspect list, even though he's being nice to me at the moment."

On Park Street, they stretched out their leg muscles. Margie said, "If you decide to leave town, let me know. I'll keep an eye on your house."

"Thanks, Margie, you are the best."

Sally made her decision—she and Paul were leaving town. Paul wouldn't be happy, but he'd have to cope for a couple of days while Sally worked out what to do next. The acrimony between Paul and her father wasn't her biggest concern. Her stalker was. Would Chester Lee follow them?

Just before 9 a.m., Sally called her boss, Olivia, and explained the situation.

"I'm so sorry about the late notice. I had a nasty experience last night." Sally explained about the masked man at her back door. "I'm frightened and I need to get away for a few days."

"Don't worry about us. We'll manage. You must look after yourself," Olivia replied. By "us" she meant her and her cat. "Oh, I forgot. A woman came into the store yesterday. Asked for you. What was her name? I've got it here somewhere." Olivia always wrote things on pink sticky notes, which she then plastered all over the counter. "Here it is. Becca. She said, can you call her? I've got her number." Olivia read it out.

The shower invigorated Sally and after a light breakfast she dialed Becca Watts' number.

"Sally, thanks for calling me back. I need to talk to somebody. First it was Carolyn. And now Lauren. Who's next? The police won't tell me anything. I don't know who to turn to."

Sally had hardly spoken to Becca and she had no idea if she could be trusted, so she wasn't prepared to tell Becca anything more than the police had already made public. "All I know is that in Lauren's case it was a hit and run. She's badly injured."

"I heard. I went to the hospital, but they won't let me see her."

"Nobody but the police and her husband are allowed to see her."

"But you managed to."

"Because I was asked to by the police."

"Why you? We can't even call her."

"Because it was attempted murder, they have to keep her isolated."

"Did she say who did it?"

"No." *And I wouldn't tell you if she did*, Sally thought.

"It's Daisy. It has to be. Do you know if she's been in Matt's house?"

It was an odd question.

Sally did glimpse someone at a rear bedroom window on the day after Carolyn passed away, but she didn't know who it was. "I don't know. I'm in and out a lot. Why do you ask?" Sally said.

"Matt said some things were missing from the house."

"He and Nicole packed a load of boxes."

"I know about those. Have you been in Matt's house?" Becca's tone was accusatory.

"No, how could I? I don't have a key?"

"I thought you did, being a neighbor and all."

A prickle of disquiet ran up Sally's spine. What did Becca really want? "What does Matt say is missing?"

"This and that. Personal stuff. It doesn't matter. Are you seeing Lauren again?"

Becca sure was nosy.

"No plans to."

"If you hear anything about her progress, can you call me? I just want to know that she's okay."

THIRTY-EIGHT

Sally had packed two duffel bags—one bag for her and one for Paul—and put them in the trunk of her car. The clothes Paul had with him wouldn't be enough for their time away with her parents. She felt lighter just at the thought of leaving her troubles behind.

Then her phone rang. Sally knew it was the cell number Foster was using. She told herself to ignore it, but she couldn't.

"What's up?" she asked, sounding harried.

"And good morning to you! I have good news." Foster sounded happy.

"Which is?"

"Come and see me today."

"How do I know it's worth the journey?"

"I'll give you a clue." Yet another game. "Someone has a history of poisoning."

"Who?"

"Come and see me. There's a slot available at 10:15 a.m."

The serial killer was in an exceptionally good mood when she arrived. Was it because he was using his detective skills once more? Did he crave the sense of purpose? Foster sat straighter and his eyes glistened. He even cracked a joke. It was a lame joke, but he chuckled at his own punch line.

"Why did the picture go to jail?" Foster asked from where he sat behind the Perspex screen.

"I don't know," Sally replied.

"Because he'd been framed."

When Foster laughed his face became all mouth, his eyes receding beneath his bushy eyebrows.

"Tell me a joke," Foster said.

"What's gotten into you today? Do you know who killed Carolyn?"

"Maybe." His bony shoulders bobbed. "A joke. Tell me a joke."

Sally had never been good at telling jokes. She always managed to become tongue-tied and ruin the punch line. She thought back to when she was a kid, when she and Margie shared jokes in the school yard.

"Okay, here's one," Sally said. "What do you call a fish wearing a bow tie?"

"So*fish*ticated," he replied without missing a beat. "Give me another."

Sally was grasping at straws. The only joke she could come up with was really bad.

"Knock, knock."

"Who's there?" Foster said.

"Figs."

"Figs who?"

"Figs the doorbell, I've been knocking forever!"

Foster didn't groan as she had thought he would. He laughed long and hard.

"God! That reminds me of my childhood," Foster said.

"Peckham was a shithole back then, but we had such a laugh. We played soccer in the street, threw stones, broke windows, dared each other to do stuff."

"Is Peckham in London?" Sally asked. She knew Foster had been with the UK's Metropolitan Police before he was sent to Franklin PD on an exchange program in the 1990s.

"Yes. It's very different now." He sighed. "I guess I won't get to see it again."

"Do you have family there?"

"Sister. She disowned me years ago. She knew, you see. She knew I liked young girls. She never went to the cops, but she left the city and wouldn't tell me where she went. I regret to say there will be nobody crying over my grave, that's for sure."

"What happened to your mom and dad?"

"Don't know about Mom. Dad died twenty years ago, and good riddance! He had a mean temper and he beat the shit out of me." Richard gave her a crooked smile. "And before you try to connect my dad's behavior to my taste for young girls, don't bother. I was born this way, and I like who I am."

It was time to get on to why Sally was there.

"You said one of the suspects has a history of using poison. Who?"

"This information is gold. I'd like you to do something for me first."

"Richard, we agreed that if I came to see you, you would give me information." Sally planned to tell Foster at the end of their session that she wasn't able to drop in for a day or two because she was going away.

"That was the price for the identity of your stalker," Foster said. "And I delivered. Now I want you to do something else. I know which of your suspects has used poison as an MO before."

Okay, that's new, Sally thought. If Clarke and Lin knew that someone in Carolyn's inner circle had used poison before, they'd have pulled them in for questioning, wouldn't they?

Should she talk to Clarke first or find out the information first? Richard's mood could shift on a whim. He was ready to talk today. What if he changed his mind tomorrow? And besides, Sally was leaving town. No more visits for a while.

"What is this favor?" she asked.

"It's nothing and everything. I want you to buy a rose tree and plant it on Aiden's grave. One of those miniature roses in red will do nicely."

Sally reeled back. "You can't be serious!" she shrieked. "Aiden tried to murder me, for God's sake."

"So? He's dead. Plant the rose bush, take a photo, show it to me. Then I'll tell you about the poisoner."

"Forget it. I won't tend the grave of a serial killer."

"That's harsh." He looked hurt, but he could impersonate emotions without feeling anything at all. "The Sally Fairburn of yesteryear would do it. What happened to the compassionate and sweet Sally I used to know, speaking up for the victims of crime?"

"Life happened. You happened. And the answer is still no. Get one of your pals to do it."

"What pals?"

"Don't give me that. You must have someone you connect with in the outside world." Sally was thinking about the person who ordered the flowers she received.

"Do I?"

"Okay, as I've said, the answer is no. Whatever it is you think you know, I'm guessing the detectives working the case will work out eventually."

"Maybe, maybe not."

She stood. "I won't be around for a few days." She headed for the exit.

"Sally! Sit down, will you?"

"Are you going to tell me who has dabbled with poison before?"

"What's got you in such a cranky mood? Yes, all right, I'll tell you."

Sally sat on the plastic chair. "Go on."

"Nicole Slavik isn't the squeaky-clean middle-class lady she pretends to be. She was born on the wrong side of the tracks. Her mom has a record for shoplifting, her dad was a night club bouncer who got done for assault. Nicole played truant at school. Disrespectful to teachers. Fiery temper. At fifteen, she fell out with a girlfriend over a boy she fancied and exacted her revenge. She wasn't charged, which is why cops like Clarke will probably miss this detail."

"Why wasn't she charged?"

"There wasn't enough clear evidence, and her parents promised to send her to anger management classes, so the case was dropped."

"What did she do exactly?'" Sally asked.

"Poisoned her friend. Gave her unripe elderberries mixed in with yogurt."

"Elderberries? I don't understand."

"If they're unripe they have lectin and cyanide in them. Causes diarrhea and vomiting. Unlikely to be fatal but can cause serious illness. The girl ended up in ER."

"Let me get this straight. Nicole used elderberries to give a friend the runs. I don't see this as intent to kill."

"Agree, but it shows she has history. If I were investigating Carolyn's death, I'd take a long hard look at Nicole Slavik."

Sally was quiet for a moment. "I'm not sure I see the connection. It's like kids who trip up another kid in the playground. They don't mean to seriously hurt the victim, just to make them suffer a little."

"Did Nicole have access to Carolyn's house?" Foster asked.

"She helped Matt pack up some boxes. I don't think she has a key."

"There you have it!" Foster exclaimed. "That's when she removed the poison."

That was what Sally thought too.

"That's possible, Richard. But I'm still not putting a rose bush on Aiden's grave."

"Help me out, here. I can't plant the rose. I can't even see his grave. Come on, Sally, do me this one kindness."

Sally thought of the girls he had abducted, raped, and killed. He hadn't shown them any kindness.

"No."

Sally walked out of the room.

THIRTY-NINE

It was like Detective Clarke sensed where she was. As she collected her purse and phone from the guards at the prison and walked out of the entrance, her phone rang.

"Lauren's conscious, but she's refusing to talk," Clarke said.

"She's afraid. She knows who killed Carolyn and who ran her over, and she's too frightened to say."

"There's a cop outside her door."

"That's not enough. She almost died. If she tells you the truth, she and her husband will be in danger. If you want her to talk, you may have to put her and James into witness protection."

Sally walked across the vast parking lot to her car. The sun's heat on her head was intense.

"As you know, Sally, witness protection has to be used judiciously, usually when the witness has firsthand knowledge of the killer's actions. Do you think she witnessed the killer poison Carolyn?"

"Perhaps at the time Lauren didn't realize that was what the killer was doing and now she does?"

"I want to hear what she has to say first. Can you come to the hospital? She might talk to you."

"I was about to leave town with my son. I don't feel safe. There was an intruder in my backyard last night. He wore a Joker party mask, stood at my back door as bold as you like, stared straight at me."

"Did you call the police?"

"Yes, and he was gone by the time they arrived."

"Is there something you know about the case that you're not telling me? Because it looks to me that the murderer thinks you know too much."

This was the perfect moment to pass on Foster's information.

"This is secondhand information, but it might be worth looking into Nicole Slavik's background. When she was fifteen, she supposedly used unripe elderberries in yogurt to make a girl sick. Very sick. It was all about a boy Nicole fancied. She wasn't charged."

"Explains why it didn't come up when we searched for suspects with criminal records." Clarke exhaled like an angry bull. "And where did you get this information?" His tone suggested he had guessed.

"Foster told me."

"How the hell does he know?"

"He has sources, people who still do his dirty work."

"Be careful you don't become one of them. He's as slippery as a snake."

"I won't."

Clarke muttered something rude about Foster under his breath. Then he said aloud, "I get why you want to leave town, but come to the hospital before you go? Talk to Lauren. She's the key to solving this case."

Sally unlocked her car. The interior was like an oven. She got in and opened all the windows. "I'll be there in thirty minutes. I'll talk to her, then I'm leaving."

The doctor gave Sally ten minutes with Lauren.

"She's badly concussed and in a lot of pain. She'll be prepped for surgery for her broken hip shortly. She may be sleepy. She's on strong painkillers."

Clarke and Lin could also be in the room providing they didn't make Lauren agitated.

Sally entered the room feeling nervous. Clarke had a lot riding on this conversation, and she was feeling the pressure. James sat on a chair next to the bed, holding Lauren's hand. They were looking at each other but saying nothing. It was an intimate moment and their arrival shattered the beauty of it.

James noticed them first, turning his head to look at them. "I don't want you in here."

"We just need a few minutes. Sally is going to talk to her," Clarke said, remaining by the door.

He eyed Sally. "She's frightened. Don't you see? I don't want any more harm coming to her."

Lin said, "There's an option of witness protection, which depends on what Lauren tells us, but I'd like to take you through it. Would you step outside with me?"

James looked down at his wife. "I'm staying right here."

Lauren parted her lips. Her voice was husky. "Go with her. I'll be okay."

James asked, "Are you sure? You don't have to tell them anything."

"I know."

James followed Lin from the room and the door was closed, leaving just Sally and Clarke behind.

Sally stood close to the bed.

"Hi, Lauren, it's Sally Fairburn."

"Hey," Lauren said weakly.

"What happened, Lauren? Who knocked you off your bicycle?"

She screwed her eyes up and tears seeped down her pale cheeks. "They know. They're going to kill me."

Sally looked up at Clarke who stood in a corner. *They?* He nodded encouragement for her to continue.

"Who is going to kill you?"

"I can't say," Lauren replied.

"Okay, I know you're afraid. How about you tell me *why* they want to kill you?"

More tears ran down her nose and over her lip. "Can you pass me a tissue?"

Sally had a fresh pack in her purse. "Here." She placed the tissue in Lauren's hand. The poor woman could only use one arm. She used the tissue to wipe her eyes and blow her nose.

"You okay to tell me why they want to kill you?" Sally said.

"Because I know who did it."

Sally wasn't getting anywhere, apart from Lauren's suggestion that there might be more than one. Or was she using "they" to avoid saying "he" or "she"?

"We know Carolyn was poisoned with oleander. Do you know how it was administered?"

Fresh tears leaked from Lauren's eyes. "The tea. Carolyn loved this weird rooibos tea."

"And where is the rooibos now?"

"We didn't know what we were doing. Please, you have to believe me! She lied to us. She made us do it."

Sally glanced at Clarke, who mouthed the word "who?"

"Who made you?"

Lauren shut her mouth.

Sally asked, "Are you saying you killed Carolyn?"

Lauren's lips stayed tightly together. There was a knock on

the door and Lin asked to speak to Clarke. They went into the corridor, leaving Sally with James and Lauren.

"This stops now. My wife is having surgery. She needs to be calm and you're agitating her."

"James, can you answer a question?" Sally led him to a corner of the room. "Lauren mentioned that the poison given to Carolyn was in her tea. Has anyone brought tea to your house?"

"My wife is not a killer. She wouldn't hurt a fly."

"I think she's afraid of the killer. Have you seen any canisters or boxes of tea in your house that you don't normally buy?"

A look of fleeting recognition across James' face told Sally that he had. "There was a box full of nonperishable stuff, including some wine, I think. I heard the bottles clunk," he said. "Nicole took that one away and left the other boxes in our garage. I thought it odd at the time, but Lauren got upset with me, so I didn't mention it again."

FORTY

Lauren was being framed—at least that was how Sally viewed it.

Lauren was the perfect scapegoat. Vulnerable, easily pushed around, trusting.

But who was framing her and why did Lauren talk about "they" and then later on speak about a "she"? Lauren was concussed and in shock, but Sally suspected that the truth was mixed up in her confusing answers.

Sally drove onto her street. She tried to shift her focus to the journey ahead, but she found it hard to put the case behind her. Their bags were in the trunk, but she'd forgotten to include camping gear. If Paul found his grandparents drove him crazy, she and Paul could go on a camping adventure instead.

As she came to a halt outside her house, she saw a middle-aged man hammering his fists on Matt's door with a woman who appeared to be pleading with him to stop. The man was tall and angular with thinning hair. The woman was of a similar age, had blonde hair, and bore a striking resemblance to Carolyn.

"Can I help you?" Sally asked, approaching them.

"We're looking for Matt Tate." The man had an English accent.

"If he's not home, he might be at the pharmacy," Sally said. "Are you Carolyn's parents?"

"Yes. And you are?" he said brusquely.

"Sally Fairburn. I live here," she gestured to her house. "I'm so sorry for your loss. Carolyn was a wonderful person."

Carolyn's mother said, "I'm Gina and this is Charles. We don't know what's going on. Matt was supposed to meet us at the undertakers this morning and he didn't turn up and he's not returning our calls."

"I saw him this morning on the running trail, but that was about seven a.m. Would you like to come in? I can call the pharmacies and see if anyone knows where he is."

"That's very kind," Gina said. "Thank you."

"Darling, we have things we have to do," Charles objected.

"We can't do them without Matt and quite frankly I need to sit down."

Gina followed Sally into her home, leaving Charles little choice but to follow. She offered them a drink.

"Do you have English breakfast tea?" Gina asked. "The motel doesn't have tea-making facilities."

A tea lover, just like her daughter, Sally thought, and smiled at the memory of her and Carolyn at Olivia's Bookstore.

"I don't have tea, I'm sorry. I can make you a coffee though. Or I have juice and homemade lemonade."

They both took a lemonade and while they drank them Sally called the Pioneer Heights and the Lincoln pharmacies. She managed to speak to Lachlan Slavik at the Lincoln pharmacy. Sally relayed what she had learned to Carolyn's parents.

"Matt hasn't shown up for work. His business partner says he thought Matt was with you."

"He's utterly unreliable. Always was," spluttered Charles. "He can't even organize his own wife's funeral." He removed his glasses and pinched his nose. Sally guessed that he was trying to mask his tears.

"Darling, please," Gina remonstrated. "There's no point getting upset."

"Upset!" Charles said. "Carolyn was poisoned and we both know who did it. The bastard married her for her money."

"Darling, it's ill-advised to make rash accusations."

Gina gave Sally an apologetic grimace.

"When did you last see Matt?" Sally asked.

Charles scratched a wiry eyebrow. "The day we arrived. Yesterday. He picked us up from the airport and took us to a motel, which, quite frankly, is cheap and nasty. The penny-pinching sod couldn't even put us up in a decent motel."

Gina said, "I assumed he'd have us to stay at his house. It's big enough, after all. And it's Carolyn's home too."

"And she bloody well bought the house!" said Charles. "That good-for-nothing squandered his money on a wretched pop group, so our daughter had to pay the deposit *and* she covered the mortgage."

"He means band. Pop band. Matt's hobby," Gina said.

So the rumors about Carolyn having the money and Matt having the debts were true.

Sally took a seat. "I should tell you that Carolyn came to me and asked me for help because she believed she was being poisoned. I want to do all I can to help the police find who did this to your daughter. This may not be something you want to tell me, and I quite understand if you don't, but do you know who benefits from her will?"

"That monster," Charles said.

"No, darling, that's not right."

Charles stared at his wife. "Gina, we don't know if she changed it."

Gina looked at Sally. "This probably isn't making much sense to you. You see, Carolyn told me she was changing her will and when she made up her mind about something, she got on with it. What Charles is saying is that we can't be certain the new will was made."

"Are you saying that Carolyn may not have left her money to Matt?" Sally asked.

"That's right," Gina said. "Two weeks ago, she rang us. She sounded miserable. She wouldn't tell us what was going on, but she said that Matt wasn't the man she thought he was and she was going to change her will."

"Do you know who she was leaving her money to?"

"She said she'd leave her savings and shares, and the town-house, to us. It's in her name, you see. She also wanted us to have her antiques. They're in storage in England. Our daughter Julie was to inherit Carolyn's London flat."

"So nothing was to go to her husband?"

"That's right, and nor should it," Gina said.

"Did Matt know about this new will?" Sally asked.

Charles answered, "I doubt it."

Sally's brain was racing. If Matt did know that Carolyn intended to cut him out of her will, that was one hell of a motive to kill her before she had time to change it.

"Does she have a lawyer here?"

"We wouldn't know," Gina said.

Charles said, "There'd be a copy in the house, I'd expect."

Not if Matt found it and destroyed it, Sally thought, thinking about the firepit.

"In the previous will, did Carolyn leave everything to Matt including the London apartment?"

"She did," Charles said.

"And what would you estimate the London apartment is worth?"

"It's in Chiswick. Very expensive these days. I'd say two million pounds."

Plenty of motive for murder, Sally thought. "Have you told the detectives this?"

"Well, no," Charles said. "We spoke to them yesterday, but they didn't ask about the will."

"We were jet-lagged. Oh, Charles, we should have told them. How could we have been so stupid?"

"You're not stupid," Sally said. "You're grief-stricken. I'd like to get Detective Clarke on the phone and for you to tell him exactly what you've just told me."

FORTY-ONE

Down the other end of the line, Clarke listened to Gina and Charles tell him about Carolyn's intention to change her will so that Matt received only his share of the townhouse. They both leaned forward so they were close to the phone. Sally felt terribly sorry for the grieving parents. Not only had they lost their daughter, but they were now involved in a murder investigation, in a country that wasn't home.

"Mr. and Mrs. Sears," Clarke said, "We have a copy of Carolyn's will dated April 17th. It was found in the house. To our knowledge there is no other will."

"There is!" Gina said. "She was meeting a lawyer, wasn't she, darling?"

Clarke asked, "Which lawyer?"

"I wish I knew," Gina said.

"That bastard must have destroyed it," Charles said. "Why haven't you arrested him?"

Gina gave her husband a pleading look. His aggression wasn't helpful.

"We don't have evidence Matt Tate killed your daughter.

We'll bring him in for questioning, but he is a hard man to track down. Sally, when did you last see him?"

"On the Falls Trail around seven a.m. this morning."

"So he's done a runner?" Charles said.

"We don't know," Clarke said. "If he contacts you, Mr. Sears, please get in touch with me immediately. Sally, was Matt with anyone else when you saw him on the trail?"

"He was alone."

"Was he carrying anything? Did he have a backpack?"

"A small backpack."

"When you reached home, was his car outside his house?"

Sally closed her eyes and tried to recall what she saw. "I think so." Sally walked to her living room window and looked out. "His car's still across the street. So if he's gone somewhere, it has to be local."

"Or someone gave him a ride," Clarke said.

That somebody had to be Daisy Sheene, or perhaps Nicole Slavik. Sally glanced at Gina and Charles, wondering if they knew that Matt was having an affair. She didn't want to distress them any more than they already were, so she asked the detective if she could have a private word.

Sally then took the phone to her study and closed the door. "Do you think Matt has run away with Daisy?" Sally asked Clarke.

"It's possible. Daisy isn't home and she didn't turn up for work either."

"That makes them look guilty."

"Daisy's car has gone, so my best guess is that Matt pretended to go for a run and then deviated off the trail to meet Daisy."

Sally thought back to Margie's comment about Matt being so good looking. What else did she say? Then it came to her. "He didn't stick to the Falls Trail. He took the Scenic Trail.

That leads to a parking lot two miles from Pioneer Heights. Could Daisy have met him there?"

"Are you sure he took that trail?"

"I can check with Margie, but I'm pretty certain."

"Give me Margie's phone number."

Sally did.

"About the will," Sally said. "Even if Matt destroyed the copy in the house, the lawyer might have a copy."

"Locating her lawyer, if she even had one, could take a while. You have any idea how many lawyers there are in this city?"

Too many. "What about Carolyn's phone? Does she list a lawyer?"

"Her contacts list is gone. Sally, you've been helpful and I thank you. Now I want you to focus on staying safe."

"I'm going to stay with my parents in North Bend."

"Good idea."

"I'll drive Gina and Charles back to their motel first." *Then a quick visit to the cemetery*, Sally thought.

FORTY-TWO

Aiden Foster's gravestone was made of a cheap stone and the corners had been chipped away with what might be a chisel. Fans perhaps, wanting a slice of his horrific legacy? There were people sick enough to think that Aiden was a god. The kind of freaks who write love letters to serial killers in jail.

The headstone had also been defaced. There was a gash of red graffiti on the front that read,

Go to hell.

Sally had stopped twenty or so feet away, unable to get any closer. She probably knew who had used the spray paint. Perhaps the parents or siblings of one of Aiden's victims. Sally couldn't blame them for wanting to destroy Aiden's memory. A killer's legacy lasted a lifetime for the loved ones left behind.

Sally battled with her revulsion. Aiden was an abomination, like his father. How dare he have a headstone? But killers needed burying or cremating like everybody else. It was just that Sally didn't want to be there. She didn't want to be reminded of the moment she fled for her life through the forest surrounding Richard and Aiden's home. She could still remember the cracking of twigs and the rustle of leaves behind her. She still saw as clear as day Aiden running after her, a gun in his hand. The bullets zinged and thumped into tree trunks or hit the ground. He chased her to a house and killed the father living there in cold blood. Sally would always regret her decision to seek refuge there. But her survival instinct had led her there. At least inside the house she was able to call the cops and hide for as long as possible. It hadn't even occurred to her that she was putting another family in danger.

A trickle of sweat ran down the back of her neck. She wore a sunhat, but the sun was scorching. In her hand was a plastic pot containing a velvety dark red miniature rose called Daddy Frank. In her other hand a trowel and a water bottle. She had done what Richard Foster had asked. She chose a red rose, and it was beautiful, but she hated it. She hated it because it would grow on the grave of a monster. If Foster hadn't demanded a photo, she might have planted it near the grave, near enough so she could look Foster in the eye and tell him she had done his bidding. He was too smart for her to lie and tell him she had planted the rose when she hadn't. He was like a poker player, looking for the ticks or mannerisms that betrayed a liar.

Sally looked around the cemetery, fifty acres of graves and cremation stones and monstrous mausoleums and statues. The ancient, the ugly, the beautiful, and the new tributes to the dead were cheek-by-jowl—literally. Far away, in another section of the cemetery, her daughter rested. Her darling Zelda, who lived just thirteen years. How dare monsters like Aiden get to be buried in the same cemetery as angels like Zelda?

Her anger burst from her in a scream. Loud and long, she screamed until she ran out of breath, the sound lost in the dry heat.

Gulping in a new breath, Sally looked around, but there were no other mourners nearby. Midafternoon on a searingly hot day was not the time to tend to graves, and the wretched rose would probably die soon after she had planted it. What did she care?

"Get it done," she told herself, and took a step forward and then another, like a robot, until she had the tips of her running shoes on the ground above Aiden's remains.

She kneeled down, leaving the pot and the water bottle near her, then she angrily slammed the trowel into the turf. It was rock hard. The dry earth cracked and broke into grassy, dusty chunks. She threw them aside. The sun on her back burned, even through her cotton T-shirt. She kept going, deliberately keeping her eyes off the words on the gravestone. She tried to forget whose grave it was and just focus on the task. Her palms grew sore, but she kept chipping away at the hard ground until the hole was just deep enough for the miniature rose. Taking the rose from the pot, she placed it in the hole, used the trowel to scrape the grassy soil over the roots, then patted it down. Finally, she poured the bottle of water around the rose. She doubted anyone would tend the grave and if nobody watered the rose it would surely die, but she had given it a first drink and that was all she would do. She kneeled back on her haunches and took a couple of photos.

Her knees were sore and dirty. She took some more photos, this time from a distance so Foster could see the whole grave. Taking the water bottle and trowel with her, Sally walked away, her stomach churning and a vile, bitter taste in her mouth.

———

The walk to Zelda's grave gave Sally a chance to sweat out some of her anger and disgust. In her hand now was a bunch of fresh flowers and a fresh water bottle. She had left the trowel and empty bottle in her car.

Just the sight of her daughter's grave softened her heart.

"I'm sorry it's been so long," Sally said, resting her hand on the top of the rectangular headstone. "I've been a little busy." Sally looked down at the browned and drooping tiger lilies. Many of the petals were on the ground and the vase was empty of water. She quickly refilled the vase and put the bunch of yellow lisianthus, strawflower, and carnations in it. "That's better."

Sally sat with her back to the headstone and tapped the hand of the marble girl next to her. "It's good to be with you. I feel kind of dirty after what I've just done." Sally stared at her muddy palms. "And I don't just mean my hands and knees. It feels like a betrayal to you, my angel." Sally turned her head so she could view the statue of Zelda. The marble face was but a few inches from hers. "I planted a rose on the grave of a vile serial killer. I did it because I want information from his father. I really have made a deal with the devil. My fear is that he's gaining power over me, making me do things I don't want to do. But he's proving useful." She paused, deep in thought. If Carolyn did make a new will through a lawyer, it might take Clarke's team weeks before they found which one. She had a feeling that Foster might be able to speed up that process, but should she use it?

Sally leaned her head against Zelda's statue and closed her eyes. "We're leaving town for a few days. We have a stalker. A bad man by all accounts. He turned up in our backyard last night with a Joker mask on. It scared me half to death and I'm concerned about Paul, so we're going to stay with Mom and Dad." The edges of her mouth twitched into a wry smile. "Yes, I know. There are bound to be arguments and Paul really doesn't want to go, but we need to get away. I hope our stalker doesn't follow us."

Sally took out her book and read chapter three aloud. When she was done, she stood up.

"I'll come back as soon as I can, I promise. I love you, Zelda."

As she walked away, tears stung her eyes. "No time for tears."

She needed to steel herself for her meeting with the devil.

FORTY-THREE

Outside the visitor's entrance to the Walla Walla Correctional Facility, Sally took a deep breath. She had met with Foster once today already and every cell in her body screamed at her not to see him again.

Just show him the rose photos and ask him to find Carolyn's lawyer, she told herself. *In and out in ten minutes max.*

Once she had been through the security checks and escorted to the visitors' room, she felt lightheaded with the strain. Her day had started in the small hours of the night, terrified, a man at her back door. Meeting Carolyn's devastated parents had upset her. And having to tend to Aiden's grave was almost more than Sally could take. Yet here she was, hoping to persuade Foster to help her, yet again.

Foster shuffled into his room on the other side of the brick and Perspex wall with a self-satisfied smile on his face that made Sally wish to God that she didn't need this monster's help. A different guard was with him this time, a man Sally didn't recognize, looking at her with a look of disdain on his face. Did he think she was a serial killer groupie?

"This must be important," Foster said once he was seated.

"It is."

Upon arrival, Sally had asked if she could have special permission to take her phone with her to meet Foster. Initially the guard managing the visitors reception area said no, then a second guard had gone away and came back with a yes. Who he spoke to, Sally hadn't a clue, but the exchange served as yet another example of Foster's power.

Sally peered through the smudged Perspex at the guard watching her like a hawk from the back of the room. "I have permission to show Richard some photos."

The guard nodded, but from his hard stare Sally could tell that he wasn't happy about it. She found the best photo of Aiden's grave with the miniature rose in front of the headstone and then pressed the phone's screen against the Perspex. Foster took his time to stand, then shifted closer. His face was about ten inches from the Perspex and even though there was a wall between them, Sally's heart raced with fear.

"Enlarge it," Foster said. "I want to see the roses."

Sally did as he asked and again pushed her phone's screen against the Perspex. "Nice," Foster said. "Like the color. You'll water it, won't you?"

"I did as you asked. Now I need you to do something for me," Sally replied, not answering his question.

Foster walked back to his chair and sat facing her. "You have to water it, Sally. No point if it dies."

What more does he want?!

"I told you this morning that I'm leaving town for a while. When I get back, I'll see what I can do. Now I need you to find a lawyer for me."

Foster barked a laugh. "Why? You broke the law?"

"No, it's about a will. Carolyn Tate's will. Two weeks ago, I believe she made a new one. But it can't be found. The lawyer who drew it up may have a copy, but we don't know who the lawyer is. Can you contact your network on the outside?"

He tilted his head to one side. His smile was gone. "Why? Because twat-face Clarke can't do it?"

"Because I asked you to. In the new will she disinherits her husband, the man I suspect was involved in her death. In the new will, she leaves all her money to her parents and sister."

"I'm with the husband. Why shouldn't he get away with murder and reap the reward?"

Sally tried not to react. He was looking for a rise from her.

"If Matt is the killer, he's also the person who employed Chester Lee. If anything happens to me, your visitor list goes down to zero."

"Hmmm. You're not giving me much choice, are you? Ever played chess?"

She shook her head.

"Shame, you'd be good at it. Okay, I'll see what I can do. I still know a few lawyers who'll talk to me." He rose from the chair. "Sally?"

"Yes?"

"Thank you for the rose."

Foster left the room. Sally watched him leave, wondering why he had made that so easy for her.

It was getting dark by the time she left the prison. Sally had yet to pick up Paul and then drive to North Bend. Once she was there, she could finally relax. For over a week, Sally had felt unsafe, as tightly wound as a ball of rubber bands. She had done all she could to solve Carolyn's murder. It was time to put herself and Paul first.

FORTY-FOUR

Chester Lee was restless and his eyes were watery. He needed a fix.

He hadn't tried heroin until he was consigned to Walla Walla. A bitter smile stretched across his sallow face. All the years he'd been dealing, he'd never tried it. But prison had been hell on earth and drugs were only too easy to come by. He tried some, and then some more, and before he knew it, he was hooked. Through a shared syringe, he was infected with HIV. When Chester entered jail, he'd been a cop with wife, kids, house, and career. He left jail with an addiction, HIV, no family, and no house—his wife had moved out of state and she wouldn't allow him near the kids.

There were very few job options for a man with his history and he had his smack and HIV medication to pay for. So he set himself up as the guy who could make your problems go away.

Chester rubbed his watery eyes, keeping one hand on the steering wheel. He was in a stolen Ford Transit, tailing Sally Fairburn and her boy. He didn't know enough about Sally to guess where she was going, but they were leaving Pioneer Heights. He guessed she was trying to get away from him.

His employer had told him little, except to watch her and report back on where she went and who she spoke to. Then the brief had changed. Now the intent was to scare her. It had all gone well until Sally's annoying son challenged him. The boy had seen Chester's face. So Chester had to change it. The beard went. His bushy head of hair went. He now had a shiny bald scalp. He dumped the black cap and stole the Lincoln Town Car. That was a mistake; it was like trying to drive a boat on the road and it was far too conspicuous. So he'd dumped that too. The Transit van was much less conspicuous.

He had to hand it to Sally—she sure got about. Although, right now, he wished the bloody woman would stay put. He was out of smack and his dealer was in downtown Franklin. Sally was heading in the opposite direction, which meant Chester had a problem. His need for a hit wasn't his only issue. He had to ensure that he kept his car far enough behind so Sally didn't spot him tailing her. Chester made sure there was always one car between them. The difficulty with that was that he had to really concentrate. And when he was getting withdrawals, his concentration was shit. And the watery eyes didn't help either.

They were heading north. Chester wasn't being paid enough to cover long-distance driving. He passed a drive-through KFC and a gas station. The smell of greasy chicken wafted in through the open window. He could do with a meal inside him. Glancing at his fuel gauge, he saw he only had a quarter of a tank. He hoped she wasn't going far.

"No point fretting."

Chester tapped a finger on the steering wheel in time to the music on the radio. The station played music from the seventies, eighties, and nineties. At the moment it was Guns N' Roses' "Sweet Child O' Mine."

Sally braked at an intersection, then took a left. The car ahead of Chester indicated right and then sat there. *What the fuck!* Why didn't he move?

"Come on, you asshole. Get out of the fucking way!" he mumbled.

If the driver didn't move soon, he would lose Sally. Sweat trickled down the back of his neck.

"Enough already."

Chester pulled out onto the other side of the road and sped past the dawdling idiot. A car heading for the intersection honked a horn aggressively and Chester gave them the finger. A rush of panic hit him when he realized that he couldn't see Sally's white Honda Civic. A truck with a big load in the back blocked his view of the road ahead.

Shit!

He swung out and overtook the truck. Ahead of him was a taxi with a passenger in the back and the driver seemed to be going as slowly as possible, assumedly wanting to max out the fee. Too much traffic coming the other way had Chester swearing—he was stuck behind the wretched taxi. By now he could feel sweat trickling off his shaved skull and under his shirt collar. He'd drunk his Coke and his tongue was bone-dry. *God damn it!* If he lost Sally, he wouldn't get paid.

There was a break in the traffic heading toward him, so he pressed down hard on the accelerator and moved out to overtake the taxi. But the Transit van's engine was piss-poor weak and the bus heading his way wasn't slowing. Chester felt his ass muscles weaken and he almost shit himself, only just pulling in front of the truck in time.

He was now directly behind Sally's car. Nightfall had set in and Chester was banking on the darkness to keep him and his van off Sally's radar. His phone rang. During one of the many hours of tedium watching Sally from the car, Chester had changed his ring tone to a roaring lion, just for the hell of it. Now he realized how ridiculous it sounded.

"Where are you?" his employer said.

"Following Sally. Heading north. Looks like she and the boy are leaving town."

"Where's she going?"

"Don't know yet."

"It's your fucking job to know!"

"I'm doing my best, boss."

"Change of plan."

"Okay."

His employer described his new task. Chester shifted in his seat.

"That's not what we agreed," Chester said.

"I want it done."

"Not by me."

"How much?"

"It's not about the money," Chester said.

"It's always about the money," his employer said.

"Pay me what you owe me and find someone else to do it."

"You're pathetic, you know that?"

Chester wanted to tell the caller to get fucked, but he needed the five grand they'd agreed. "You want me to keep following or not?"

The caller was quiet for a couple of beats. "You have access to her house, right?"

"No problem. Craig, the locksmith guy, is at your service."

He was very pleased with how his locksmith act had gone. Sally hadn't been the least bit suspicious. The blonde wig had done the trick.

"Okay, keep with her for now," his caller said. "If she heads home, call me. All I need from you is access to her house."

FORTY-FIVE

Their arrival in North Bend had Ellen running out of the house and down the steps to greet them, enveloping them in her plump arms. George stood on the porch, his lips in a tight line, his arms folded. He gave Sally a nod and shook Paul's hand but no smile.

"I'll take that," George said, nodding at the duffel bags.

It was after ten o'clock at night by the time Sally locked her car and walked up the porch steps. She paused on the front deck, enjoying the familiar sounds of the night, hoping to forget the stresses and fears of the last week. A bat chirped as it flew overhead, and the giant conifers in the backyard whistled as the warm night breeze shook the needles. Even though this was one of the main streets into the town center, the traffic was sporadic and people drove in a leisurely way—such a contrast to the high-pressure driving and traffic jams of Franklin.

A warm golden light poured out of her parents' windows and open door. Her childhood bedroom window looked onto the street and the sky-blue drapes her mom had made were still hanging. Sally smiled. The last time Sally had visited, it had been snowing. Sally and Paul threw snowballs and made a snowman. Then Paul had helped her dad shovel snow off the driveway and porch steps. It had taken all of thirty seconds before George found fault with Paul and her son had stormed off in a huff.

Her smile disappeared.

"Please, no fighting," Sally whispered to herself.

The small town of North Bend—population 4,702—was located on the bend of the River Winona and was backed by the Winona Ranges, and she was looking forward to going for walks and perhaps swimming too.

Sally shivered. They say that animals and humans instinctively know when they are being watched and Sally had that feeling now.

She stared into the night, into the road, and at houses opposite. People here had big blocks of land and plenty of driveway, so there was no need to park on-street. Yet there was a car parked across the road, or perhaps it was a van because of its boxy shape. There was no engine noise and the headlights were off, the interior dark. An elderly widow, who Sally had known her whole life, sat on the swing seat of the house directly behind the van. The old woman raised an arm and waved. Sally waved back.

"He's not here," she told herself. "It was just the neighbor."

Ellen, her sixty-six-year-old mom, appeared at the door, the warm lighting giving the impression that she was glowing. Ellen married George when she was twenty and gave birth to Sally, her only child, at twenty-one. Ellen later told her that she felt bad that Sally didn't have a sibling and had worked tirelessly to ensure that Sally was never lonely, taking Sally with her wherever she went and encouraging Sally's friends to stay over. Some of Sally's fondest memories were of baking bread and tending to the garden with her mom clad in her straw hat.

"What are you doing out there, Sally? Come on in and make yourself comfortable."

Sally followed Ellen inside, inhaling the familiar smell of furniture polish, baked bread, and the sweet scent of freshly washed linen. Ellen hugged her daughter again, then led her into what Sally had always regarded the heart of the house: the kitchen.

"Are you hungry, my love? I'm happy to cook something."

Ellen's kitchen never changed. Pine storage cupboards, pine chairs, and large dining table. Flowering pot plants covered every available surface. The six-burner gas cooktop and oven must have been there for twenty years and despite their age the cooktop and door sparkled.

"Thanks, Mom. We're good. We stopped on the way and picked up burgers from the drive-through."

Ellen was generous to a fault. Sally thought back to all the times her mom had waited up for her dad to come home, no matter how late, so that she could cook him his dinner. It was a thankless task.

"An omelet would be great, Grandma," Paul said. "Or some of your amazing cake?"

Sally frowned at Paul. They had eaten their fill only thirty minutes ago.

"Coming right up," Ellen said, putting on an apron.

"Don't you go spoiling that boy," George growled from where he sat on a dining chair, nursing a mug of cocoa.

George had taught at the town's only school, which at the time had about thirty kids attending. Sally had no choice but to be taught by her dad and he had been ultra-critical of her performance and gone out of his way to demonstrate that she received no favoritism.

"It's no trouble," Ellen said, taking eggs and butter from the fridge.

"I'll help," Sally said, keen to spend time with her mom. "Paul, why don't you tell Grandma and Grandpa about your trip to Tampa Bay?"

Sally hoped it was a safe topic.

Paul pulled out a dining chair and sat. "I stayed with Cousin David and his family. It was amazing. He has his own Optis and we took it out every day. I can sail one on my own now."

George stared hard at Sally over his mug of cocoa.

Sally knew that look of disapproval.

"You paid for this boy to fly to Tampa!" His nostrils flared. "You spoil him!"

George left the kitchen with a shake of his head.

Paul rolled his eyes and shook his head. "I told you, Mom."

"Don't take any notice," Ellen said. "It's past his bedtime and he gets grumpy when he needs his sleep."

"I heard that!" George called from the living room. "And I'm not grumpy."

There was the familiar creak as George settled into his mushroom-colored leather recliner chair. She didn't have to see what he was doing to know that the TV's remote control would be resting on the right arm of the recliner, and heaven help Ellen if it was ever moved. George controlled the TV viewing, much as he controlled everything in the house, including Ellen. The kitchen was the only place where Ellen was allowed to be in control.

"Go talk to your father," Ellen urged Sally. "He's excited you're here. I'll bring you some peppermint tea and a slice of chocolate mud cake. Off you go now."

Reluctantly, Sally left the kitchen and sat on the couch, leaving Paul in the kitchen with Ellen.

"How've you been, Dad?" she asked.

"I'm good. How are you coping without Scott? Must be hard."

"Dad, life was bad when Scott was around. Now he's out of our lives, we're happy."

It didn't matter how many times she tried to explain that

Scott emotionally and mentally abused her, George didn't understand.

"I always liked Scott. You were a fool to let him go."

Sally balled her hands and tried to keep her tone level. "You forget, he walked out on us. He made me deeply unhappy, and he bullied Paul and Zelda."

"Nonsense. He kept Paul in line."

Sally bit her tongue. Her patience was being sorely tested. She stroked a crocheted blanket her mom had made that lay folded on the couch's arm.

"Why are you so late, anyway?" George said. "We thought you were coming earlier. We have lives, you know. Commitments."

At seventy, George was retired. His only commitments were to fishing every day with his longstanding friend Anthony and to completing a crossword every day, leaving Ellen to do the groceries, clean the house, do the laundry, run errands, cook all the meals, read story books to the kindergarten kids twice a week, and bake cakes for the church tea every Saturday afternoon.

"I was helping the police with a homicide investigation and comforted the deceased's parents."

"I thought you'd stopped that namby-pamby victim bullshit."

Her skin prickled liked she'd lain down in poison ivy. "How's Anthony these days?"

"Getting old like me. I never understood why you moved to Pioneer Heights. Why didn't you come here? I could do with some help around the house."

It was her mom who needed the help.

"I like living in Pioneer Heights and Paul is doing well at school. His teacher says he could get a football scholarship to college. Isn't that great?"

George mumbled a response, and Sally excused herself, too tired to cope with her father's belligerence.

In the kitchen, she found Paul whisking eggs and Ellen cutting a loaf of seeded bread.

"Mom," Sally said. "Is the farmers market on tomorrow morning?"

"Sure is. Every Wednesday and Saturday morning."

"I'd love to go. Paul, like to come?" Sally said.

George called out from the living room. "He's coming fishing with me."

Paul called out, "Thanks, Granddad, but I think I'll sleep in."

"Youth of today!" George moaned loud enough so they all heard. "Lazy!"

FORTY-SIX

Lauren Duthie woke with a start.

At first, she thought it was her husband, James, in the room. He'd promised to stay with her, even though there was a police officer seated outside the room. The opioid drugs they had given her to dull the pain also made her drowsy and she had fallen into a deep sleep. She was groggy and the room was dark. Was he sitting in the chair in the far corner?

"James?"

Her mouth and lips were dry and sticky, and she didn't recognize her own croaky voice. She turned her head and it throbbed like the worst hangover. There was a jug of water and a plastic cup on the overbed table. She raised a hand, but even such a simple movement had her whining. Even the needle taped to her hand, which enabled her to stay hydrated, throbbed. Her hip surgery was tomorrow morning. Or was it today? She wasn't sure. There was no clock in the room, so she had no idea what time it was. It could be the small hours of the morning, because there was no light coming in through the window. Until her hip surgery was done and she was on the road to recovery, she was unable to move her lower body and the only way she could go to the toilet was through a catheter.

Someone had tried to run her over and had very nearly killed her. It was no accident. No drunken driver. No one had lost control of their car. Lauren could think of only one person unhinged enough to do it, yet still she couldn't believe it possible. What had Lauren gotten herself into? How had she been so blind? It was too late to extricate herself now.

Where was James? Had he nipped out to the restrooms or for a coffee? She was so vulnerable. Was it possible the maniac would try to finish her off? Her eyes grew watery, and her breathing became rapid. She just needed to see her husband's face—his reassuring smile, his loving eyes, his wild hair. There had to be a call button for the nurse. But where was it? Turning her head a fraction, her neck pulsed with pain that felt like a knife stabbing her eyeballs. Gasping away some of the pain, Lauren moved her hands slowly across the sheet, hoping to feel the call button. From the time when her father had to have his appendix removed, Lauren remembered that the call button was on a long cable, at the end of which was a bulbous section, a bit like the remote for the garage at home.

Her pinkie finger touched a solid device. She tried lowering her eyeballs, but the pain was excruciating, so she kept moving her fingers. *Yes*, she thought, *this has to be it.*

Lauren ran a finger over a bump that must be the button.

And then it was gone, and her hand felt nothing but sheet.

"You don't need that, Lauren."

The voice came out of the darkness. Lauren would know it anywhere.

Her eyes darted around, wide with terror.

She parted her lips to scream for her husband. "Ja—"

A hand covered her mouth. The inside of her lips hit her teeth. "Owwwww."

Lauren wriggled her head, despite the pain, trying to free herself from the hand.

James! Where are you?

A salty tear spilled out of one eye and slid down her temple. *Oh, Carolyn. I'm sorry. I'm a coward and now it's my turn.*

Then the hand and arm had a body and a white coat. "Scream and I'll break your neck." Lauren stared into remorseless eyes. Ruthless eyes. There was blood in her mouth from the pressure on her lips. Lauren stopped trying to speak through the palm on her mouth and the killer lifted the hand away. "What did you tell them, Lauren?"

"Nothing, I swear."

"I'll end James's life if you're lying."

Lauren squeaked, tears flowing. "Please don't. He doesn't know anything. They think I did it."

A creak of shoes. Then the brush of her IV line on her lower arm. The maniac had merged into the blackness of the room. Lauren clenched her eyes shut, then turned her head to see why her IV line had moved.

A burst of cold liquid entered her vein and ran up her arm. The shock made her gasp.

"No, please!" Lauren begged. "I didn't..."

She fought a longing to sleep, but the desire was overwhelming. It swept over her in a wave, and she closed her eyes. She felt the killer's breath on her face. She heard the words, "So long, Lauren."

The sedative had relaxed Lauren, but the killer knew that she was still able to hear.

"You're lucky, Lauren, it's over for you. Night, night."

The syringe of sedative was put back in the box and another syringe made ready.

Into the IV line, the killer injected the overdose of anes-thetic. Lauren's breathing slowed. Her eye movement stopped, then her heart. Ten seconds passed by. The killer touched Lauren's wrist and, satisfied there was no pulse, walked away without so much as a backward glance.

Now to tie up one other loose end.

This one was going to be truly enjoyable.

FORTY-SEVEN

There was no point spending yet another night inside a vehicle, Chester thought. His back ached and he could smell his own rank body odor. He was sweaty and shaking and if he didn't get a fix soon, he'd go crazy.

North Bend was one of those dull country towns where people spied on their neighbors and the highlight of the week was a punch-up at the only bar in town. Jesus! How could people live in this dump?

Chester switched on the van's engine. His employer wouldn't have a clue if he drove back to Franklin, picked up some smack, then drove back, maybe stopping at a bar on the way. Sally and her brat were tucked up all cozy in their beds.

"To hell with it!"

He did a U-turn and headed down the street and out of North Bend. Cranking up the music and motivated by his addiction, Chester made it back to Franklin in record time. He called his dealer and arranged to meet him downtown. There was one problem. He didn't have enough cash to pay the dealer. He had already blown the five-hundred-dollar advance his employer had given him. But Chester knew how to get hold of some more.

Turning into the street where Sally lived, he slowed the vehicle to a crawl. The house lights were out. The houses on both sides were also in darkness, although he'd kind of expect that at 12:38 a.m. He double-parked outside Sally's house, the engine ticking over, and observed the street for a while. All was quiet, so he parked in an empty bay and walked up to her front door as if he owned the place, used a duplicate key to the one he had given her, and opened the door.

He shut it behind him. He was wearing gloves and used a small flashlight to navigate his way up the stairs. The first bedroom on the left was Sally's. He went to her dresser. There was a leather jewelry box. He opened it. The earrings looked nothing special. There were no rings of any value. He slid open a drawer.

"That's more like it."

A silver chain and a single sapphire, plus a pair of sapphire drop earrings. He put them in his pocket, then kept searching. In the next drawer down was a watch. Looked antique with a rose-gold-plated centipede-link bracelet with fold-over clasp. The watch had a cushion-shaped white dial with gold Arabic numerals.

"Has to be worth a bit," he mumbled, and put it in his pocket.

The three pieces of jewelry should get him a few hundred bucks, enough until he got paid.

Chester closed the jewelry box lid, crept down the stairs, and locked the door.

There was a pawn shop in the city where he'd get a fair price for the jewelry. Then he'd meet his dealer.

FORTY-EIGHT

Daisy Sheene didn't know what to do. Her photo was all over the TV news, Facebook, fricking everywhere! "Wanted in connection with the murder of Carolyn Tate," the news anchor said. She wasn't the only one. Matt's photo was also plastered everywhere, wanted in connection with the murder of his wife.

Holy crap!

How had it gone so wrong? How could Matt have let her down like this, the low-life skunk! And she had believed he loved her!

Daisy couldn't go back to her condo and she couldn't go to her parents' house either. Cops would expect her to do just that. She had received one voicemail from her mom, which simply said, "Darling, please hand yourself in. Whatever you've done, we love you."

Typical! They always thought she was a loser. If she sought sanctuary with them, her dad would insist on doing what he regarded was the right thing and take her to the police.

And Daisy wasn't going to jail. No way!

After waiting and waiting for Matt to turn up that morning, she guessed Matt had left town without her. The rat! Freaking out, she had finally opted to drive to her dad's hunting cabin in the Cascade Mountains. She and Matt had used it a few times so they could be alone, but it was never long enough. His nagging wife ruined every moment together, leaving phone messages, wanting to know where he was.

If he had killed Carolyn, she wouldn't blame him.

But she wasn't going down for his crime. No way! Uh-uh!

Daisy looked around her hiding place. The cabin was one room with very few amenities. Gas for the hot water and the stove came from a bottle outside. Water came from an outdoor tank. A composting toilet was in a separate outhouse. No shower. But it had a bed and a pantry of canned food, and it would do for now, as long as her parents didn't mention the cabin to the police.

It was past one in the morning and Daisy sat on an uncomfortable pine chair, tapping a kitchen knife on the tabletop, watching a spider in a roof corner dart at a trapped fly. On the table, a tin plate, the remnants of the beans she had for supper, now cold and congealed.

Why hadn't Matt stuck to their plan? He could have been with her now, safe where nobody would think to look.

They had arranged to meet in the parking lot at the start of the Scenic Trail at 7 a.m. It had been his idea. He was terrified of someone, but he wouldn't tell her who. Was that why he didn't meet up with her? Okay, so Carolyn was dead and one of his friends had been injured in a hit and run. Daisy wasn't going to shed a tear over Carolyn. Now that she was out of the way, Matt and his inheritance would become hers once they were married. But Matt was freaking out, saying all sorts of crazy stuff. He even thought that someone was trying to kill him.

It was Matt's idea to run and hide. Daisy had thought it a dumb idea. She kept telling him that it would make them both look guilty, but he wouldn't listen. He was leaving town, he had said, and she therefore had to go with him, or she'd lose him altogether.

And here Daisy was, alone, in a dirty cabin, with nothing but a camping lantern to light the room. The nighttime forest sounds were freaking her out. Screeches and cracking branches and strange huffing sounds. And her cell phone had no reception. If Matt was trying to get in touch with her, she wouldn't know until the morning, when she would have to drive back to the main road where she could pick up a phone signal.

Snap.

A stick had cracked. Who or what had broken it? Daisy listened, her eyes on the only door. She had slid a bolt across, but it was rusted and the screws were barely holding the mechanism in place.

Was it a deer or a person? Could Matt have found his way to the cabin without her? She doubted it. Each time they had come here, she had been the driver.

Snap, snap.

Daisy's stomach plunged with fear. It was getting closer. She stared at the cabin's only window. No drapes or blinds. She was clearly visible to anyone on the outside. Daisy stood and switched off the camping lantern that hung from the wooden beams. The cabin was plunged into a thick darkness. There was not a chink of light. It was so dark that Daisy was disoriented and almost fell over when she turned in what she hoped was the direction of the bed, with her arms out front to feel her way. Her phone was in her bag on the bed. Her boot hit the solid base and she patted the bedcover for her bag. *Where's the fucking phone?* She found it.

Snap! Thud!

Daisy hadn't reached the bed when the door flew open, a metal clank the only sound of the useless bolt giving way. The legs of the wooden chair scraped across the floor. Daisy froze. A flashlight beam darted about the room and when it landed on her, she was blinded. Daisy raised a hand to protect her eyes from the stinging brightness.

"Who are you?" Daisy said.

"Your executioner."

Daisy wanted to scream, but she couldn't. Behind the flashlight beam, a baseball bat rose up. Daisy tried to step back. The bed stopped her. The bat swung at her. She raised a second arm. The bat broke the arm. The pain was instant and excruciating. The bat continued into the side of her jaw. The agony of the smashed bones and teeth were too much. Daisy collapsed onto the bedcover and almost passed out.

The killer loomed over her. The final blow hit Daisy so fast, she was dead in an instant.

For the first time in a while, Sally had slept soundly. Her childhood room felt so safe and cozy, she had fallen asleep as soon as her head hit the pillow. The next morning, she found her mom in the kitchen frosting a chocolate cake. The table was laid for breakfast and Ellen had a pot of coffee brewing.

"May I have some coffee?" Sally asked.

"You certainly can, I brewed it just the way you like it. Extra strong."

Sally poured herself a mug and added cream. Out of the kitchen window Sally could see her mom's incredible flower garden: echinacea flowers in red and oranges, hydrangeas in blues and pinks, purple bee balms, mauve lavender, and penstemons in fuchsia pink, as well as Ellen's prized roses. The lawn, which she tended with such care, was like green velvet. "Your garden looks so beautiful."

Ellen smiled furtively. "Don't tell your father. He thinks he's responsible for its splendor."

Her mom would never say that if her dad was around. "Dad gone fishing already?"

"Left a few minutes ago." Ellen stopped smoothing the

frosting and grimaced. "He's upset Paul wouldn't go with him. It would mean a lot to him if Paul joined him tomorrow."

Ellen was the peacemaker. The mender of bridges. The provider of comfort. As a child, Sally learned to do as her mother did, or else George would complain and criticize more than ever, not just targeting Sally but also his long-suffering wife. It wasn't until Sally was a teenager that she began to notice that other men didn't treat their wives the way her dad did. At sixteen she vowed to her friend Margie that she would never marry a bully and yet that's exactly what she did. And Scott was a hundred times worse than George.

"Mom, you know what'll happen if Paul goes with him. Dad will tell Paul that he's not doing it right and Paul will get angry. You know Dad can't stop criticizing."

"George means well. It's just that he's a perfectionist," Ellen said, as usual making excuses for him. "What if we all went together and had a picnic? He's less likely to be difficult with us around."

Sally wasn't so sure, but she could see that Ellen was excited by the idea of a picnic, so she agreed.

"Do they go to the same spot? By the big willow?" Sally asked.

"Always the same place and always with Anthony. Your father likes his routine."

"Sounds like a plan," Sally said. "Why don't we sit on the porch and chat? Paul won't be up for a while."

"What about breakfast?"

"Don't worry about it."

Ellen placed a mesh dome over the cake to keep the flies off. Then they sat on the wicker chairs on the back porch, nursing mugs of coffee.

"It's so lovely to have you here." Ellen seemed to study Sally's face. "There's something different about you. More confident, maybe?"

"It's taken six years to get this far, Mom, but I think I'm on the road to recovery. Scott almost destroyed me, Paul too, and his actions brought on Zelda's suicide. I'll never forgive him for that."

"We didn't know," Ellen said. "He told us you were mentally ill. That you needed time away from us. We thought that you didn't want to see us."

"Quite the opposite. He wanted me isolated so that he could control me and the kids. The day he walked out on us was the best day of our lives, although I didn't know that at the time."

"I know your father is a difficult man, but Scott was something else. He pretended to be nice, but deep down he cared only about himself."

Ellen hardly ever criticized anyone, and Sally was relieved that finally her mom understood, even if her dad didn't.

Inside the house, a cell phone rang. Sally recognized her ringtone. "Damn! That'll wake Paul."

Sally rushed into the house and picked up her phone, which was recharging in the bedroom.

"Detective?" Sally said, "Has something happened?"

"It's about Lauren Duthie," Clarke said. "I'm sorry to say she died in the night. We suspect murder. Her IV drip was tampered with."

The bedroom felt as if it closed in on her. She sat heavily on the bed's edge, trying to take it all in.

"Sally?" Clarke asked.

"She was murdered in a hospital?" Sally couldn't believe it possible.

"Yes. The officer assigned to watch her had gone to the restroom and her husband was getting a coffee."

"But how? I mean, didn't a nurse see a stranger walking about?"

"They saw nothing unusual. We're checking the hospital's CCTV."

Sally's hand trembled. "The poor woman. She was so afraid. Why did she have to die?"

"She knew something. Listen, Sally, I don't want to alarm you but watch yourself. Keep Paul close. Carolyn's killer is tidying up loose ends."

FIFTY

The walk along the trail had given Sally some time to recover from her distress at Lauren's murder. She stayed quiet while Ellen and Paul chatted, lost in her own thoughts about the killer. The picnic would prove a welcome distraction and by the time they arrived at George and Anthony's fishing spot, Sally found that she was hungry.

Her father and his friend had set up their fishing rods on the soft bend of the Winona River where the water was shallow and where small pebbles provided a relatively flat surface for their folding fishing stools. They had a large umbrella on a long pole set up so that it gave both men some shade.

"Yoohoo!" Ellen called out, attracting the men's attention.

Sally laid picnic blankets on a patch of ground under the ancient willow while Ellen laid out the food: two BBQ chickens they had purchased at the farmers market, cooked sausages that were still warm, Ellen's freshly baked bread, creamy potato and egg salad, strawberries, and slices of Ellen's chocolate cake.

"Well, ain't this something," Anthony said, taking a paper plate from Ellen.

Anthony was in his mid-seventies and had worked for the

local lumber company all his life. He now lived in an in-law apartment in his daughter's backyard and liked to get out as much as possible so that he didn't get under his daughter's feet.

"Did you bring pepper and salt?" asked George, tearing off a chicken leg and taking a couple of sausages. "And BBQ sauce?"

"Certainly did," Ellen replied, handing the condiments to him.

"Who wants some of Mom's watermelon juice?" Sally said.

"I will!" said Paul, who was already munching two slices of bread in the middle of which was a sausage.

"Did you catch anything?" Sally asked.

"Sure did. I caught two trout and Anthony hooked a yellow perch." George nodded in the direction of a bucket filled with water.

"Yup, that's my supper sorted." Anthony chuckled.

Sally remembered coming to this part of the river to paddle. Margie was a daredevil and she'd encourage Sally to climb trees and go skinny-dipping when there was nobody around.

Sally let the talk wash over her. She tuned in to the soothing sound of the running water and the rustling of the willow's swaying branches. A few walkers followed the path through the trees, but none stopped where Sally's family was picnicking. After eating her fill, she took a book from her backpack and propped herself up against a tree. Paul was talking to George and Anthony about his hope that his team would win the state championship. She tuned out the voices and opened *All the Light We Cannot See*. She read the first few lines, but something bulky protruded from the pages at the back. It was an envelope, and it was addressed to Carolyn Tate.

Sally's heart rate quickened.

The envelope had been opened, the jagged edges at the top suggesting it had been torn open in a rush. Sally flipped it over and on the back was printed the name and address of City

Lawyers. Sally blanched. Was this Carolyn's newest will? Did Sally have it in her possession all the time?

She carefully slid the folded pages from the envelope. It was the Last Will and Testament of Carolyn Patricia Tate.

Sally searched for the date and found it. It was signed and dated June 20, 2016. It had to be the most recent will.

Sally went back to the beginning and skim-read the contents. In it, Carolyn left all her worldly belongings, properties, and shares to her parents and her sister. There was no mention of Matt Tate. Carolyn had totally cut Matt out of her will.

"What have you got there?" Ellen asked.

Sally was in shock. Why had Carolyn given a copy of her will to Sally? Had she feared that Matt might find it and destroy it? The stab of guilt she felt had her clutching the will to her chest. "I'm so sorry I didn't believe you," she whispered.

"Your mother asked you a question," George said sharply.

Sally looked up. "Oh, um, sorry, Mom." She stood. "I have to go."

Paul stood too. "What's wrong? Is that another threat?"

"Threat?" Ellen asked, worry in her shaky voice.

"No, it's Carolyn's last will. I must get this to—"

Before she could complete her sentence, a figure burst out of the trees and dove into the middle of their circle, snatching the letter, ripping it from Sally's hands. It happened so fast that Sally didn't have a chance to see his face. He was already running away, taking the path they had taken earlier, which led back to the parking lot.

"No!" wailed Sally.

She'd had the key to the Carolyn Tate case all along and now it had been literally snatched away from her.

Paul sprinted after the thief.

"Wait, Paul, don't tackle him!"

But Paul was gone, running after the guy as fast as he could.

She dove for her backpack and took out her Glock, cursing herself for not wearing it, then she ran in the direction her son had taken. If the will had been stolen from her by Chester Lee, then Paul was in grave danger.

"What the blazes...?" George muttered.

"Call the cops!" Sally shouted over her shoulder, taking in the stunned expressions of her parents and their friend.

Adrenaline sped through her body. She jumped over sticks and undergrowth. Paul was up ahead, and in front of him was a man with a shaved head. The thief looked back over his shoulder as he ran. He looked familiar. It was a flash of a face, that's all. A shaved head, no beard, so it couldn't be Chester, right? The path meandered and the forest on both sides thickened. In the distance, a young couple was ambling toward them, holding hands.

"Get out of the way!" Sally shouted, but they were engrossed in each other's company and didn't hear her.

The thief plowed through the middle of them, sending the young woman flying. Her boyfriend stumbled backward in the other direction. Paul kept running, bypassing the couple, his arms and legs pumping like pistons. She didn't stop either.

"Call the police. Say 'Carolyn Tate murder.'"

The couple watched her run by, wide-eyed.

Up ahead, Paul had closed the distance between himself and the thief. He lunged at the man's back and grabbed a fistful of the man's shirt. The thief stumbled and almost fell over. Sally's heart was in her mouth. She didn't want him to get hurt.

"Paul, let him go!" she cried.

The thief elbowed Paul's gut. Paul flinched but hung on. That's when Sally saw the glint of a knife in the assailant's right hand.

"Knife!" Sally screamed.

In that split second, Paul's assailant swiveled on his heels and brought the knife around, aiming for the side of Paul's ribs. Paul dove to one side and landed hard in the dirt.

"Stop!" she shouted.

Sally stood stock still, her pulse pounding, her breathing heavy. She raised the pistol, aimed. Chester raised the knife, ready to plunge it into Paul's stomach.

Not my son, she thought.

Boom!

The gunfire reverberated through the woods. Birds squawked and flew up into the sky.

The assailant fell forward, staggered, and landed on his knees. He held on to the knife, but Paul kicked it out of his hand, then scooped it off the ground.

The man sat on his haunches, clutching his right shoulder. "You fucking shot me!"

Sally kept her gun aimed at him and positioned herself so she was facing him. "Raise your hands."

"I can't."

"Raise one hand," Sally said.

He stayed as he was. Paul kicked him in the thigh. "Do as she says."

He raised the uninjured arm and glared at Paul.

To her son she said, "Take the copy of the will from his back pocket."

Paul whipped it out of the man's jeans.

"Have you got your phone?"

"Yes," Paul said.

"Call 911."

Paul stepped away to make the call. She studied the man's features. He was familiar in more ways than one. He might have shaved away his head and beard, but his beak of a nose was a giveaway.

"You're Chester Lee."

"So?"

He'd worn a blonde wig when he'd come to her house to change the locks.

"You're also Craig from Abbott's Locksmiths."

"Nah, not me."

"Give me a break. I expect the police will find the wig in whatever stolen car you're driving these days," Sally said.

"No comment."

"Why did you want keys to my house?"

He gave her a wicked smirk.

FIFTY-ONE

Sally and Paul sat side by side on the trunk of a fallen tree watching two deputies escort the man Sally now knew to be Chester Lee from the crime scene. He was handcuffed to one of the deputies and accompanied by a paramedic, loudly claiming that Sally had attacked him unprovoked.

"He certainly knew how to disguise himself," Sally said, shaking her head. "Bushy hair and beard one day, then shaved head and no beard, then a blonde wig when he was the locksmith."

"And don't forget the cars. A Sonata, then a Lincoln, then a Ford van," Paul said.

"What I want to know is who he's working for," Sally said.

Paul nodded in the direction of Detective Clarke and Sheriff Alford, heads bowed together. Alford was in a beige and khaki uniform, Clarke in a dark gray suit.

"What's going on with those two?" Paul asked.

"I hope Clarke's speaking up for us. He knew I had a stalker and he knew I suspected he was Chester Lee."

"Maybe he's telling him that you're one cool mom! Seriously, that shot was amazing!"

It hit the mark and she was thankful for that. Sally had wanted to incapacitate him, not kill him. The leg was too hard a shot. If she'd hit an artery, he might have bled out.

Sally put an arm around her son. "Thank you. The shot saved you. That's all that matters."

Paul was buzzing with adrenaline. He could barely sit still, engrossed in the activity around him. He seemed to be coping better than Sally, who was feeling cold and her hands hadn't stopped trembling since she took the shot.

"You were so brave chasing after him and this may all seem exhilarating right now, but later on you might feel different. Don't bottle it up. Come to me if you're feeling overwhelmed or anything, okay?"

"Sure, but I'm good."

Ellen and Anthony sat on fishing stools just outside the crime scene tape as if they were at an open-air movie theater. Her dad was talking to a deputy, leaning over the crime scene tape. *Please, Dad*, Sally thought, *don't go saying the wrong thing*.

When Ellen noticed Sally looking at her, she waved and mouthed, "Are you okay?"

Sally nodded at her mom and smiled, hoping to reassure her.

A small crowd had formed along the trail, and some had their phones out, shooting videos. A cameraman and a reporter pushed their way to the front of the onlookers and within seconds they were recording the scene.

Paul jerked his head in their direction. "I guess we're going to be on the news."

The TV camera was pointed at them and the female reporter was gesturing their way.

"Come on," said Sally, "I don't want us to be on TV." Sally turned her back on the TV camera and Paul followed her to where the sheriff and Clarke were deep in discussion.

"Sheriff Alfold. Detective. I'm sorry to interrupt, but I'm

feeling very shaken. Can we go to the station and make our statements there?"

"I don't see why not, Ms. Fairburn. Detective Clarke here has been filling me in on Chester Lee," Alfold said. "He's also told me about your capabilities with a pistol. That was quite some shot you took. But I'm going to need your Glock as evidence." He looked down at the Glock 19 tucked into the side of her waistband. He held up an evidence bag and Sally dropped it in there.

"Sheriff," said Clarke. "I need some time with Sally. It okay with you if I drive them to the station?"

"Suits me fine, my friend. I won't be long behind you."

"Could do with some help keeping those newshounds at bay," Clarke said.

Alford called over a deputy and told him to escort Clarke, Sally, and Paul to the parking lot and to keep reporters away.

The deputy took them on a wide loop away from the crowd. When the hubbub was distant Clarke spoke.

"Did you give Alford the copy of the will?"

"I have it here," Sally said, taking the folded will out of her pocket. "Carolyn's current will, dated June 20th." Sally handed it to Clarke.

"You read it?" he asked.

"I skim-read. She leaves nothing to her husband."

"How did you come by it?" he asked, putting it in his jacket's inner pocket.

"Carolyn gave me a book as a gift. I didn't open it until today's picnic. The envelope was wedged between the back pages. Chester must have followed me here and seen me reading it."

"Well, you don't have to fear Chester anymore. With your testimony and all the witnesses, he's going down for attempted murder."

"He posed as a locksmith. I just didn't recognize him in his wig and without his beard. And he had the official van and the clothing, and it just didn't twig that he was my stalker. I feel such a fool."

"Don't beat yourself up about it. He's in custody and I'm going to find out who sent him, believe me."

"Do you think it's Matt and Daisy?"

"They have motive, means, and opportunity, plus they've disappeared."

"It makes sense that they murdered Carolyn so Matt would inherit," Sally said, working through their crimes out loud. "They killed Lauren because she was going to tell us who did it. Then they discovered the new will Carolyn had made but they didn't know how many copies there were, and they suspected I had one, which is why they asked Chester to watch me. How am I doing?" Sally asked.

"Good, except we have no evidence. If Chester is willing to testify against the killer or killers, he may receive a lesser sentence."

"What puzzles me is how Chester knew there was a revised will. Whoever employed him to follow me must have told him to search for it. From what I know only the lawyer, Carolyn and her parents knew about the second will."

"Carolyn must have confided in someone," Clarke said. "I'll get Chester to talk."

"I feel it's time to go home. Paul isn't happy here and after what's just happened, I think he'll be better off at home, near his friends. Although I'll have to update my locks—again. I hate to imagine who Chester gave keys to."

"I know a locksmith," Clarke said. "I can highly recommend her. Do you want her number?"

"That would be great."

They had almost reached the parking lot. Another news crew had just arrived, tumbling out of their van and racing toward her.

"What about Nicole?" Sally asked. "I think she knows more than she's letting on which could mean she's also in danger."

"I'm pulling her in for questioning, and if needs be, I'll get a patrol car to watch her house."

The killer observed Sally in conversation with the detective, the son trailing behind and the deputy up front, telling onlookers to move away. The deputy was focused on keeping media crews at a distance and didn't pay any attention to the stranger walking through the forest within hearing distance.

Sally was too close to the truth and was clearly not the type of person to give up. Which made her a problem.

FIFTY-TWO

It was all over the TV news. Chester Lee had attempted to stab Paul Fairburn, and Sally Fairburn had shot him in the shoulder to save her son. Foster clapped. The sound of his dry palms coming together was like a series of gunshots. *Clap, clap, clap.* Faces appeared in the cells opposite.

"What you clapping for?" said Benny, who had killed his four wives, then fed them to his pigs.

"My protégé."

"Come again?"

Benny, a short tubby guy with receding hairline, wasn't a sophisticated kind of serial killer. He'd gotten away with the murders through luck, rather than judgment, and some hungry pigs.

"My rookie. I'm training her to be a detective."

"What you doing that for? Ain't there enough detectives already?"

"Ah," said Foster, "but she's *my* detective. And she's helping me to oust someone I don't like."

"Who's that, then?" Benny asked.

"Never you mind."

Benny scratched his crotch. He scratched it so often, the rumor was he had a nasty rash down there. Or maybe it was herpes.

"Come on, man. Tell me. I ain't got a TV like you."

"Shut up, Benny, I'm busy."

"Fuck you!" Benny snarled, then turned away from the bars, lay on his bed, and started to jerk off.

Jerking off was Benny's primary entertainment.

Foster ignored him. The news anchor talked about the police search for Matt Tate and Daisy Sheene, the prime suspects in the Carolyn Tate and Lauren Duthie murders. Their photos were shown. Foster flared his nostrils.

So far, Foster's person on the outside had gotten nowhere discovering which lawyer had assisted Carolyn with drawing up a new will. Irritated at the failure, he had asked them to turn their attention to the murder suspects. He saw the prime suspects as Matt Tate and Daisy Sheene, Nicole Slavik (born Nicole Chambers), Becca Watts, and Nicole's husband, Lachlan Slavik. One, or a number of them perhaps, was responsible for the murders. He wanted dirt on them. Their secrets. The stuff that you didn't find on databases or in bank accounts or on lists of phone calls made. Foster had to ensure that Sally solved the case. He wanted Clarke to fail, and Sally would unwittingly help make it happen.

Benny's moaning was getting loud, loud enough to interfere with Foster's TV viewing, so he upped the volume. So engrossed was he with the news coverage, he didn't notice Tank outside his cell calling his name.

"Phone call!" Tank said.

"Who is it?"

"I'm not your secretary, Foster. Get up and put your hands through the bars. Now!"

Foster switched off his TV and ambled over to the bars and

did as he was told. Tank handcuffed him, then opened the sliding cell door.

Benny had finished jerking off and sat up in his bed. "Hey! Why can't I have phone calls?"

"'Cause nobody wants to speak to you, Benny," Foster said over his shoulder.

Tank escorted him to the phone on the wall, told him to make it quick, and then stood five, six feet away.

"Yes?" Foster said down the phone.

The receiver stank of bad breath. Why didn't the lazy guards clean it?

"I got something," the caller said. "Thought you'd want to know straight away."

"And?"

"They were best buds at college. Matt and Lachlan studied pharmacy; Nicole was studying medicine. Becca, veterinary science. They dealt drugs. Mostly dope, but ecstasy and cocaine too."

"So? Kids at college do all sorts of shit. Where are you going with this?"

"I spoke to some people who were at the same college. Doing the same courses. Told them I was investigating the Carolyn Tate murder. Anyway, they said that one of the gang was the linchpin for the group. But the leader was clever. Was never seen dealing. They fell out over something; there were rumors the leader took photos and used them to blackmail the others. You get what I'm saying?"

"One of the group had a hold over the others. Blackmail, maybe?"

"Exactly," the caller said.

"Which one?" Foster asked.

The caller told him.

Foster stared at the scratched wall where countless prisoners had picked away at the paint with their fingernails.

"Okay, keep digging."

"Yes, boss."

After the call, Foster was led straight back to his cell. He pondered what his source had told him. The blackmailer could destroy the friendship group's lives if the drug-dealing photos were to go public. But how did this link to the murder of two of the group, especially to Carolyn, who only became part of the group just a year ago? Nevertheless, it was a lead, and he wanted Sally to follow up on it. Carefully, of course. He needed her alive. Sally was shaping up nicely. Toughening up. She had bought into the give and take of information between them. Perhaps, as he had hoped, she was becoming reliant on him? Seeing him as an ally? And from the news bulletin he had watched earlier, he was certain that Sally was more than a match for this killer.

FIFTY-THREE

Nicole Slavik was about to click "send." Her hand rested on her mouse, finger poised for the right click that would send her application for the position of doctor at a highly thought-of medical practice. Her twin boys, Zac and Joe, were in the backyard, chasing each other with water guns. She'd tried to put sunscreen on them, but they wriggled like little fish and ran off, so she'd have to get them inside soon or they would burn. She'd get no peace once they were inside.

Bring on the first day of school, she thought longingly.

Not that she'd had a moment's peace since Carolyn died. Why did the detectives keep asking questions? Why did they suspect her, after she had been so careful?

"Forget them. They have no evidence. Move on," Nicole said to herself.

She clicked her mouse and the email to the High Point Medical Clinic went.

There! She'd achieved something today, at least.

It wasn't that Nicole didn't love her kids, but she craved more intellectual stimulation. She'd enjoyed the mothers groups, but she was done talking about kids' and parent issues. It was time to get back to what she loved. If she was honest, it wasn't just about using her brain. She loved being in the public eye. She was pretty and dressed well and she wanted people to admire her looks, not just her skills. It was about time she was appreciated because it sure as hell wasn't happening at home.

Lachlan ignored her most of the time, too busy at the pharmacy or playing golf or drinking with his buddies. Perhaps she should see the upside of his lack of attention. He didn't suspect a thing, not even when he found her in the kitchen, rubber gloves on her hands, emptying bottles of wine down the sink. The place stank of bleach, which she was using to clean out the bottles and wipe away fingerprints. She wouldn't take any risks. She had to be certain that all traces of the oleander were gone before she took the bottles of Chardonnay to a public glass-recycling depot.

Nicole looked out of the tall windows of her living room at Zak and Joe in the backyard. The rooibos tea, also containing the oleander, was buried under the stone birdbath at the far end of the garden. She'd broken a nail moving the birdbath, but once the tea was in the hole she'd dug and fresh soil was layered on top, plus the birdbath was back in place, she was confident that even a police search wouldn't find it.

She owed Lauren that much, at least. Stupid, stupid Lauren might be dead, but she'd almost spilled the beans to Sally Fairburn and the detective before she died. Nicole had never really liked Lauren. She was too weak, had too much of a conscience, and Nicole found such people repulsive.

However, the cops kept coming back to her. It was difficult to keep her story straight, no matter how often she rehearsed her lines. Now they knew about the time she deliberately made a girl at her school sick with unripe elderberries, they seemed to have latched on to her in a way that had her on edge. Why didn't they take the hints she had dropped about Daisy, who was the obvious suspect: the jealous lover, who wanted the wife out of the way and to share Matt's fortune. Now that Daisy had disappeared, it should be blindingly obvious that Daisy was guilty.

Nicole stared at the one broken fingernail. The others were perfect, professionally manicured and polished. She'd have to get a false nail put onto the broken one. But first she must give the cops one last nudge in the right direction. She dialed Detective Clarke and put the call on loudspeaker.

"I've remembered something," she said. "It could be nothing but..."

"Tell me anyway," Clarke said.

The murmur of voices in the background were cut off. Perhaps Clarke had closed a door.

"I popped in to see Matt on Sunday. He was in a terrible state. Mumbling about Daisy. Said he thought Daisy had something to do with Carolyn's death."

"Did he say why he thought that?"

"Daisy had been on him to leave Carolyn, but he couldn't afford to leave her because he was technically bankrupt. It was Carolyn who was keeping his business afloat."

"Why did Matt think Daisy was responsible?" Clarke sounded impatient.

"Right, well, Matt told me that Daisy said she had found a way to free them of Carolyn *and* he'd have her money too. It was obvious to me what he was thinking, but he didn't come right out and say it: Daisy poisoned Carolyn."

"Was anyone with you when Matt said this?"

Clarke sounded as if he didn't believe her.

"Just me."

"You say Matt told you this Sunday and today's Wednesday. Why didn't you tell us this before?" Clarke asked.

Good question. "It's all been such a shock. First Carolyn, then Lauren. I guess I just didn't think."

"Can you come in to make a statement?"

"Can I do this tomorrow? I have the kids with me all day."

"I'll send Detective Lin. Expect her within the hour."

Had Clarke bought her lie?

Time would tell.

FIFTY-FOUR

JULY 21, 2016

Sally smiled. It was good to be home again.

Chester Lee was under arrest and Clarke's locksmith had already been and gone. She had replaced the locks Chester, aka Craig, had installed. Clarke clearly had some clout because the locksmith was keen to keep the detective onside and invited Sally to call her anytime should she need help.

It was lunchtime Thursday and Sally had unpacked her belongings. She hoped Paul had done the same. His bedroom door was shut, and it was quiet. On the drive home, Paul had been chatty and upbeat about taking down Chester, reliving the scene where he chased the man through the woods, and then, when he drew a knife, Sally had shot him. He'd then phoned Reilly and every friend he knew to regale them with his adventure, as he saw it. But as they had reached home, he'd grown increasingly sullen and noncommunicative. Had the euphoria finally worn off and the trauma set in?

She vacillated outside Paul's door, in case he was sleeping, then she quietly knocked. No answer. So, she crept downstairs and called Margie's work number from her study, where she could close the door and not disturb her son.

"I'm so pleased you called," Margie said. "I must have left fifty messages. Are you guys okay?"

Sally smiled at Margie's exaggeration. "We're good. A bit shaken." She looked up at the ceiling. "Hope Paul will be okay. He was pumped afterward, but now he's shut himself in his room."

"The adrenaline's dissipated by now and the ramifications of the assault are sinking in," Margie said. "Talk to him. Listen. Let him know he can talk to you anytime. Maybe ask him if he'd like to see Dr. Kaur."

"Thanks for the tips. Dr Kaur is a good idea. He's a resilient kid, but he's just been through a traumatic event."

"Getting your life back to normal is important."

"Now our stalker's been charged, that's exactly what I'm hoping to do. Hey, I was thinking, would you like to join us for dinner tonight?"

"I'd love to. Will Paul be okay with that?"

"I asked him as we drove home. He loved the idea. And stay the night. Then you can relax and enjoy your wine."

"I don't mean to be rude, but are you sure it's safe?"

"I have new locks—once again. We'll be totally safe."

"Great. See you later."

Sally rolled her shoulders and then moved her neck from side to side, trying to loosen the tension.

Her phone rang and she knew the number. It was the cell phone Foster sometimes used. She sighed. She didn't want to speak to him. She let the call go to voicemail and switched her phone to silent. Then she went upstairs and knocked on Paul's door again. She waited for a count of ten and when there was no response, she entered quietly. Paul was curled up on his bed, his back to the door. Perhaps he was asleep after all.

"Mom?"

"Yes? Are you okay?" Sally said.

He took a while to answer. "No."

Sally's heart almost broke. He sounded so vulnerable. Moving quickly to the other side of the bed so she could see his face, she saw the tear marks down his pale cheeks. "Hey," Sally said, "I'm here."

Sally sat next to him and brushed some hair away from his forehead.

He sniffed. "I keep seeing the knife."

"Me too. We were both running on adrenaline, but now we're crashing. I've got the shakes, look."

Sally held a hand out so he could see her trembles.

Paul moved his head so he could see her better, the back of his skull resting on the pillow. "It's over, right? He's in a cell?"

"Chester won't come near us again. He's in a police cell, then he's going to jail for a very long time."

"But Chester didn't kill Carolyn, right? So her killer's out there somewhere. What if he comes here? Tries to kill us."

"I won't let anything happen to you, I promise. And besides, the Joker guy was Chester, the guy watching us was Chester. The killer has no reason to come near us."

Paul thought for a moment. "Can I have a gun?"

"Paul, you're too young and one of us with a gun is enough. Trust me. I'll keep you safe."

Paul sat up and hugged her.

"Do you want to see Reilly?" Sally asked, thinking he might feel better with some company his age.

"Nah, I'm not in the mood. Feeling beat."

"You still okay with Margie coming to dinner? I can cancel."

"Sure. She's fun." Paul gave her a smile. "Can we go to the movies? Now? *Central Intelligence* is good."

They had nothing to do that afternoon. "I can find out if it's still showing."

"Thanks, Mom."

"I'll see if I can get tickets." She stayed where she was, wondering if now was the time to broach the subject of the child psychologist. "Would you like to talk to Dr. Kaur about how you feel? You've always found her helpful."

"Maybe. I'll think about it."

Sally managed to book two tickets for *Central Intelligence* and they set off for the IMAX. Sally took her phone with her but didn't look at her voicemails. All she wanted to do was enjoy the movie with Paul. By the time they left the movie theater, it was late afternoon and they both blinked at the bright sunshine after spending two hours in the dark. On the way home, Sally did a quick grocery shop so she could cook a salmon dish and a cheesecake for dinner, plus she picked up some wine. Only when they were home again did Sally glance at her list of messages. There were three from Foster.

Her curiosity got the better of her. She played them.

"Sally, call me. I have some information."

Then, "Sally, this is important. Phone me."

The last one, "For Christ's sake, call me!"

The last comment angered her. He acted as if she were at his beck and call. For a fleeting moment she thought about calling him to tell him that she wouldn't visit him again. He had been helpful, but Foster was a serial killer and she feared that his vile view of life was rubbing off on her. Her priority was her son and she wanted to enjoy the rest of the summer with him. She deleted the three messages. Her heart was pounding. She had broken the tie to Foster, and she was so relieved that she wanted to dance around her house.

FIFTY-FIVE

The cops had granted Chester one phone call, but who the hell would he call? He had no friends, and his family wouldn't speak to him, and he couldn't afford a good lawyer anyway. He'd end up with an attorney appointed to him, some snotty-nosed kid with acne who had no effing idea what he was doing.

His employer was his only hope. He dialed.

"What are you doing calling me?" They sounded livid.

"If you want me to keep my mouth shut, you get me a good lawyer."

"Don't try blackmailing me, you piece of shit. This burner phone's going in the lake. I paid you with cash in a paper bag left in public trash bins. If you claim I did it, the cops won't believe you."

"I'm not going down for murder. You did that all by yourself."

"Like I give a shit about you. Goodbye."

That hadn't worked, damn! Without a decent lawyer he was truly fucked. He had one ace card up his sleeve, however.

"No, wait! Help me out and I'll tell you why the cops are going to knock on your door, real soon."

A pause. "Okay. Tell me."

"Sally knows," Chester said.

"Knows what?"

"Knows you blackmailed the others." There was no sound for a beat or two. "You there?" Chester asked.

"I need details."

"Okay," Chester glanced across the room at the cop watching him. But he was beyond hearing distance. "I heard Foster was asking questions about me."

"Who the hell's Foster?" his employer asked.

"In jail for serial murder. Anyway, for some goddamned reason he's helping Sally to find you." He let that land for a while, then continued, "Anyway, he knows that you have photos of Matt and his mates, selling drugs when you were at college. He's told Sally, and she'll tell the cops. They'll want to talk to you."

"How would he know that?"

"He's got connections, see?"

Another silence. "If Sally had already passed that on to the cops, I'd know. Maybe Sally doesn't know yet, or she's sitting on it."

"Yeah, but either way, she's going to do something about it, right? She's not the type to sit on information like that." Chester glanced at the cop who was gesturing at him to wind up the call. "I did my part. Now you do yours, okay. Get me a real clever lawyer."

"Listen here, you cockroach, you're going to keep my identity to yourself and take it to your grave. Otherwise, your son is going to meet a tragic accident. You understand?"

Chester's son was the only person in the world he loved, even if his mom wouldn't let him go near him. "I won't say a word, just leave my boy alone."

Chester put down the phone, resigned to his fate. No lawyer was going to save him.

He wondered if Sally knew what was coming her way. He kind of hoped that she could outwit his employer.

He had made Sally a problem and, knowing his employer, that problem was going to be eliminated.

FIFTY-SIX

JULY 22, 2016

Sally's eyelids snapped open. A sound in the house. What was it? Voices?

She threw off the sheet and was out of bed so fast she swayed and had to find her balance. A slice of moonlight was visible through her partly closed drapes, but the rest of the room was in darkness. Her digital clock said 2:09 a.m.

On her nightstand, her Glock 19 was loaded and ready. Her pistol had been returned to her by the sheriff. Clarke had sped up the forensic process so she could have it with her tonight. Without it close at hand, Sally wouldn't have been able to sleep. Wrapping her hand around the cold steel, Sally unlocked the safety and slid her finger close to the trigger. But not on it.

The noise that woke her might well be Margie or Paul moving about the house, unable to sleep. She had heard of too many instances of people shooting a loved one, mistakenly thinking they were intruders. Sally had to be certain she was facing a genuine threat before she discharged her weapon.

Her bedroom door was closed. She kept the bedside lamp switched off. Too risky if an intruder was outside the door.

Feeling her way with her free hand, she walked around her room. No one was hiding there.

At the door, Sally pressed her ear close to it.

Muffled voices. Angry? *Boom, boom!* It sounded like one of Paul's violent video games. Would he play a video game in the middle of the night?

Looking down, she noticed a weak light under her door, too weak to be the bright light on the landing, but a light none the less. Then for a couple of seconds that light was broken. Someone had walked past her door. Fear flooded through her body. She gasped, then shut her mouth fast. Had she been heard?

If a killer was in her house, Paul and Margie were in terrible danger.

Sally crept back to her nightstand for her phone. She didn't dare make a 911 voice call in case she was overheard. She texted a 911 message:

Sally Fairburn, 9256 Pioneer Drive. Police. Home invasion.

If her 911 call proved to be a false alarm, so what? She'd rather her loved ones were safe.

Leaving the phone on the bed, she grasped her Glock in both hands and headed back to the door.

Her heart almost stopped when the door handle started to move. Millimeter by millimeter, the metal handle began to drop until the lever was free from the doorplate. Adrenaline rocketed through her veins. Who was on the other side of the door?

Sally glanced at her bed, the sheet thrown back. The person coming through the door would know that Sally wasn't asleep.

She mustn't forget that it could be Paul or Margie, she reminded herself, her finger next to the trigger, but not on it. Sally flattened her back against the wall. With any luck, as the door opened, she would be hidden.

She waited. All she could hear was her heart thumping. The door began to move. They were coming in. Sally braced, her arm muscles tight, the gun pointing straight ahead. She shifted her finger to the trigger. *Wait, just wait*, she told herself. The door moved some more.

A dark figure stepped into the room. Sally could just see the side of the face and the upper body. She knew that profile and the smell of him. A teenage-boy sour smell, coupled with cheesy food.

Her son walked over to her bed. "Mom?" he whispered.

Sally released the breath she had been holding and lowered her gun.

She whispered his name and stepped forward.

He wheeled around. "Shit!" he said. "You scared me."

Sally beckoned him to her. "You scared me too. What are you doing?" Sally whispered.

"I saw someone. In the house."

It had to be Carolyn's and Lauren's killer. Chester was in custody. Who else would it be? Cold dread almost froze her limbs. But she had to be strong, for Paul's sake. For Margie's sake.

"Where?" She pulled him by his T-shirt away from the open door, so she could better protect him.

"Passed my room. Like a shadow."

"Where are they now?"

"Don't know." His eyes dropped to her Glock. "You heard him?"

"Stay here, you hear me?"

"But—"

"Hide under my bed."

Sally waited. He threw his arms up, but then he headed for her bed and lay down on the ground, flat on his stomach. Then she raised the gun and stepped out of her room, moving her weapon horizontally from side to side. Paul's bedroom door was open, light on, and a video game had been frozen on-screen.

"I know you're here!" Sally shouted. "I'm armed. Show yourself!"

Nothing. Sally walked into her son's bedroom. Checked under the bed and in the wardrobe. This left the bathroom to check on this level.

She threw the bathroom door wide. It was empty. She prayed the intruder hadn't gone upstairs to where Margie slept. Sally left the bathroom and peered up the dark staircase. Taking the stairs slowly, Sally aimed her Glock at the next landing. A bad feeling settled on her shoulders like a wet towel. Why hadn't Margie stirred after Sally had shouted? There was only one room on the top level and beyond that room was the roof terrace.

Margie's door was open. When she had said goodnight to Sally, she had closed it so the air conditioning would work better in the bedroom.

"Margie?" Sally called out.

No reply. This was bad, very bad.

Sally's arms trembled, her grip on her pistol loosening with the sweat on her palms. She kicked the door wide open and raced in. Margie's bed was empty. She spun to her right. The sliding doors were open. A figure straddled the glass fence between her roof terrace and Matt Tate's terrace. The intruder's head was covered in something black and they paused for a moment, looking straight at Sally. The blade of a long knife glinted in the moonlight. Sally gasped. Then the figure ran into Matt's house.

It was as if the knife had severed Sally's ability to think. Her mind raced with images of the horror that knife could inflict.

"Margie!" Where was she?

Sally ran into the guest room and switched on the light.

Squinting at its brightness, she shouted, "Margie! Where are you?"

"Has he gone?" Margie's voice came from the walk-in wardrobe.

"Yes, thank God, are you okay?"

Sally rounded the corner and found Margie huddled at the back of the wardrobe. Sally lowered the gun and kneeled in front of her friend. "Did he hurt you?"

She shook her head. "Are you sure he's gone?" She was shaking like a leaf.

"Yes, he's next door. The house is empty."

"Then go after him. He's got a knife. I saw him pull it out of his jacket. I was so afraid. I'm sorry, Sally, I was too frightened to warn you."

"Paul!" Sally yelled. "He's gone. Can you come up here?"

"Go!" Margie said. "Chase him."

Paul ran up the stairs.

"I can't leave you," Sally said.

"Yeah, go after him, Mom."

"Are you sure?"

"I'm sure."

Even then she hesitated.

"Call 911," she said to Paul. "Stay with Margie and lock the sliding door behind me."

Rushing onto the roof terrace to pursue the killer, she easily vaulted the glass partition. Then she heard a car engine growl from the street. It had to be him. The killer was about to get away. She couldn't wait for the cops to arrive. Vaulting back over the partition, Sally ran back inside and down the stairs, grabbed her car keys from the bowl on the coffee table, and shot out of the front door.

FIFTY-SEVEN

The asphalt was cold and slick beneath her bare feet. She raised her gun, but the intruder was too quick. He accelerated away, burning rubber, the headlights blinding her. She didn't see the license plate. It was a long heavy-duty SUV, a Ford Excursion maybe? Sally dived into her driver's seat, turned the engine, and sped after the killer.

The SUV was going at full pelt and skidded as it took a left. Sally pressed down hard on the accelerator to catch up and felt its roughness on her bare soles.

Only then did Sally remember that she was in her summer PJs and had no shoes. She cursed herself for not grabbing some on her way out. Worst of all, she had left her phone behind. How could she alert the police without a cell phone? She swore under her breath. How could she give them her location?

And she had no driver's license. No credit card.

She shook her head but kept driving, her grip on the steering wheel tight.

I can't lose him.

The killer was driving at double the speed limit, screeching around corners, overtaking like crazy. Thankfully, in the early hours of the morning, the streets held very little traffic. Sally trailed the SUV up the ramp and onto the freeway, heading north. The driver sped up to one-hundred-twenty miles per hour. Sally's old car struggled to match it. Headlights on the other side of the freeway stung her eyes with their glare. She dropped her eyes briefly to the fuel gauge—a quarter of a tank. That could be a problem. If the killer was fleeing cross-country in the hopes of crossing the state border, Sally wouldn't have enough gas to keep up.

As she overtook cars in pursuit of what she was now certain was a Ford Excursion, she tried to think about what she had in her car that might be useful. Her gun was in the pocket of the driver's door. That was a given. In the trunk was the jack and spare tire. Were her running shoes still in there too? She liked to keep a spare pair in the car. The last few days were a blur, but she dearly hoped they were. In the glove compartment, there was a flashlight she had put in there when she'd driven to her parents' house. Her eyes brightened when she noticed some loose change in the cup holder near the hand brake. She hoped it would be enough to pay the freeway toll five miles ahead.

The fastest way through the toll booth was to chuck coins into the unmanned collection machine. In the small hours of the morning only one booth would be manned. Was this her opportunity to ask for help? But taking the manned booth option would delay her and might result in her losing the killer's car.

Overhead signage spanned the width of the six lanes—the toll booths were one mile away. The Ford Excursion drove like a bat out of hell. She kept on its tail and then watched as it raced for the coins-only booth. Sally swerved and took the manned booth. In front of her was a semitrailer. An arm from the huge vehicle reached out to the booth window. He was paying the toll.

"Please hurry!" Sally said, watching the killer accelerate away from the toll machine.

The truck's brakes hissed, then slowly pulled away.

"Come on!" she muttered.

As soon as the back of the truck had left the booth window, Sally revved the engine and darted forward. The guy in the booth smiled.

"What's the hurry, ma'am?"

"Please call the police. This is an emergency."

He was a bald guy in his forties with a big belly. He looked at Sally's silky PJs, then back at her face. "Why don't you call them yourself?"

"I don't have a phone. Please, 911. Tell them Sally Fairburn is heading north on the F21 pursuing a Ford Excursion."

"I'm not a messaging service. I just want three dollars."

In the distance, the Ford Excursion was getting smaller and smaller. "Damn it!"

"There's no need to be like that, ma'am. Three dollars."

Sally rummaged around in the cup holder, searching for loose change. Her fingers touched a stack of quarters and a crumpled ten-dollar bill. She counted out three dollars in quarters and gave them to the booth man. "There's your money. Now dial 911, I'm in pursuit of a killer."

"Sure you are, lady."

Sally seethed in frustration. She sped away so fast that the engine spluttered for a second and then, fortunately, recovered and lurched forward. She pushed the little car to its limit, overtaking trucks and other vehicles, but the Ford Excursion was nowhere to be seen. Where had it gone?

The next turn off was to McWilliamstown. If she hadn't caught up with the Ford Excursion by then, she'd take the exit and find the nearest pay phone.

FIFTY-EIGHT

Four miles later, Sally took the McWilliamstown turnoff. She had lost the killer's vehicle. Either he had taken this turn off or he was way ahead of her on the freeway and heading north. Her gas tank was on low and the tank symbol had lit up on her dashboard, indicating that she had just twenty-two miles to go before her tank reached empty.

She had to find a gas station fast and there, she hoped, she could call Detective Clarke. She was so far out of Franklin that she was probably in some other police jurisdiction, but Clarke would be able to muster the necessary support from the local sheriff.

At a roundabout she took the second turning, signposted to McWilliamstown, figuring that the town was the most likely place to find a gas station. The land on either side of the unlit road was flat and she guessed they were open fields. This was a big farming area, known for its fruit, vegetable, and wine production, especially its small artisan wineries. A sign welcomed her to McWilliamstown. It was now 2:56 a.m. and the roads were near deserted. The food outlets and stores were shut except for a twenty-four-hour McDonald's. Sally glanced at the dashboard's tank symbol: just nineteen miles worth of gas left now. When she spied the lit-up sign of a gas station, she breathed a sigh of relief.

She pulled into it and killed the engine, then ran, barefoot, over to the cashier. The store was closed and the cashier sat behind a window, beneath which money and receipts could be exchanged. The boy looked to be not much older than Paul, and he was head down, staring at his phone.

"Please help me. I need you to call the police."

The cashier looked up. "Excuse me?" He saw that Sally was in her PJs and frowned.

"It's a long story. I need to contact a Detective Clarke. Can you call 911?"

"Hey, lady, what's the problem?"

"A man tried to kill me earlier. It's related to a case. Maybe you've seen it on TV. The Carolyn Tate murder."

His acne-covered face lit up with recognition. "Yeah, I seen that on the news."

Sally was trying to keep her voice measured, but her frustration was beginning to show. "This is an emergency. Just dial 911. Please."

"Oh-kay, lady. I'll do it, but if this is some hoax, I'm not taking the rap for it."

"It's no hoax."

The boy dialed 911, asked for police. "I'm at the McWilliamstown Chevron. Lady here says she's got information about the Carolyn Tate murder." He then put the phone onto speaker and pushed it under the glass but held on to it. Sally leaned forward and explained she needed to get a message to Detective Fred Clarke from Franklin homicide. She gave the details of the Ford Excursion and the man in her house with a knife. The operator said they would pass on the details and asked Sally to stay put so that she could be contacted on the cashier's phone. The local sheriff's department would be notified.

"Thanks," Sally said to the cashier once the call was over. Then it hit her. How was she going to pay for gas? From memory, there was a ten-dollar bill in the cup holder in her car. It was better than nothing. "I have ten dollars for gas. I'll go and fill up."

"Don't do a runner on me, lady. I don't want no trouble with the cops."

Sally wandered back to her car. How long would it take for the sheriff's office to dispatch a car to meet her? She filled her tank, then paid. All was quiet. No sign of a sheriff's vehicle. No sign of anyone.

The McDonald's was over the road, lit up like a Christmas tree. Even from the gas station forecourt, she could smell the food. A vehicle exited the drive-through. She did a double take. A black Ford Excursion crossed the road and headed into town. The driver wore a hoodie. There was no way of identifying them. How many Ford Excursions could there be on the road in this town at three in the morning?

"Phone the cops, tell them I'm pursuing a Ford Excursion that's just left the McDonald's drive-through."

She bolted for her car, got in, and set off. The cashier yelled at her to wait.

Two roundabouts later, the SUV turned onto a road that led out of town and in the direction of some of the larger wineries in the region. Soon the wide roads got narrower, and she was driving through sloping vineyards, the gnarled and twisted vines heavy with ripe grapes, almost ready for harvesting. There were no streetlights and Sally feared that, as she was the only driver on this stretch of road, the killer would notice that he was being followed. She couldn't turn her headlights off. All she could do was keep her distance. She passed signs to some vineyards and she recognized the name of a large estate that was known for its excellent red wines. Two miles later, Sally was driving through woodland. The road started to bend like an S. By the time she came out of the S-bend, the vehicle was gone. She pulled over to the side of the road.

Where had he gone?

She did a U-turn and drove slowly. How could he have disappeared? She would see headlights, wouldn't she? It was deciduous woodland either side. Sally's head moved from side to side, searching the darkness.

A brief flash of white light, then it was gone. She slammed on the brakes and reversed the car. An unsurfaced road headed into the woods. There was a sign nailed to a tree. She reversed some more and switched on her high beams, which lit up the hand-painted sign:

Ghost tour.
McWilliams Wines.
1 mile.

The car engine ticked over as Sally considered what she should do next. If she followed it and found the Ford Excursion , what would she do then? She didn't have a phone. Her only choice would be to return to the gas station, where, by then, the deputies would have hopefully shown up. Sally was at a huge disadvantage. She knew nothing about the layout of the winery or the area. It was possible that the killer was luring her into a trap. Should she turn back?

Sally was close to the truth. She could feel it.

She considered the ghost tour sign. Why would a killer hide at a winery that conducted tours? She couldn't even research the place on her phone. Sally thought back to the conversations she had had with Matt, Nicole, Becca, and Lauren. It was Nicole who had said that Matt first met Carolyn at a winery. Could this be that same winery and was this therefore where

Matt and Daisy were hiding from the police because nobody would dream of looking for them here?

Sally looked down at her Glock, stashed in the driver's door compartment. From what Sally knew, the killer had a knife, or at least that was what Sally had glimpsed when he fled her house. Sally, on the other hand, had a gun. If it was a trap she was walking into, she felt confident that she could keep the killer at bay. But could she handle two of them?

Sally almost turned back, then, in her mind's eye, she saw Carolyn begging for her help.

She turned into the unmade road and drove into the woods.

The lane wound left, then right, then left again. There were no houses, no other lights but her headlights. The necklace poplars and the green and white ash swayed in the wind, like skeletons waving bony arms in the air. She began to feel very isolated.

Turning a blind corner, she came upon a towering building with a jagged roofline. Her headlights illuminated the large stone blocks that made up the walls. The windows were tall with a pointed arch at the top. Suddenly afraid that she had just alerted the killer to her arrival, she switched off the lights and the car engine, pulling on the hand brake.

Fear throbbed through her. The place was truly creepy. No wonder they did ghost tours here. It had to be the most bizarre winery she'd ever come across.

As her eyes adapted to the darkness, she looked up at the sky and the stars and then down to the undulating and jagged roofline. The building had two towers and, incredibly, it looked like a feudal castle.

"I must be imagining it," she mumbled, blinking and refocusing.

There was no sign of the killer's SUV. The road went around the side of the building. Had he parked there instead?

There was only one way to find out.

She took the flashlight from the glove compartment and opened the car door, stepping out. Leaving it open, she picked up the gun and walked to the trunk. Sharp little stones dug into the soles of her feet. Sally was relieved to find grubby pair of running shoes inside a plastic bag in the trunk. They had gotten coated in mud a while ago and she hadn't yet cleaned them. It was such a relief to put the shoes on and tie the laces. It also gave her confidence to feel she could now run if necessary.

Switching on the flashlight she kept the beam focused on the ground just ahead of her.

Nature had virtually reclaimed the building, but the pale stone walls seemed to glow a ghostly white in the moonlight. From what she could tell, the arched windows had lost their glass. The towers were square in shape, like an English bell tower, and in the middle of the building was an arch that was wide and tall enough to allow a truck through it. The doors or gate were gone but above, there was a sign with the name of the winery: McWilliams Wines.

A crack of twigs in the wood behind her had her spinning around. She raised the flashlight, her breath coming thick and fast. Something or someone screamed. Sally jumped, and her flashlight fell to the ground. Her pulse skyrocketed.

"What was that?" she whispered.

Peering through the gaps in the trees, a pair of golden eyes looked at her, then with a flick of a bushy tail, the fox was gone.

"It's okay," she soothed herself.

Her body was soaked in sweat and her PJs clung to her. She had to gain control of her fear.

Sally kept going, through the main entrance. She looked up. There was no roof: she could see the stars. She lifted her flashlight. Stones had fallen to the ground, leaving the roofline uneven. The courtyard was overgrown with ivy and weeds. There were even trees growing there. But no sign of the killer or his car. She stood still and listened. She thought she heard the crunching of sticks underfoot or was it a wild animal? She followed the sound, which led her out of the courtyard and around a corner to the back of the building.

There was the Ford Excursion, the roof's paintwork glinting in the moon's white light. The warm engine ticked over. Sally inhaled a few calming breaths, raised the Glock, and approached the car from the rear. There was no movement inside the car. Closer now, she peered in the driver's window. On the passenger seat was a black balaclava.

She spun around.

Where was the killer now?

FIFTY-NINE

The only way for Sally to know who was hiding in the derelict winery was to see them with her own eyes. So far, she hadn't had a good look at the killer's face. She must keep searching.

But where did the killer go? The bizarre building, built like a castle, had no roof and therefore did not provide shelter to the fugitive, or perhaps there was more than one fugitive? Sally was guessing, but she suspected it was Matt who had tried to kill her earlier and he and Daisy were using this place as a temporary hideout.

Sally looked around her for anything that would indicate which way to go. Behind her was dense dark woodland. Before her was a building that was barely holding together. Rectangular stones the size of supermarket baskets littered the ground. They must have fallen from the top wall. The building was fraught with hazards. If ghost tours were being conducted here, they had to be unlicensed and the organizer was trespassing. The risk of someone getting seriously injured was far too high.

The driveway, potholed and overgrown with vines, had been trampled underfoot and a leafy path had formed. Perhaps this was the way the ghost tour company took its guests when they explored the place, and if so, where did it lead?

Sally set off.

The path stopped at a small arch at the base of the exterior wall, barely more than four feet high. Sally crept closer. Beyond the arch were eight or more steps down into darkness, perhaps the cellars where the wine was fermented? Sally had a problem with dark and enclosed spaces, and she recoiled from the entrance, her flesh crawling. Memories of seven-year-old Sally trapped inside a dark barn had her breaking out in a sweat.

She shook her head, trying to shift the memory to the back of her mind. She failed.

Margie and Sally had ventured onto an old man's property on a dare. The kids in her school called the old man Dr. Death, because he'd once been the town's doctor. Rumor had it that he killed some of his patients with a lethal injection. Margie and Sally had dared each other to go into his barn, where he had supposedly buried the bodies of his victims. The old man caught them trespassing. Margie ran like the wind and escaped. Sally didn't. He shut the barn door so she couldn't escape and no matter how much she screamed and begged, the old man wouldn't open the door. Day turned to night and Sally was terrified. At last, her father and Margie's father demanded that Dr. Death release her from the barn. To this day, Sally could still hear the creak of the old wooden door.

I was a kid then, Sally told herself. *It was just a barn, and this is just a cellar.*

Still, she hesitated, psyching herself up.

She shouldn't use the flashlight, in case the killer saw her coming, but there was no way she'd go down there without it.

The light revealed the steps were mossy and damp. She trod carefully down the slippery surface, a voice inside her head warning her to turn back. She ignored it and kept going. *I just have to know who's here.* The temperature dropped noticeably and, despite the hot summer, the air in the basement was dank and rotten.

Her feet finally touched an uneven cobblestone floor. In a corner, waist-high wine barrels were stored, and the damp wood had an oaky smell mixed with a vinegary stench. Some of the barrels had been smashed into pieces. The metal hoops that had held the wooden staves in place were scattered around the floor. Some of the hoops had snapped in two or three pieces, as sharp as a scythe's blade. More hazards to avoid.

At first, Sally's labored breathing was all she could hear in the echoey void. Then she heard a tapping. No, not tapping. More like the slap of shoes on stone. Someone was down here.

Ahead there was an arched doorway and more darkness.

Something small and rodentlike scurried across the floor. Sally flinched.

It's gone, she told herself, gulping rapid breaths at the thought of rats.

Recovering her composure, she crossed the room, sidestepping the sharp pieces of metal. She cringed at the squeaky sound her running shoes made on the damp cobblestone floor. Peeking through the archway, this part of the cellar had an alcove with shelves, and on one shelf were three stocky white candles, the wicks black from use. On the floor, empty wine bottles lay scattered about. An upright barrel had been used as a table and was covered in more empty bottles. There were one or two wineglasses, the surfaces smudged. Did the ghost tour organizer offer winetasting as part of the tour package?

Sally found the scene before her unnervingly familiar. Why was that? Had it been in one of the burned photos Sally had saved from the firepit? She tried to remember each one in turn. The last one had two people stepping through a pointed arch just like the one before her. There had been candles flickering. Most of the photo had been lost in the fire, but Sally had suspected the blonde woman and the muscular man to be Carolyn and Matt.

They had met nine months ago. This place would have been just as derelict back then as it was now. Why would Carolyn and Matt come here to this dank and dangerous place? Nicole told Sally that Carolyn and Matt had met at a winetasting. Was this where it happened?

Why on earth would anyone hold a winetasting here?

A voice. Distant and echoing. A woman.

Sally swung her flashlight in the direction from which the voice had come.

Through the next archway, Sally saw a glimpse of a row of enormous oak barrels, each one as large as an SUV. They were resting on their side on stone supports. The wood beneath the taps was stained a dark reddish-brown. The woman's voice had come from the room beyond that.

Sally didn't want to lose the light. It kept the darkness of this cramped and dank place away from her. But if she was to remain undiscovered, she must switch it off.

She took a deep breath and pressed the "off" button.

A shudder ran up her spine at the all-enveloping blackness. She would have to feel her way along the length of the six giant barrels to the next archway. The only way she could do this and have her pistol at the ready was to leave the flashlight behind— one hand out front to feel the way, the other gripping the gun. Sally hesitated. The flashlight was like a crutch, even when it wasn't used.

Then she thought of Carolyn disoriented and desperate on the day she died. She thought of Lauren, murdered in the hospital because she knew too much about the people on the other side of this cellar wall. She thought about the intruder in her house, and fury began to build inside her, giving her strength to continue.

This ends now, Sally thought. *I'm the only person who knows they're here. It's down to me now.*

Leaving her flashlight under the last barrel's tap so she could locate it later, Sally held the Glock in her right and felt her way forward with the left. Her fingers smacked into a barrel's hard edges as she counted each barrel as she passed them. At last, she reached the sixth barrel and the archway to the next room.

With her heart feeling like it was in her mouth, Sally peeked through the archway.

A soft light from a Coleman camping lantern was on the floor. Down one side of the cellar were six more huge barrels, positioned on their side and held off the ground by stone supports. Matt Tate had his back against the fifth barrel. The woman was crouched down near him, her back to Sally. It was impossible to be certain who she was because there was a hood over her head, but given Matt's affair with Daisy, who else would be with him in this dismal place?

"This is your fault," the woman said. "All of it."

Sally stood stock still, the hairs on the back of her neck prickling. She didn't know the voice.

"My fault! *You* did this. Christ! You're insane!" Matt said.

Was he accusing the woman of murder?

"I had to. Don't you see?" the woman said. "Now we can be together."

Her voice didn't sound like Daisy. It was too deep.

"No way," Matt said, angrily. "I can't do this anymore. Get out of my life!"

"You don't mean that. You need me. I've always been there for you."

"You didn't give me a choice. You blackmailed me!" Matt shouted.

"Shut up!" she screamed.

A scuffling.

"No! Don't, please!" Matt said. Then a muffled "Mmmmmmm."

Panic surged through Sally's body. What was the woman doing to him?

The woman shifted position slightly and this enabled Sally to see Matt's wrists were tied to the barrel's solid tap with rope and he was now gagged.

Sally took a step back, shocked at what she saw. How had she gotten it so wrong? Matt was the captive!

He was dressed in the same running shorts and singlet he'd worn on the morning that she and Margie had passed him on the running trail.

The woman spoke, "I'd have done anything to make you happy. But you never chose me. First Carolyn. Then Daisy! You had your chance, and you blew it!"

Sally's mind was racing. If this woman wasn't Daisy, then who was she? Sally looked back the way she had come and into pitch blackness. Down a line of huge wine barrels was her flashlight. She was underground, in a vast cellar, with one, possibly two killers and she was way out of her depth. Doubt whispered to her. *You'll get yourself killed and nobody will ever find your body. Your son will never know what happened.*

If Sally was quick, she could make her way through the various cellar rooms to the exit.

"Wuuuuuuuuuv." Matt tried to speak through his gag.

"Love?" the woman said. "You don't know the meaning of the word. But don't worry, my love. This will be painless."

Sally's head whipped around. Matt was a nasty piece of work. He had married Carolyn for her money. He'd been unfaithful. She didn't like the man, but she couldn't let the woman kill him. She raised the gun and aimed at the woman's back.

Sally was about to shout a warning for the woman to put her hands up when Matt slammed his forehead into his captor's face. The woman screamed. The impact of the blow had her scurrying backward, cupping her nose.

"Fuck!" she seethed. "Fuck!"

Blood seeped through her fingers. It looked black in the shadowy light of the camping lamp. Her moaning reverberated through the room.

"You'll pay for that!" she mumbled.

She picked up the lantern with her free hand and turned toward the archway that Sally was hiding behind.

Sally ran and hid behind the nearest barrel in the adjoining room.

The woman strode through the arch and straight past Sally, a hand cupping the blood dripping from her nose. Enough of her features were caught in a flash of light for Sally to recognize her.

It was Becca Watts.

SIXTY

Sally watched Becca disappear into the blackness. The shock had Sally unable to move. Even her breath seemed stuck in her throat.

Becca Watts? Why hadn't Sally seen it coming?

The woman's dark hair was dangling from the hood. It was definitely her. Becca was tall and broad. She could easily be mistaken for a man in a baggy jacket and with a balaclava over her head.

What had Becca said just then? That Matt had ignored her. He'd chosen the wrong women. She and Matt could now be together. Dear God! Becca had murdered Carolyn and Lauren, and she was going to kill Matt because he didn't want her.

Hurry, she told herself, coming out of her stupor. Becca must have gone to her car to deal with her nosebleed. And she would be back. Sally had a frighteningly small window of opportunity to free Matt and get them both out of there.

Without the glow from the gas lamp, the cellar was pitch black. Sally felt her way back to where she had left the flashlight. Twice she stumbled into one of the giant barrels, bruising her hand. When she had reached the last barrel, she bent down and, with splayed fingers, she felt the ground until she touched the flashlight.

It was a relief to switch it on. Sally hadn't realized she'd been holding her breath until she released it and raised the flashlight in her trembling hand. It took just a few seconds for Sally's eyes to adjust then she ran to where Matt was tied to the tap of a barrel.

He cringed in the bright light.

"Matt, it's Sally," she whispered. "I'm getting you out of here."

His forehead was smudged with Becca's blood. The scarf in his mouth was filthy, and his skin was dry and puffy around his bloodshot eyes. He must have been held here, maybe, forty-eight hours, and he had the look of a man deprived of water.

Sally reached out to lower the gag, then paused. "Keep your voice down. She could come back at any time."

Tugging the scarf down she found the corners of his mouth were cracked, his lips dry and flaky.

"She's going to kill me," he hissed. "Hurry!"

Sally put the flashlight on the ground beneath the tap, with the beam pointing upward so she could see the rope. She left the pistol on the ground next to her. The rope was thick and heavy, and Sally found it difficult to shift the knot.

"Who killed your wife?" Sally asked, her voice low.

"Becca. She's crazy!" Panicking, Matt yanked at the rope.

"Don't pull," Sally said. "You're tightening it."

He stopped tugging at it.

"Is Daisy here?"

"I don't give a fuck about Daisy! Free me!" Matt barked.

Nice man, Sally thought.

The knot wouldn't budge and the greasy quality of the rope made it hard to grip.

"Why did you run away with Becca?"

"I didn't. She tricked me. She found out I was leaving with Daisy. Becca turned up in her place. Told me to hop in the car and she knew where Daisy was."

A fingernail tore off and Sally winced at the pain, but she was getting closer to freeing him. A piece of rope was now loose. She worked the other piece loose. Matt tugged his left hand free.

"Look out!" he said.

Too late, she saw the bottle swinging at her head. It smashed into her skull, and everything went black.

When Sally came to, it felt as if her head had been cleaved in two.

Beneath her, the ground was damp and hard. She lay on her side. The pulsing pain in her head and neck was beyond anything she'd experienced before. When she tried to open her eyes, she saw stars and her skull throbbed. Her stomach heaved and bitter bile surged up her throat and spilled out of the side of her mouth. If she had been gagged like Matt, she might have suffocated on her own spew.

She counted to three in her head and then attempted to open her eyes once more. Through the half-open lids, she saw double. Walls moved. Light danced. The barrels seemed to wobble. She tried to move her arms, to use them to sit up. Her wrists were bound together and held at an angle. When her wobbly vision settled, she saw that her wrists were raised and tied to a barrel's tap by a scarf. It wasn't a rough material, perhaps chiffon or silk, but they were bound tightly.

She had to sit up, but even lifting her head a few inches had her vomiting with pain again, the spew pooling around her cheek. The acidic smell of it made her throw up more.

Something touched her leg. Sally flinched, thinking it was a rat.

Sit up! she told herself. Sally wrapped her fingers around the base of the tap, clenched her stomach muscles and then used the tap as leverage to pull herself into a sitting position. The room spun. Her skin was cold and clammy.

Another knock on her leg, this time her ankle.

She looked down at Matt's running shoe. "Mmmmmmmm," Matt mumbled though his gag.

He used his eyes to direct hers.

He stared at a pile of broken hoops, which lay in curved strips perhaps four or five feet away. Matt was secured to one barrel and Sally to another, some ten or twelve feet apart. She understood what he was doing. He wanted her to use the sharp metal to free herself and help him. She stretched out her leg and reached her shoe for the nearest strip of metal, but it was beyond her reach.

Neither of them was in any doubt about what would happen next. If they didn't escape, Becca would kill them and leave their bodies there to rot.

The sound of shoes on stone chilled Sally to the bone. There was no time left.

Through the arched doorway, a flashlight's beam danced across the adjoining room's floor. Sally wiggled her hip so that one arm rested over the barrel's pipe leading to the tap. It helped her to stay upright.

Then Becca appeared through the archway. Her hood was down. The skin around her nose was inflamed and swollen, although the nosebleed had stopped. Her eyes were cold with fury.

In Becca's hand was Sally's Glock 19. Sally's blood froze.

"Ah, you're awake," Becca said, the hoodie lowered so her dark hair was clearly visible. "Welcome to the party."

"The police are on their way." Sally's defiant words failed to mask the tremor in her voice.

"That's a lie. I checked your car. No phone. Nobody knows where you are, right?" Becca gave her a sympathetic tilt of the head. "Look at the state of you. Vomit on your cheek. We're quite a pair."

"I used a pay phone."

Becca laughed. "There isn't one for miles. I should know. I know everything about this place."

Each beat of Sally's racing heart might be her last. All Sally could think about was staying alive and to do that she had to keep Becca distracted. *Keep her talking. Buy some time.*

"You used oleander, right? How did you get Carolyn to ingest it?"

"I didn't. Lauren and Nicole did it all."

Becca lifted her chin, proud of this revelation. And it was a revelation that turned all of Sally's assumptions upside down.

Matt tried to scream through his gag and failed.

"I don't believe you," Sally said. "Why would they want to hurt Carolyn?"

"They didn't want to. My plan was so simple and so perfect. They would plant the oleander in Carolyn's kitchen and they had no idea they were doing it. When Carolyn died of poisoning, I told them what they had done. They couldn't go to the cops because *they* had planted the poison and it was *their* fingerprints all over the wine bottle and the rooibos tea canister. Technically, *they* were the killers and there was nothing linking me to Carolyn's murder."

Sally was speechless. Becca manipulated her two best friends into committing murder. Matt writhed to be free of the rope that held him fast. A vein in his neck bulged and his eyes were enraged.

Becca smirked, seemingly finding Matt amusing. "Don't pretend to be angry, Mattie. I did you a favor. You inherit her money and you're free of your fucked-up wife with all her mood swings and medication. You should be grateful!"

Becca was getting mad again. *Keep her talking, keep her calm.*

"How did you know that only Carolyn would consume the poison?" Sally asked.

"That was easy. I went to a specialist tea shop that stocks Carolyn's favorite tea. Rooibos. They sold it in this neat little tin canister. I suggested to Lauren that Carolyn was a bit down and she should give the tea to her to cheer her up."

"And she did?" Sally asked.

"Oh, yes. Lauren was a pleaser. Always trying to make people happy. It made me sick! And she knew Carolyn was miserable. Carolyn had told us that she suspected Matt was having an affair." Becca glanced at Matt. "Story of your life, right? You just can't keep it in your pants."

Matt glared at her.

"And what about the wine?" Sally asked, appalled by what she was hearing but eager to keep Becca talking. Becca had turned Lauren's kindness into a weapon. What a truly hideous thing to do.

"The same deal with the wine. Carolyn drank Chardonnay. We all hated it. Matt too. The only person who'd drink it was Carolyn. I bought a top-of-the-range bottle, gave it to Nicole, and planted the idea that she should give it to Carolyn, which she did. It was only a matter of time before Carolyn drank the tea or the wine, and I just had to watch and wait."

Sally stared at Becca, imagining her formulating this terrible plan.

"If you had Lauren and Nicole under your control, why murder Lauren?"

"She had a conscience. I hadn't taken that into consideration. She would have talked at some point. Nicole never had that problem. She's self-centered through and through. Nicole would never implicate herself."

Becca's scheming was horrifyingly Machiavellian. "What did you hope to achieve by killing Carolyn? He was having an affair with Daisy by then."

"Ah, Daisy. She was an obstacle I knew I could deal with, and I have."

Sally blanched. "You...?" She just couldn't ask the question.

Becca turned her hard stare to Matt. "Her death was thrilling. Like hitting a cushion, over and over."

Matt kicked out at Becca. He missed his target. She moved closer to him, goading him.

"She was after your money, you dipshit. She didn't give a damn about you."

While Becca was distracted, Sally leaned over the knot that bound her and bit down on it, determined to free her hands or die trying.

Becca kneeled, her back to Sally.

"You're so suggestible, Mattie. I planted in your head the notion that you would be the prime suspect and sent Nicole to help you clear out Carolyn's belongings. Of course, Nicole was desperate to remove the wine and the tea, so she was more than willing to do it. What she didn't know was that I had already taken the poisoned tea and wine from the house, and she took the other stuff." Becca smiled smugly at Matt. "I have your house key, remember?"

So Becca removed the items containing the poison and kept them to blackmail the two women. Sally guessed that Becca had also jumped the glass partition between the two roof terraces, entered Sally's house, and found the burned items Sally had rescued from the firepit. Fortunately, Sally had kept Carolyn's phone with her. Becca must have been the person Sally glimpsed in the upstairs window of Matt's house, watching her as she fished the phone from the pond.

The knot between Sally's teeth loosened. She took a quick look at it. Almost there. Clamping her teeth down on the chiffon again, she managed to tug one end of the knot loose.

"It was a perfect plan. All you had to do was run away with me. I had everything planned. We'd use fake names and start a new life far away."

Becca was seriously deranged.

Sally had managed to wriggle the bindings loose, but her wrists were still inside the scarf.

"And you messed it up, so now you have to die," Becca said, waving the gun in front of Matt's face. "But first, you watch Sally die."

Sally sat up as Becca turned to look at her and pointed her own pistol at her.

Keep her talking!

"Did you tell Matt to throw Carolyn's phone in the pond?"

"No way," Becca said, "He simply had to destroy the SIM and then chuck the body of the phone in a public trash bin. But that was clearly in the too-hard basket. He was lazy and dropped it in the pond. I was going to retrieve it and destroy it when you found it."

"If you blackmailed Matt, how did you stay friends all this time?" Sally asked.

"I didn't give Matt a choice."

Becca walked over to her.

"What do you mean?" Sally asked.

"I mean just that. We met on our first day of college. It was love at first sight for me. Sadly, not for him. But I waited. He fucked all the pretty girls. I waited and waited. He grew more distant. I knew he was distancing himself from me and I wasn't going to allow that."

She kneeled next to Sally. "I ran a college drugs ring. Had Mattie, Lachlan, and Nicole selling to students. It helped that Mattie was hooked on cocaine. I videoed him taking it. Took photos of them all dealing. I then blackmailed them if I needed money or their help with something."

Matt writhed and jerked his chin up and down, trying to remove the gag.

"It's too late to beg for your life," Becca said over her shoulder.

Matt kept moving his head up and down and his lower jaw finally came free.

"You blackmailed me," he shouted. "I could never be rid of you. You're like a fucking leech!"

"I kept your secret," Becca said.

"I wanted you out of my life!"

Becca swiveled to face him, her back to Sally. "You needed me!"

Matt released a sob. "You got me hooked on cocaine. You took my money, endangered my business. Everyone thought I wasted it on the band. But it went to you!"

Sally tugged her hands free. Matt glanced at her and saw what she was doing.

"Carolyn ruined everything!" Becca yelled at him. "The winetasting and ghost tour were for you! It was meant to be our special night. You'd finally realize how much you loved me."

Sally lunged at Becca's ankles and jerked them toward her, pulling them out from beneath her.

Becca hit the floor, facedown. "Ooooof!"

The gun fell from her hand and slid across the floor.

This was Sally's chance. Sally crawled on all fours toward the gun. Nothing mattered except her pistol. It blurred in and out of focus, her head pounding so badly that her eyes watered. The room felt as if it tilted, but she kept crawling. The tip of her middle finger touched the cold metal of the Glock.

"Nooooo!" Becca yelled.

Sally's index finger wrapped around the trigger.

Becca threw herself at Sally. She was heavier than Sally, but Becca only managed to latch on to Sally's legs. Sally kicked out.

"Mine!" Becca screamed.

Sally twisted at the hips and pointed the pistol behind her.

"Let go!" Sally ordered.

Becca reared up like a cobra and reached for the gun. Becca would never stop until Sally and Matt were dead. Sally fired.

SIXTY-ONE

TWO WEEKS LATER

Richard Foster sat at his desk. Glenn, a prison guard in his employ, handed him paper and pen.

Of course, Foster was not supposed to have paper and pen, because pens were dangerous weapons and if it hit the right spot in someone's neck, it could be fatal. Foster had access to a lot of things other prisoners didn't have. He shouldn't have a desk, or a TV, but he did. He wasn't supposed to have access to a cell phone, but Glenn had smuggled in a burner phone, in return for which Foster paid for Glenn's mother to be at a nice nursing home that specialized in dementia care.

"Be quick," Glenn said, stepping outside Foster's cell and closing the barred doors.

Foster didn't bother to respond. He would hand back the pen and paper when he was good and ready. He tapped the pen over his left hand, deep in thought. He wanted Chester to fully understand what the note meant, but without anyone else understanding the message too.

Chester Lee had recovered from the bullet wound to his shoulder. It had gone right through him, and the wound was relatively clean. Chester was now in the prison hospital. *This* prison's hospital. Between Foster and that hospital were two wings that housed the general prison population. Not even Foster could organize for himself to leave the maximum-security wing where he was held, unless he was grievously ill. And Foster couldn't bother to fabricate such a situation. The note would suffice.

Chester, he wrote. *You know who I am. And I know Becca Watts employed you to watch Sally Fairburn, yet you deny writing the warning note "I'M WATCHING YOU." If you didn't send it, I want to know who did. And I think you know. Someone called in a favor, right?*

Foster's pen hovered above the white paper. His contact in Franklin PD fed him updates on Becca's and Chester's confessions. Becca Watts had survived the gunshot wound. At a price. She'd lost her spleen. She confessed to the murders of Carolyn, Lauren, and Daisy, and the attempted murder of Sally. She also confessed to employing Chester to intimidate Sally.

Chester had initially denied all of it but eventually he confessed to working for Becca and to drawing a knife on Paul Fairburn, although he claimed it was in self-defense. There was one aspect of the case that Chester had repeatedly denied. Early on, Sally had received a note with the words *I'M WATCHING YOU* on it, and Chester claimed it was nothing to do with him.

Foster continued writing his note: *Answer truthfully and I'll see to it you serve a lesser sentence in a mental health facility. Lie to me and you know what accidents can happen in a jail like this.*

Foster signed off with the initial *F*. Then he folded the paper in four and handed it and the pen to Glenn. He watched Glen conceal both inside his shirt and walk away.

Foster lay on his bed, imagining Chester's reaction. He might grunt dismissively and puff out his scrawny chest. Or look up at Glenn warily, perhaps considering whether the guard was capable of arranging such an accident. It was now a question of who Chester feared most—Foster or his employer.

In forty-one minutes, Foster heard Glenn's familiar shuffling walk, his shoes scuffing the floor. He waited at the bars and Glenn handed him the same piece of paper, folded four times.

"Well?" Foster asked.

"You got your answer."

"Did you look at it?" Foster asked.

"None of my business," Glenn said, walking away.

Foster returned to the bed and when he was certain no other guards were about, he unfolded the paper. There, in Chester's almost illegible scrawl, was a name.

Foster smiled. "Perfect."

SIXTY-TWO

It was Reilly Doyle's birthday and the Doyles' house was full of noisy teenagers and relatives. Reilly's father was busy at the barbeque, chatting to the other dads, a beer in one hand and tongs in the other, using them to turn sausages and chicken kebabs. Sally was busy in the kitchen buttering bread rolls while Reilly's mom, Grace, checked to see if the miniature beef pies were cooked through and ready to hand around.

"Any idea where Reilly and Paul went?" Grace asked, taking the hot tray of beef pies out of the oven.

"I saw them in the rumpus room, but that was a good fifteen minutes ago."

"I think we should do the birthday cake soon and, knowing Reilly, he'll have sneaked out at the exact wrong time."

"Sneaked out where?" Sally asked, taking a sip of wine.

She had dressed up for the occasion. A floral wraparound dress that suited her figure.

"There's a treehouse in the woods the boys go to sometimes. I caught Reilly and Paul smoking there once."

Sally almost snorted the wine she had just sipped. "You're serious? Paul was smoking?"

Grace shrugged. "Teenagers try things. And I'm guessing they won't do it again. They were green in the face and coughing."

Sally wished that Grace had told her. But given what Paul had been through recently, a puff of a cigarette wasn't the end of the world. Provided it stopped there.

Grace gave Sally a smile. "I know you worry about him. But he's resilient. He's coping well with everything. That creep with the knife, I mean."

"He's remarkable. But I've arranged for a session with his psychologist."

When Sally had sped after their intruder's car and the cops arrived, Paul had explained the situation with a calmness and clarity that belied his years. It was only later, when the cops couldn't find Sally or the Ford Excursion, that Paul began freaking out, or so Detective Lin had told her.

"It was really sad about that girl, Daisy," Grace said.

"It was."

Daisy's body was found in a shallow grave near her parents' hunting cabin. She had been beaten to death and then wild animals had gotten to her. Becca had confessed to her murder. Her plan had been to frame Daisy for the other murders and then make it look as if Daisy had gone on the run.

"Hello, gorgeous girls!" Margie said as she entered the kitchen, all perfume and energy. She clutched a box wrapped in blue-and-white birthday paper and a bottle of red wine. "Sorry I'm late. This is for the birthday boy." Margie held up the box. "Where do you want me to put it?"

"In the corner, by the TV," Grace replied. "Did you see Reilly on the way in?"

"With a group of kids on the back deck. Paul's there too."

"Great, I'll find Eric." Her husband. "Then I'll bring out the cake. Margie, can you lead us in singing 'Happy Birthday'?"

"It would be my pleasure." Margie had a brilliant singing

voice. "But first I have to warm up the vocal cords with some wine."

Grace left Sally and Margie alone in the kitchen and Margie poured herself a glass of red. "You doing okay?" Margie asked.

"I guess. Becca is awaiting trial. Chester too. I'm not looking forward to being in court, but that won't be for months yet."

"So, the murders were all about love and jealousy." She sipped her wine.

"More like obsession and hatred," Sally said.

"She's one sick puppy," Margie said. "Was Becca the person watching you take things from the firepit and pond?"

"Yes, Becca had a key to Matt's home."

"And Foster? Please tell me you have stopped seeing him?"

"No more visits," Sally replied. "Paul and I need to move on. I want to enjoy life."

Margie gave her friend a broad smile. "As you should."

Foster had been in her thoughts over the last two weeks. He hadn't pestered her to come and see him. He had been in touch only once. A bouquet of yellow roses and one word on the card: *Congratulations!*

Foster didn't get his wish that Detective Clarke would be demoted for failing to solve the case. Sally made certain that he and the homicide team were applauded for arresting Becca Watts and Chester Lee. If anything, Clarke's reputation at Franklin PD went up a notch.

Grace came back to the kitchen, trailed by her husband. "You light the candles," she instructed. "I'll carry the cake. Margie, Sally, can you help gather everyone around?"

"Sure," Sally said. Her phone rang in her pocket. "Margie, you go ahead. I'll join you in a minute."

Sally took the phone from her pocket and saw Detective Clarke's name.

"Hey, how are you?" Sally answered.

"Good, have you got a moment?"

"I'm about to sing 'Happy Birthday' to Paul's best friend. Can we make it quick?"

"Sure. Look, we're closing off the case. I wanted to touch base with you on something."

The singing had commenced, and she was missing the party. "Can we talk about this later? I really must go."

"Let me finish. Please. It's important. Chester claims he never sent you the 'I'M WATCHING YOU' note."

"I guess he's lying," Sally said.

"Maybe, maybe not. What I'm saying is, watch your back," the detective warned. "Somebody is out to get you, and they might still be out there."

A LETTER FROM L.A. LARKIN

I want to say a huge thank-you for choosing to read *Her Deadly Truth*. If you enjoyed it and you'd like to keep up to date with my latest releases, just sign up at the following link. Your email address will never be shared, and you can unsubscribe at any time.

www.bookouture.com/l-a-larkin

Her Deadly Truth is the second book in the Sally Fairburn crime thriller/police procedural series. But never fear, it doesn't matter if you haven't read the first book, *Next Girl Missing*. There is enough backstory to fill in the gaps. This novel is about the secrets we keep and the people who know them. It's about a friendship group with a dark past and there is a killer on the loose. It's about obsession and jealousy. Sally's world is turned upside down when a neighbor asks for her help. During the story, she will need to contend with the whisperings of an imprisoned serial killer who claims to be an ally. He has the potential to take Sally down a dark path. How badly does Sally need the information he offers?

I hope you loved *Her Deadly Truth*, and if you did, I'd be very grateful if you could write a review. I love to hear what you think, and it makes such a difference helping new readers to discover one of my books for the first time.

See you again soon, I hope!

Thanks!

Louisa

www.lalarkin.com

 facebook.com/LALarkinAuthor
instagram.com/la_larkin_author

ACKNOWLEDGMENTS

Writing a series is such a delight. It gives me the chance to watch a character develop over a number of books. It's also a big task, which requires a forward vision and it's easy to lose my way. Thank goodness I have such a wonderful team at Bookouture to keep me on track. This novel's concept started with publisher Helen Jenner, and was developed with my new publisher, Lucy Frederick. Lucy, I am so thankful for your enthusiasm, your great feedback, and your attention to detail. Thank you also to Ian Hodder, Madeline Newquist, Chris Shamwana, Noelle Holten, Kim Nash, Peta Nightingale, Melanie Price, and Alexandra Holmes. You guys turn a manuscript into a wonderful novel with a gorgeous cover and then tell the book-buying world about it.

As always, huge thanks to my literary agent, Phil Patterson, and the team at Marjacq, and my first readers, David Gaylor, Carolyn Tate (yes, she shares her name with a key character, but I assure you Carolyn is very much alive and bears no resemblance to the fictional character!), Su Biela, and Anna Wallace. Writing can be a lonely occupation, so it means the world to me to have supportive friends and family. Thanks especially to my husband, Michael Larkin, all the girls from the gym, my dog-loving buddies, and Sonia Nazaretian, Katrina Bettington, and of course, my two gorgeous doggie companions, Lilly and Tigger. Thanks, Margie Clay, for allowing me to use your name for Sally's best friend.

I'd like to add that the city of Franklin is imaginary, as are

Pioneer Heights, Lincoln, North Bend, Osmandson, the F21, McWilliamstown and the lakes, mountains, and forests. There is a Walla Walla State Penitentiary in Washington State, and I have taken the liberty of transposing the jail to the fictional world of my story. The Franklin PD building, the school, the bookstore, and so on, do not exist. I chose to create this fictional world so that I could take Sally in exciting and varied directions without the limitations of a real-world city.

Finally, thank you to my readers, my friends on Facebook, Instagram, and Goodreads, and all the wonderful book bloggers and reviewers. Bye for now, and I look forward to reading your feedback on this and my future books!

Made in the USA
Monee, IL
07 July 2023

38821097R00194